CODE NAME:
PISCES

USA TODAY BESTSELLING AUTHOR

JANIE CROUCH

CODE NAME: PISCES - ZODIAC TACTICAL

To all Pisces out there…
Still waters run deep.

Chapter 1

Alyse Peterson focused on the perfume bottle in her hand. It was the only thing keeping her sane. A perfect example of everything that she was supposed to be and wasn't. Beautiful, shining, and transparent.

But the bottles had always been one of the best parts of being the spokesmodel for Endless Ivy perfumes. There was a nostalgic quality about them, taking her back to looking at the colorful glass clustered on Mom's vanity.

Behind her, the door cracked open, and the perky production assistant who had greeted her this morning before hair and makeup poked her head in. "We're ready for you, Alyse."

Her smile was open and easy, and Alyse was pretty sure she couldn't tell that she was freaking out. She hoped she couldn't. One last check in the mirror assured her she looked fine. Polished, perfect, and prepared for the role she always had to play while in public.

America's Glamour Princess.

Don't panic. She kept her internal voice calm. *You can do this. Deep breath. Game face. Let's go.*

Alyse pulled air deep into her lungs and held it, willing

her heart to slow and the sweat to magically evaporate from her palms. This wasn't her first job. It wasn't even her hundredth job. But that never seemed to matter. She always felt the same: dread and panic welled in her gut, rising until they threatened to choke her.

Usually, she could push through it, but not today. Today had felt different as soon as she woke up, and so far, she had been unable to put her finger on why.

Alyse followed the assistant down the hallway to the set, the huge, fluffy skirt of her wardrobe gathered in her arms so she wouldn't trip. Her legs were shaking, and she was glad today was only a photo shoot and not a video one. Shaking wouldn't show in the stills. She resisted the urge to bite her lip or fidget—to do anything that might give away that her heart was pounding.

Today's set was made to evoke ancient Greece. A bright-blue backdrop mimicked the color of a summer-kissed sky, and crumbling ruins were scattered across the stage. She could already imagine the different setups that were possible and could tell they would look amazing.

She had been surprised they were shooting on a set and not outdoors, as they had previously. Endless Ivy's headquarters were based in Paris, and the gorgeous streets and monuments were just steps away. But Anne Rigal—the owner of Endless Ivy—wanted something different for this campaign.

She had tried to explain when they spoke a few weeks ago, her perfectly accented voice showing her passion for the new vision. "Our upcoming scents are light and heat," she had told her. "We need for the ads to evoke that feeling. But with our same timeless style. It will be our best campaign yet. I already know this."

She would not have been surprised if Anne had decided she wanted to do this shoot in Greece in front of actual ruins. But they stopped her before she got that far, requesting that the shoot coincide with the movie promotion Alyse was already doing in Paris.

A slight hush rolled through the set when she walked in, and she took a breath, steadying herself. Every instinct in her body screamed to retreat and beg everyone to stop looking at her. But that wasn't Alyse Peterson. Alyse Peterson would always greet you with a smile. Was always pleasant and charming, even in the worst circumstances. Would always complete whatever task was before her with sophistication and grace.

Nobody knew Alyse Peterson was merely a role. One she was finding it harder and harder to play.

Jared Darenzo, her longtime manager, appeared at her side and swept her into a hug. "You look beautiful, darling."

"Thank you."

"How are you?"

The question was innocent enough, but she knew it was deeper than that. Jared was the only person in her life who knew the truth. As he was her manager, the amount of time that they spent together meant she was unable to hide it, no matter her acting skills. "I'm fine."

He smiled, mostly for the other people in the room. "This will only take a couple of hours. Then the interview, and you're home free." He didn't give her the chance to say anything about the interview and, instead, walked her over to a younger man directing the placement of some lights. "This is Henri. He'll be your photographer today."

She plastered the classic Alyse Peterson smile on her face. "It's lovely to meet you, Henri."

"You as well," he said, Parisian accent thick. "Shall we begin?"

"Of course."

Henri turned back to his assistants for the final touches before helping her up onto the set and describing the first shot. He was clear in his vision, which allowed her to relax a bit. Eyes were glued on her from all sides, but this was something she had done before.

A certain image was expected of her, and she would deliver.

"That's perfect, Alyse," Henri called from behind the camera after a while. "One more set of close-ups and we'll have everything we need."

"All right."

Someone on the makeup crew stepped in quickly to touch up blush she must have smudged. Then the camera was closer than it had been the whole morning. "Look straight at the lens, Alyse," Henri instructed. "Good. Now away. Demure."

He continued to call out emotions and directions, and she followed, keeping her mind blank. It took a moment before she realized the camera wasn't on her anymore.

"Excellent," Henri called over his shoulder. "That's a wrap."

Scattered applause echoed through the room. Not an unfamiliar sound. It made her uncomfortable. Over the last few years, Alyse had gathered a lot of modeling experience, but these jobs weren't things she'd earned. Not completely. She got lucky with a body that liked to be thin and with features that people found beautiful. And because of who her parents were—had been—she never had to fight for opportunities in this business. She didn't deserve applause for her own good luck.

The familiar ache in her chest from missing her parents weighed down on her. A whole year, and thinking about them still hurt.

She'd barely started moving back toward the dressing room to change when she heard Anne's voice behind her. "There's my beautiful flower." She placed a kiss on each cheek before pulling back to look at her. "You were stunning, Alyse. Come, I want to show you."

It had been her mother's idea to approach Anne about Alyse being the spokesmodel for Endless Ivy last year. She herself had been the face of the cosmetic line when she was her age, and she knew the media would adore the legacy aspect. A win-win for both her career and for Endless Ivy. Anne had agreed.

It had ended up being the last career guidance her mother would ever give her.

Henri smiled as they approached the large computer monitor with rows and rows of photos. "They're beautiful. It will be impossible to choose."

"We will plaster your face all over Paris, my love," Anne whispered.

Just what she needed. Her face plastered all over another country.

But she smiled and pushed aside the comment on her tongue—that too many people already knew her face. "I'm glad. This was a fun shoot."

"Which is now over," Jared chimed in, suddenly appearing. "My apologies, Anne, but we need to get Alyse changed and over to her interview."

"Of course." She leaned in and once again gave her the classic French kisses on each cheek. "Come back to Paris soon, dear. Not just for work."

Since her parents died, Alyse had been living far more privately. Without them, everything seemed far too big and too much—this career she'd been born into far too overwhelming. She had cut back on contact with everyone for her own sanity.

Alyse smiled as brightly as she could. "I'll see what we can fit into the schedule."

"I look forward to it," she whispered, hugging her one more time before Jared managed to pull her away.

"You've only got about a half hour to get changed, and then we're on the way to the hotel for the interview," Jared said, guiding her back to the dressing room at a brisk pace.

It was a trick they'd perfected over the years. Even if they weren't running behind schedule, appearing like they were being ushered places in a hurry cut down on the people who stopped to talk or ask for an autograph.

"Wasn't the original plan just to stay in the dressing room and do it here?"

Jared winced. "Yes. They wanted to do a few casual pictures of the interview setting with you—nothing fancy. But because of that, they wanted something that looked a little more glamorous than a dressing room."

She sighed. "Okay."

"I don't think you need to change your makeup. You'll be plugging the perfume anyway when they ask you what you've been doing. Plus, you look fabulous. I'll see you in a few minutes," Jared said. "Anne sent a gift. I left it in there for you."

She laughed softly. It was always the same when you worked with brands and people like Anne. They often sent you gifts and gave you things but never acknowledged that they had done so. "All right. I'll be out in a few."

Anne's gifts were always simple and lovely. And more tasteful than some overflowing baskets other clients gave her.

She looked over at the small, flat box on the bed, tied with a crimson ribbon. Possibly clothing of some kind. A tag on the ribbon read in elegant script *Love, Anne.*

She untied the ribbon and flipped open the cover. She wasn't expecting underwear, but that was what she found laid out in front of her. A delicate blue thong...

That looked eerily familiar.

Her body suddenly went cold as she saw a snag in the lace —the same snag that had occurred when she'd caught the fabric on her belt after arriving in Paris a few days ago.

This underwear was not supposed to be there. She'd thrown this in the trash at her hotel.

Chapter 2

"Jared!" Alyse stepped back from the cloth.

He poked his head around the door, phone to his ear. "Yeah?"

She swallowed, trying to make her voice function. It came out weak and watery. "This isn't from Anne."

Jared frowned and flicked his eyes down to the package in front of her. "What do you mean?"

"That's my underwear. From the hotel."

He went still for a moment. "I'll call you back," he said into the phone.

"Are you sure it's yours and not just something similar?"

"No. I snagged it in the exact same place. I was sad that I had to throw them out."

She pinched the thong with two fingers, picking it up. The feeling of being watched increased. Under the cloth was a note in the same flowing script that had been on the tag.

Her legs shook, and she had to sit down. "What does it say?"

"I need to call Anne." Jared turned away to leave.

"Jared. Read it."

He looked paler than she'd ever seen him in his many years as her manager. But she needed to know what that note said, and there was no way she could touch it.

Slowly, he picked it up. There was clearly something else in the box, but she did not move to find out what it was.

"My dearest Alyse," he read, clearing his throat. "This was not the way I wanted to introduce myself. I must have gotten your schedule wrong since you weren't here."

Her stomach dropped. Whoever wrote this had expected to find her in the hotel. She assumed it was a he. Jared kept reading. "I didn't have much time, and I couldn't wait any longer for you to know me. I noticed you changed your body wash. Everything of yours smells so different, and I don't like it. I hope you'll change it back for me. When I finally feel your skin, I want it to be the scent I've had in my dreams.

"I look forward to when we're together. I know that I'll be the one who finally understands you, Alyse. I see everything that you try to hide from the world. I'm the only one who sees. I'll meet you soon."

Jared stopped reading. She thought she might vomit.

"Jesus," Jared muttered as he dropped the note on the table.

"What else is in the box?" she whispered.

Jared tore the tissue paper back, and they both just stared. At first, it was like the underwear—easily mistaken for something mundane. Then her heart stuttered as she realized it was the body wash she'd been using up until a couple of weeks ago. A lilac scent that had been specially made for the cast of the movie she'd been promoting.

"He's been in my shower."

Whoever had left her the note not only had her underwear from yesterday, but had been in her shower twice—once to know she had that lilac body wash and again to know it was gone.

Fuck, she was going to vomit. She threw herself toward the sink just in time for the little food she'd had for breakfast to come rushing up. Her mouth burned with it. Behind her, Alyse heard Jared speaking into the phone, but she could not process what he was saying. Something about security. Something about the interview.

Her mind was spinning. Someone was following her. Wanted her. Had been inside her hotel room. Knew the smell of her skin and had before she'd even gotten to Paris.

Suddenly the way Alyse had been feeling all morning made sense. Like her body had known there was danger before there was any sign of it.

Jared raised his voice, and she sank onto the couch, tucking her feet up under her as people suddenly flooded into the room. Assistants and the security team for this building. She felt like she was the only thing not moving.

"I need you to get the security footage now," Jared snarled into the phone. "We're not coming back to the hotel until you review every minute of it."

He was talking to the hotel a few miles away, where they'd been staying for the past few days. Her mouth was dry, but she could not find her voice to ask someone for water.

"No, I can't tell you what you're looking for, but we have proof someone was in Alyse Peterson's room and took her possessions. If you don't want to be the center of an epic shitstorm of media, you'll look right now."

Someone moved the box slightly, and a dark speck peeked out from under the corner of the white tissue paper. Jared saw it and walked over, never stopping his tirade with the hotel.

When he saw what it was, he muttered a curse fouler than she'd ever heard him use in her presence.

"You're looking for a white male, average build, likely dark hair," he spat into the phone. "I can't give you a facial description, but hopefully that will help narrow it down a little."

The discovered item was a Polaroid picture of a man licking her panties in her hotel room. No details of his face were caught in the photo, but the image would forever be burned into her mind.

If she'd had anything left in her stomach, she would be sick again.

Jared ended the call with a punch of his finger and knelt in front of her. "Alyse."

Her name was hard to hear in the chaos of the room. Assistants clearing out the makeup and wardrobe while the building's security pored over their own footage on tablets to make sure the safety of the building hadn't been compromised.

All of them stole glances her way when they could, and she felt their eyes on her like those fingers of the man in the photos. Her breath was short in her chest.

Alyse couldn't look at Jared. The panic was rising under her skin. It worked its way into her throat and through her bones until she was entirely frozen. The sensation was so acute that she knew if she moved one muscle—*uttered one single word*—she would start screaming and not stop.

"We're going to get you home," Jared whispered. "Everything will be on hold until further notice. And we're going to hire you the best security team possible. Before you arrive at your house, we'll have every inch of the property secured. I know the perfect company for the job. Your father hired them a few years ago when he had an incident on set."

The mention of her father snapped her out of the haze and loosened her enough to speak, even though the horror gripped her throat to the point of pain. "Who?"

"Zodiac Tactical." He answered so quickly, she wondered how often he'd thought they might need this eventually.

"Okay."

"I'll call them now and set up a meeting for as soon as we're back in the States."

"Sorry," she whispered.

"Alyse, this is not something you need to apologize for. I —" Jared's words were cut off by the shrill ringing of his phone. "Yes?" His mouth turned into a flat line as he listened.

She closed her eyes and pulled a deep breath into her lungs. Then she counted to five before she released it. Jared kept listening, and he didn't look happy. She wanted to know, and yet she didn't.

Alyse tried to sit up straighter, hoping the movement would help her keep up the appearance that everyone expected of Alyse Peterson. Enough people still lingered in the room that it mattered, even after an incident like this one.

"Okay, thanks," Jared said. "Keep me posted."

She looked at him, waiting for the final blow. "They think they found him on the footage. Guy is brilliant at hiding his face from the cameras, but they've found the back of someone's head who's been at the hotel every day. He's in the background when you left the hotel to go jogging."

A few seconds later, images arrived on Jared's phone. It was definitely the same guy in multiple shots, but none of them was going to help them figure out who he was.

She sat on the couch and tried to keep it together.

Keep it together. Keep it together.

She'd been saying that every day since Mom and Dad died. Now she was saying it for an entirely different reason. She stared out the window.

"He was here too." A new voice came from across the room. A man in a suit who held one of the tablets was showing it to Jared. "Fits the description, hides his face from the cameras."

Everyone was looking at her to see if she would fall apart.

A couple of the lower-level assistants already had their phones out in case she lost it.

Instead, she sat up straighter. She was Alyse Peterson, America's Glamour Princess. She was never caught without looking her best, and she never gave the paparazzi or social media any fodder on her.

She needed to deflect and keep the persona. She could—and would—fall apart later. But she still had an audience. She knew the role she needed to play.

From somewhere, she managed a small smile at Jared. "See the lengths I'll go to in order to get out of an interview?"

He didn't laugh, but everyone else chuckled. As she'd expected.

Her eyes fell on the photos in the box one more time, and chills ran across her skin. He had been in her room. Touched her bed. Tasted her belongings. Those few private spaces were the only sanctuary she had left in the world, and they were drying up in front of her eyes.

Chapter 3

"After that brief scare, the rest of the trip went as planned," Mark Outlawson finished, barely containing a yawn.

Tristan Zimmerman raised an eyebrow at his friend and Zodiac Tactical agent currently on loan to their division. "You could at least pretend to be interested in the debriefing."

"Sorry, man." He made a face and laughed. "That jet lag from Dubai is seriously kicking my ass."

Across the table, Isaac Baxter, also a newer member of the ZT Guardian Unit, chuckled. He let it slide. Both men knew the importance of keeping accurate records dealing with mission parameters, and debriefs were a critical part of that.

They also tended to be boring as hell compared to being active in the field.

The Guardian Unit of Zodiac Tactical had just as many active missions as the Rescue Unit. Their division focused on body guarding and protection services, where the rescue team tended to deal with kidnappings and ransoms. They were two sides of the same coin.

And world-class at what they did.

They'd almost doubled their caseload since Tristan's boss

and friend, Ian DeRose, had asked him to take over the department. His inner team, including the two men sitting in this conference room with him now, all had the same focus and discipline he did. Almost all of them were former military —Navy SEALs, Rangers, Special Ops.

They all knew what it meant to be the ones who held the line to protect others.

But it was his job to make sure even the boring debriefings got done.

He'd run this division for two years and did a damned good job at it. His code name might be Pisces, but that didn't mean he necessarily shared those characteristics. A kind, sensitive, slightly disorganized dreamer—the traditional Pisces —he was not.

A focused, disciplined, highly aware leader, he *was*.

Mark Outlawson, known by nearly everyone as Outlaw, held up a hand before he could open his mouth to get them back to the debriefing. "Sorry, Tristan. You know I take this seriously."

"Yeah." He nodded. "Let's finish. We have other things to discuss."

Isaac launched into the final description of the trip and how they handled the client's anonymity in the country. Both the men in front of him were at the top of their game, physically and mentally. He trusted them without question.

"And that's it," Isaac sighed. "We got the confidentiality forms from them to sign, and I'll have them sent by messenger before end of day."

Tristan scrubbed his hand across his face. "Good. I'm glad it's over."

Political clients were always tricky and stressful when it came to physical safety. So many things could go wrong quickly. He always heaved a sigh of relief when the contracts were complete.

"Before you guys go slip into a coma, let's talk about proposals."

"Only a couple." Isaac pressed a few buttons on his tablet so they could see upcoming potential jobs. It was good to be in a place where they only needed to take the jobs they wanted. "Standard stuff. Tech company wants a top-to-bottom security evaluation and upgrade after a failed physical break-in."

Tristan nodded. "That sounds reasonable. Good training work for some of our newbies."

Isaac clicked more. "Agreed. Second one, you're not going to like so much."

"More politicians?"

Isaac shook his head. "Worse. Actress."

He barely refrained from rolling his eyes. "I doubt we're a good fit for that case."

Models and actresses were a no-go with him. Not after their last high-profile client in that field. They often paid well above their standard rate, but it wasn't worth the hassle.

More than one actress had wanted headshots and physical stats of their team members so she could pick which one would be the best fit for security. *Best fit* meaning most likes on social media.

"I don't know." Mark pulled the file up on his tablet. "This one might be worth looking at, at least. Urgent security request for an actress who may have a stalker."

Tristan rubbed his eyes. "You weren't here for what went down with Victoria Thorpe."

Isaac let out a groan. "Trust me, you don't want to know."

Victoria Thorpe was an up-and-coming actress who'd hired their team to catch a stalker that was escalating quickly —which sounded like this prospective client. But Victoria hadn't taken their protection seriously. She'd demanded to be guarded only by the male members of their team and kept them busy by sending them on errands like getting coffee or picking up her dog.

Her reasoning had always been clever—spun in a way that made those tasks necessary for her security. But once she'd sent them, she'd often gone off on her own, forcing the team to spend valuable time and energy to catch up with her so they could do their job.

Then it was somehow "leaked" on social media that she was romantically involved with more than one of her bodyguards. It had been easy enough to combat those rumors, until one of them became true, and Michael—the youngest and greenest member of the Zodiac Tactical team—fell into bed with Victoria.

Tristan ended up having to step in personally for damage control. They caught her stalker and terminated the contract the next day. And Michael was still on semi-permanent assignment guarding some warehouse in Alaska—where there were no beautiful clients anywhere in the vicinity.

"Whoever the actress is, let's try to direct her to another firm. There are plenty who'll be happy to help."

Isaac didn't immediately agree.

"Problem?" He asked.

"Potential client is Alyse Peterson."

Fuck.

Tristan knew who she was. Everybody knew who she was. He clicked on his screen, and the picture that stared up at him confirmed the image he'd already formed in his mind.

Brown hair fell around her shoulders in waves that belonged spread across a pillow, and sapphire eyes made you feel like she was seeing you, even through the camera. A Mona Lisa smile that contained every feminine secret ever created.

All of it perfect. Not a hair out of place. Not a blemish to be found anywhere on her skin. Ever. Thus dubbed America's Glamour Princess.

He didn't think any male in the country could say they hadn't had some kind of fantasy about Alyse Peterson.

The details of her case jumped out at him from the tablet, and he cringed. This wasn't a run-of-the-mill fan who had gotten too enamored like with Victoria Thorpe. This was deliberate. Alyse was being targeted in a clinical, neatly sophisticated way.

Given her public profile and level of fame, the fact that she had a stalker was hardly surprising.

"Zodiac did some security work for her father a few years ago. I met her briefly."

"Lucky bastard," Isaac muttered under his breath.

"It looks like she only has a few individual security members working for her. I would have thought her father would have made sure she had a full team." Alyse's father—Alden Peterson—was a celebrated Hollywood film director, and she had followed in her family's footsteps into that life with the ease only someone born to it could manage.

Alden Peterson's high recommendation of them had helped grow the Guardian Division to the point where they only took the cases they wanted.

Mark looked surprised. "You don't remember? Parents died a year ago. Car crash near the Toronto Film Festival. Really unexpected."

Tristan nodded, studying the info flashing up on his tablet. He did remember that vaguely. "Someone of her level of celebrity should still already have a full security team. The fact that she doesn't already means there're probably hidden issues."

Maybe she was like Victoria Thorpe and liked to give her own security team the runaround.

Isaac gave him a grin. "I'm happy to get to the root of any hidden issues. You don't have to do a thing."

He raised an eyebrow. "You looking for a job guarding a warehouse?"

Mark looked at him, practically pouting. "You wouldn't actually deny your friends the opportunity to guard America's Glamour Princess, would you?"

He already knew they were going to take the case. Alden Peterson had helped out the Zodiac Tactical Guardian Unit back when they were first getting on their feet—taken a chance on them. Tristan wasn't going to hang his daughter out to dry, no matter how much of a headache he knew she'd end up being.

Mark got up and poured himself what Tristan was sure was at least his third cup of coffee. "You saw the file. That's not a stalker who's going to stop, and if she doesn't get protection, something worse is going to happen to her. But being able to say I'm Alyse Peterson's personal bodyguard would be fine with me."

"Same," Isaac grinned. "It does have a nice ring to it, I have to admit."

"We'll have to let her choose. That's the only way it will be fair." Mark sat back down. He leaned his head back on his chair and closed his eyes. Tristan doubted he would make it through that cup of coffee.

These two were just going to continue to fight over who got to head up this case. "You both need sleep."

"Yes," Mark groaned. "Yes, I do. But you wanted to talk about proposals, and I can't go to sleep until you finish with them."

"Okay." Tristan raised his hands in surrender and fought against the grin that threatened to crack. "Get more details from the tech company. And I'll meet with Alyse. If only to get the two of you off my back."

The two of them shared a conspiratorial smile, and he pointed to each of them in turn. "If we accept her as a client, you are not allowed to fight over her. This cannot turn into another Thorpe situation. Got it? Because I will send both your asses to Antarctica if needed."

"Got it, boss." Isaac stood and stifled a yawn. "Free to go?"

"Please. Get some sleep before you collapse on the table."

Mark pushed himself up with a groan. "I think the table would feel like a pillow at this point."

Tristan smiled as they left the room. Twelve hours of sleep and they'd be good as new.

When he was alone, he opened his tablet again, found Alyse's file, and once more reviewed the details of her case. Both Mark's instinct and his own had been right. This woman needed help.

For the sake of her father and what he had done for the company, Tristan would meet with her and her manager, Jared Darenzo. Hopefully, he'd be able to gently refer them to a different company that could better serve her long-term needs.

He looked down at those blue eyes piercing him from her picture on the tablet. She really was perfect—not a single wrinkle dared lay on her impeccably fitting dress, every curl of hair rested with unnatural grace on her shoulder.

Too perfect to be real. Definitely too perfect for anyone like him.

Chapter 4

Alyse looked up at the exterior of the high-rise in the middle of downtown Los Angeles. Slick, glossy windows shone in the sun, and the paparazzi were in full force outside the car.

The flight from Paris had been long and sleepless. Usually, she could ease off into a few hours of rest, but this time, every movement of the plane had her nearly crawling out of her skin. She couldn't seem to stop looking around, and every time she thought that she'd relaxed, she felt invisible eyes on her back and felt compelled to search for them again.

She was grateful that Zodiac Tactical was gracious enough to fit them in at the last minute, even if that meant they came straight there from the plane. Jared must have known that she would not want to go home since it hadn't yet been secured. She'd used the first-class bathroom on the airplane to freshen up.

After all, it was imperative she keep up the polish that everyone expected from America's Glamour Princess.

Alyse did not feel glamorous. She felt worn and on edge and shaky. But that did not matter. The paparazzi did not care how she felt. If she looked like she was falling apart, it was only better for their business. So she changed her clothes. Put on a fitted gray suit with a flirty pink tank top under the jacket. She refreshed her makeup, added coral lip gloss and dry shampoo to combat the airplane hair. Then she pasted on a smile.

LAX security had been kind enough to have them escorted directly to the car. And now she was there, staring through the car window at a sidewalk full of flashing cameras. Alyse never knew how they managed to find out where she was going to be before she knew. For her own sanity—especially in the current situation—she had learned to stop asking those questions.

Her fingers would not stop moving. They fidgeted, the frayed edges of her nerves beginning to show. And she was expected to talk to strangers about being stalked. Would they want to know everything? Would they have to show what had been sent to the dressing room? She shuddered at the memory—and the idea of baring her embarrassment to someone else. This was already bad enough.

"Do you want to take something?" Jared asked. "Just to knock the edge off?"

Of course he could see that she was losing it. When this was over, she owed Jared a gigantic bonus or raise or fully paid vacation with his husband, Derek. That was the least she should do for the way he'd handled the last thirty-six hours. Every concern that she'd had, he'd thought of before she'd had a chance to worry about it. It had helped, even if she wasn't currently capable of showing it.

Alyse shook her head. "No. I don't like the way it affects me."

The medication she sometimes took to help with anxiety made her feel like she was seeing the world through a glass wall. She was interacting, but muted. It was horrible, even on her best days. With someone watching her, she wanted to be able to react fast if she needed to. She would need to find another way to deal with the jumpiness and phantom eyes on her back.

When this was over, she needed to eat. She hadn't been able to stomach the thought of food since they'd received the "gift." But hunger compounded all the negative feelings, and Alyse knew it was a contributing factor in her anxiety as well. As soon as this meeting was finished, she would force herself to eat a full meal.

Two men in suits approached the car, forcing the paparazzi back and making a path to the front door.

"Ready?" Jared asked.

"No," she said, as the first security guard opened the door.

Somehow, she never seemed to be ready for the noise. The wave of shouts coming from reporters and the clicks of shutters always set her on edge. She remained in between the guards as they guided her through the crowd.

Alyse had never been more grateful for sunglasses. The dark lenses made it so that no one could see how she couldn't keep her eyes still. How she searched every face for a sign of the man who had invaded her life. Being ushered through the crowd masked the fact that her breath had gone short and she had started to shake in the proximity of so many people.

It was maybe thirty feet from the car to the door, and those thirty feet felt like an eternity. Once they stepped inside and the noise quieted a bit, she took a deep breath, trying to steady herself.

"Miss Peterson, Mr. Darenzo," one of the guards said, turning to her. "We'll show you to the conference room, and Mr. Zimmerman will be with you shortly."

"Thank you," Jared answered for her. She tried to give the man a smile, but she wasn't successful. The classic Alyse Peterson glamour wasn't something she could muster at the moment.

One silent elevator ride later, Jared and Alyse were shown into a spacious room with a glorious view of the Los Angeles skyline. From there, everything seemed...serene. Like her world wasn't completely falling apart. But if she'd learned anything living in Hollywood most of her life, it was that things always looked better from a distance.

"Do you think they'll be able to help?" She asked quietly.

"Absolutely," Jared said without hesitation. "Zodiac Tactical is the best in the business. A lot of these guys are former Special Forces, and they have a reputation for handling difficult cases with ease and discretion. Your father spoke highly of them."

She barely remembered the incident that had required her father to hire outside security for one of his movie sets. He'd done his best to hide the full scope of it from her and her mother. But she did remember Tristan Zimmerman from a few years ago. He had been striking.

Their meeting had only been a brief interaction—a simple introduction. But she would never forget those blue eyes. They were piercing and added to the air of quiet, utter certainty that he projected.

In that five-minute conversation, Alyse felt as if Tristan Zimmerman saw more of her than most other people who'd known her for years. It had been disconcerting and enough to make her avoid him for the rest of the time he'd been on set.

But she never forgot him. Someone like Tristan Zimmerman was impossible to forget.

"I can see if Dr. Elliot has an opening," Jared said softly as she stared at the door of the conference room.

Alyse had already had that thought multiple times in the last day. But she wasn't sure she wanted to sit in an office and attempt to process all this. Dr. Elliot knew everything about her, and she was great about her boundaries and also knowing when she needed to be pushed. Even so, the thought of trying to speak about this was too raw to even contemplate. She already felt battered to the point of breaking.

"I'll think about it," was the only answer she could give him.

The door behind her opened, and Alyse whirled to face the unexpected sound. Her heart was in her throat until she saw Tristan Zimmerman step through the door.

It was as if he stepped out of her memory. The same piercing gaze and confidence that rolled off him like a wave when she'd met him before were present now. He took in the two of them in a moment, and she again felt like he saw everything.

And judged it. Had he been that way when she'd met him before? She didn't think so.

"Miss Peterson, Mr. Darenzo, thank you for thinking of us." He crossed the room and extended his hand to her. She shook it, unable to ignore the strength there. This was not a man who failed. If he put his mind to something, he accomplished it. She had no words to say.

"Thank you for fitting us in so quickly," Jared said as he shook Tristan's hand.

"I hope your flight was good?"

Alyse tried to smile, to show anything that was a part of her normal persona. If anything, she managed a flicker. "As good as it could have been, I suppose."

Tristan looked at her carefully, and she did her best to meet his stare with confidence. He managed to look through her like she was an open book—which wasn't possible since the man didn't know her at all. But his gorgeous blue eyes seemed to break through her walls without any effort.

He laid the file he was carrying on the table and pressed a button on the intercom. "Rebecca, can I see you for a moment?"

Jared and Alyse took seats next to each other across from

Tristan, and the receptionist they had passed on the way in opened the door. Their host spoke a few hushed words to her before returning to the table and sitting. He seemed unhurried, but not dismissive. If anything, the fact that he was treating this as a normal meeting, without any reflection of her celebrity status, was almost comforting.

He opened the file he'd brought in with him. "We've dealt with stalkers before, so there's a possibility that we can help you. If you can give me a more detailed account of the Paris incident, I'll have a better idea if we're the right security firm for you."

Panic flared inside her. It wasn't a done deal? Walking out of here without protection made every nerve in her body feel like it was on fire. Outside of herself, she could hear Jared giving the details of Paris, from the gift to the pictures to the faceless man on the security videos.

Once again, Alyse felt eyes on her like the stalker was inside the room with them. She fought the instinct to turn around and look, even though she knew there was nothing behind her but windows. Her fingers flared out and back into fists.

Breathe, Alyse.

She remembered the way Dr. Elliot had trained her to control her breath. Inhale for four, hold for four, exhale for four, hold for four. Like a square. And every time you repeated the cycle, you made it longer. Until your heart rate settled. In theory.

This time, it wasn't doing shit. Her thoughts felt fractured and jittery. She was barely inside her own mind. The opening of the door made Alyse jump again, but it was just the receptionist. She was carrying a large tray with glasses of water, a giant bowl of salad, and a platter of vegetables, cheese, and fruit. Plates were already made up with an assortment of each.

"Thank you, Rebecca," Tristan said. He immediately picked up and slid one of the plates in front of her. "You should eat something."

The idea of taking orders to eat from a stranger made frustration rise in her chest, but he was right. Alyse had already admitted to herself that she needed food, and the lack of calories was definitely affecting her focus.

"Thank you," she whispered, keeping her eyes on the plate.

Jared continued with the details of Paris, including the list of everywhere her stalker had been tracked, answering questions as Tristan asked them. By the time Tristan had all the details he needed, she had finished the food on her plate without even realizing it.

Alyse looked up to find Tristan watching her. Not judgmental, just observing. He nudged the plate of cheese and fruit toward her, while at the same time making a note in the file. She wished she could act like she wasn't still hungry, but she was.

She took the second plate, pushing away the thoughts swirling in her head that she shouldn't be eating this much in front of Tristan. That if he decided to harm her reputation, he could tell the media that she did nothing but eat. Instead, she tried to focus on the fact that she already felt clearer and less panicked because of the food.

Eating a second plate was not unacceptable when she hadn't been able to force anything down in over twenty-four hours.

"I do have some questions for you, Miss Peterson," Tristan said. "Take your time with the answers. The more detail we have, the faster we can narrow down who's coming after you."

Alyse nodded. "All right."

"Oftentimes, stalkers of this nature can rise out of

previous relationships. Do you think any of your past boyfriends might be the cause?"

Cold ran down her spine. She honestly hadn't considered that it could be someone she already knew. But she shook her head. There was no need to tell Tristan that her relationships had been few and far between. She only had three exes, and she didn't think any one of them was capable of the violation she felt in that dressing room.

"They have busy schedules," Alyse said. "As far as I know, none of them were in Paris, and that can be easily checked."

Tristan made a note. "Any shorter relationships that may hold a grudge?"

She raised her eyebrows. "Meaning what?"

"Hookups and one-night stands." Tristan didn't flinch when he looked at her. "I apologize for the bluntness, but your public profile is well-known. There's rarely a week that passes without an appearance at a party or in the various tabloids. Even someone who may not pay attention to popular culture knows who you are. So anyone you may have encountered and spent the night with is someone that we need to know about."

Alyse looked down at the table, fighting a blush. That wasn't her. That could never be her. But people didn't want to read about the girl who stayed home in her pajamas, watched movies, and fell asleep on the couch. They wanted to read about America's Glamour Princess. The woman who was constantly on the move. The girl who mingled with the world's elite and only visited the most exclusive places.

It was all an exquisitely crafted lie. Every party or shopping trip was designed by her PR team—rarely what it seemed when it showed up in the media. Every detail was planned beforehand so that she could manage the anxiety that bombarded her each time she stepped out her door.

But that wasn't why she was blushing. Most of the time,

Alyse didn't care that people thought she was a party girl. That was just a role she played. But somehow she hated the idea that Tristan would think of her like that.

"There's no one," she said quietly.

He stared at her for a silent moment before he spoke again. "If my team and I are to protect you, Miss Peterson, you need to be honest with me. Surprises do not help us here."

Alyse stiffened. "There have been no hookups. Zero. And the implication that I'm lying about it isn't welcome. And stop calling me Miss Peterson. My name is Alyse."

Their gazes clashed in a stare, and, while she was uncomfortable, she couldn't help but be relieved that at least her irritation was chasing back her fear.

Meanwhile, Tristan sighed and made another note in his little notebook, like he was letting it go but didn't believe her when she said it. It stung more than she expected.

Alyse was used to people judging her. That was part of being a Peterson—you didn't get to own your own life. People created who they thought you were, and that guided their opinion of you. It was rare that anyone got close enough to know who she truly was. But even when she let people through the walls, too often, they still expected her to maintain that perfect image the media and public had created.

Her parents had never cared about perception, but they were gone now. And Jared, as great of a manager he was, had his own life with Derek. He loved her, but she was his job. She was alone and had accepted that.

Alyse wasn't going to let Tristan Zimmerman unnerve her.

She finally dropped her gaze from his and found a second empty plate in front of her. She had eaten everything. When was the last time she'd eaten until she felt comfortably full without having to force herself?

More the question, how had Tristan known she'd needed food? She hadn't wanted it. It couldn't be his normal operating procedure to provide meals for potential clients coming in for brief meetings. He hadn't offered Jared anything.

Something hung in the air between them. She wasn't sure what it was. Not quite a power struggle, but something similar.

As Tristan shifted his gaze to Jared, Alyse realized whatever it had been between them, she'd lost. "What does Miss Peterson's schedule look like the next few months?"

Jared was already pulling up the calendar on his phone. "Movie shoot here in LA. Starts next week. I can forward you the exact details."

"Excellent," Tristan said. "And home security? We need to evaluate your current system for upgrades." His eyes focused on her again, that perfect confidence overwhelming. "Eventually, the system will be enough. But for the foreseeable future, while the threat is imminent, I would recommend an in-home presence."

Dread wrapped around her chest. Alyse didn't want anyone in her space. Her home was the only haven she had, the only place where she could breathe without any trace of fear.

She shook her head. "No."

Nothing changed in Tristan's face, but she could still feel the sudden change in mood. His voice was as cool and collected as it had ever been as he pulled a photo from the file.

"This is a targeted attack." She could hear the invisible edge to his words as he slid a photo across the table to her. It was a catalog of all the Polaroids the stalker had left behind. "And a camera watching you sleep does not stop someone from doing this again. An in-home bodyguard does. Why are you here if you're not going to take your security seriously, Miss Peterson?"

Alyse felt better enough to keep a hold on herself—and to grasp for the Alyse Peterson smile she could pull around herself like armor whenever someone fired at her. And that was what Tristan was doing, even though his demeanor stayed cool. Especially with her name. He hadn't forgotten she'd asked him to call her Alyse.

She relaxed her jaw so her smile could fall into place. She had way more experience than him at this game. "Alyse, please. And if that's what you think is best, then I'm sure it's appropriate."

He reflected her smile back at her, but it felt like a mockery. Like he knew, inside, she wanted to get away from him, despite her agreeable words. "I'll review your schedule with my guys and see who's available."

Jared cleared his throat. "Mr. Zimmerman, if there's an in-person presence needed, it should be you. Alden Peterson knew you and trusted you. It's why we came here, and I'm sure it's what he would have wanted if he were here to choose protection for Alyse."

"Alden Peterson was a good man," Tristan said, standing and observing them both coolly. "But he isn't here. And Alyse seems to not care very deeply about her own security, safety, or that of those around her."

She couldn't believe the words she was hearing. "*What?*"

He shrugged nonchalantly. "Given your reluctance to tell the truth about your sexual history and dismissal of valid suggestions, what else can I believe?"

Red crossed her vision, and Alyse found herself standing to her feet, a vortex of fury that was begging her to let loose. "You're unbelievable."

He faced her calmly, still completely in control of his

emotions. "Honesty is the best policy, Miss Peterson. I hope you'll come to understand that if we work together."

She took a breath, shoving the urge to scream down into the pit where she kept all the emotions that she couldn't show. Grief and pain were rearing their heads, chased up by exhaustion and stress, and she didn't feel like she could contain any of it.

One thing Tristan was right about. Her father wasn't there. And if he had been, Alyse didn't know what he would have wanted. But she knew he would have trusted her to take care of herself and know that she was not this vapid and selfish woman Tristan Zimmerman was suggesting she was.

"Whatever you may think about me, *Mr. Zimmerman*"—she spat out his name—"do not assume that you know me."

His nostrils flared just the slightest bit. "I'll send in the contract shortly. Sign it or don't, it's your choice."

He didn't look at her again as he walked out of the room, dismissal evident in the action. This was her life in his hands. At the very least, he could be respectful of it, no matter what he thought of her.

Alyse looked over at Jared, shaking her head, trying to figure out exactly what had happened in the course of the last hour. Because honestly, she had no idea.

She said words she would've never dreamed she'd say anywhere in public. America's Glamour Princess wouldn't dare. But America's Glamour Princess wasn't currently here.

"That bastard is a cold, fucking asshole."

Chapter 5

Tristan didn't bother stopping by his office on the way to the security suite. Restless energy hovered under his skin, and all he wanted was to review everything that had just happened with Alyse Peterson through the outside eyes of their cameras. It was a habit he'd developed over the years: watch client meetings back, because everything was amplified on film.

That included his own behavior. Because he wasn't sure he recognized it.

The only stop he made was asking Rebecca to bring their standard contract to the conference room for them to consider. Regardless of whether Alyse decided to take them on, he was glad that Jared Darenzo was by her side. He had a good head on his shoulders, and Tristan could tell he cared about Alyse.

Alyse. Her insistence that he call her by her first name had caught him off guard. Almost as much as his refusal to do so. The whole damned meeting with her had left him…unsettled. That was not a familiar feeling. He prided himself on keeping calm and collected no matter the situation.

Tristan didn't like the way the meeting had gotten under

his skin. He shouldn't feel this way—like he pushed too hard, too fast. That was his job. Too many clients lied from embarrassment or fear, and those lies could put both his people and the client in danger.

But that hadn't made pushing Alyse any easier. For the first time, it hadn't been what he'd wanted to do.

Walking through the door, she'd looked fragile, brittle, like she might shatter at any moment. The urge to feed her had nearly swamped him, and he'd had Rebecca get the food before he could think better of it.

Who the hell offered food to a woman known for her impeccable figure and flawless complexion? For all Tristan knew, she existed on a diet of tofu and baby whale skin.

But something about the way she'd sat there, nearly jumping out of her skin at every sound, arms wrapped around herself as if she might fly apart any second… he couldn't *not* do anything. Maybe it was his parents' hospitality in him, but he'd had to get her something to eat.

Or pull her into his arms and promise her he was going to make her feel safe again.

That would've gone over well.

Ended up food was the right call. She'd eaten all of it, which had seemed to surprise her even more than it did him. He didn't care who it surprised as long as she lost that tension in those blue eyes.

But his feeling of protection was something he needed to channel into making sure that her stalker was caught and that she was safe. Nothing more than that.

Voices buzzed in the security room. Tristan should have known his team wouldn't be able to resist seeing the celebrity on the cameras. Who didn't want to get a close view of Alyse Peterson?

Alyse's delicate voice poured from the speakers as he

stepped into the doorway. "That bastard is a cold, fucking asshole."

It seemed like half the Zodiac employees were in the room. Every single one of them laughing at Alyse's words.

"Play it again, please." Mark's laughter was the loudest of everyone. "Nothing like watching Tristan get taken down by America's Glamour Princess."

Isaac backed up the recording and let it play.

"That bastard is a cold, fucking asshole."

Tristan watched silently from behind them. On the video, Alyse's eyes were pure fury, staring at his retreating figure. There was more energy in her when she said those words than she had shown the entire meeting. He liked it much better than the polite facade she'd erected when he'd pushed her. And he damned well liked it better than the brittleness from when she'd first entered.

Besides, she wasn't wrong. He was an asshole.

He had to smile just the slightest bit as the guys played it again. Alyse had more fire than he originally thought.

Tristan watched the flames in her blue eyes, her face for once *not* the perfect reflection of glamour in that moment, and the inexplicable urge to protect her rose up once again.

Protection was not only his career; it was in his blood. Made up a big chunk of who he was. It was why Ian had chosen him to run this division. He always felt protective of whomever they were guarding.

But none of their jobs had ever made him feel the need to protect a client from anything that would hurt them like he did with Alyse. This was visceral—deep and physical. Alyse Peterson was beautiful, but she was so much more than that. Even in the state she was in, she had something that drew you in. He had no trouble understanding why people flocked to follow her. Ten minutes in her presence and the curiosity was overwhelming, even for him.

Whistles and more laughter follow Alyse's replayed outburst. Isaac shook his head. "Maybe Tristan has met his match."

"Maybe," Tristan said. Everyone spun to look at him, more than one guilty face. He rolled his eyes. "You're allowed to make fun of the boss from time to time, so I won't fire you all. But now get back to work."

Almost everyone shuffled out, most of them grinning. He grabbed Mark's arm as he went by. "Need your help for a second."

He nodded and stepped to the side. Once the room was empty, Tristan turned to Nathaniel Grubber, their resident tech expert. This was his domain, but he needed privacy with Mark. "Nate, will you give us a few minutes?"

"Sure thing, boss." He grinned before stretching. "Needed a coffee break anyway after that show."

Tristan sank into the chair Nathaniel vacated and looked at Mark, who might only be a temporary employee for the Guardian Unit but was one of his best friends.

He was staring back at him with an absolutely shit-eating grin on his face.

"Shut up."

"What?" He made the very picture of innocence. "I didn't say anything."

Tristan shook his head as he backed up the recording to the beginning of the meeting. "Yeah, keep it that way."

They watched the meeting play out again, and he closely watched Alyse's transformation. When he first walked in, she was so jumpy, it almost felt like she was an animal backed into a corner. In a way, she was, between her stalker and the paparazzi that followed her around everywhere.

"What do you think?" He asked him.

Mark cleared his throat. "You going to give me your take too?"

"Of course."

He sighed. "She's definitely not Victoria. She's not looking to hire us for cosmetic purposes."

Tristan shook his head. "Agreed."

"And I think she's telling the truth. She's terrified."

"And exhausted." He watched her accept the plate he pushed toward her on the footage. "I've seen that look before. She's close to breaking."

Mark shot him a look. "You gave her food."

"They came straight from the airport," Tristan said, shrugging. "I thought she might be hungry."

Mark might be a friend, but Tristan still didn't want to admit feeding Alyse had been an instinct he didn't understand and hadn't seemed to be able to control.

"It was a good call. But then you overcompensated by being pretty fucking hard on her."

The recording showed him exactly that. He listened to himself tell her that she was, in essence, a selfish brat.

He cringed. "Felt necessary at the time. Trying to force the truth out. Her hiding one-night stands isn't going to do anything but give the stalker an advantage."

"There's more than one way to get the truth out. I know you know that."

He did. And he should've tried gentler methods before jumping into brute emotional force.

Watching himself prod her, Tristan realized "cold, fucking asshole" had probably been a little too tame of a response from her.

He'd brought her dead father into it. Tried to use him against her. Unforgivable. Especially since Alden had helped build this division when they first started.

He owed Alyse an apology. A big one. If she decided to sign with them after all.

"…cold, fucking asshole."

"Honestly, I don't think I'll ever get tired of hearing that." Mark laughed and slapped him on his shoulder. "But you can fix this, Pisces. You're too professional to let someone else's mistakes influence how you treat Alyse Peterson."

He was right. Tristan just needed to remember it.

He watched the playback he hadn't yet seen. Alyse standing still after he'd left the room, and Jared doing his part to smooth over the damage he'd inflicted. If he salvaged the contract, Tristan owed him a thank-you along with Alyse's apology.

He scrubbed a hand down his face. "I wouldn't blame her for going with another firm. I pushed way too hard."

Mark shrugged, leaning back in the chair. "It is what it is now. If she does sign on, we need to secure her property immediately. She's already unraveling at the seams, and that will bring her some peace of mind."

"Let's see, then." Mark hit a button that flipped the cameras live in the room where Alyse and Jared were talking. Tristan pressed the button to mute the feed so they couldn't hear what they were saying. This part of the conversation was private, and they didn't have a right to listen.

The contract he had Rebecca take in was sitting on the table in front of Jared, but Alyse wasn't where he'd left her. She was standing and looking out the window at the LA skyline. Her back was stiff, arms crossed around herself once again.

Cue his need to rush back into the room, take her into his arms, and promise everything was going to be okay.

Wouldn't that take everybody by surprise? They never promised a client everything was going to be okay in a case like this. They calmly and rationally discussed how specific protective measures could add levels of safety. But they never carte blanche promised *everything okay* rainbows and unicorns. All that did was provide a false sense of security.

But Tristan wanted to promise Alyse that. Just to take off some of the weight that seemed to be crushing her slender shoulders.

He could see Jared's mouth moving, but it didn't seem like she was interested. He continued to speak, and Alyse's shoulders finally slumped in defeat.

After a few moments, she looked back at the contract on the table. Resignation and determination painted her expression, and she crossed the distance to the table and signed on the dotted line.

Chapter 6

The affluent outskirts of Los Angeles weren't where Tristan normally hung out. But this was where Alyse lived. The gated community was admittedly a touch more casual than he had expected from someone of her celebrity, but in this instance, he was happy that she had neighbors. Some giant estates that the rich and famous owned and wanted secured had acres and acres of unattended land that could take an army to patrol. This should be easier, at least.

It only took a few minutes to be waved through the gates, but the man at the station did his due diligence in checking Tristan's ID and his name against the list and making sure that his face matched what was on his ID. Good. One less thing to worry about.

Inside the gates, however, there were problems. The neighborhood was beautiful, with perfectly manicured landscapes and decorations, and what looked like a full park in the center. Even though each of the individual houses had fences and its own gates, there were plenty of places for a stalker to hide.

He could see at least three places within sight of Alyse's

gate that could be made into a hideout if someone wanted to do so. They would have the team do regular sweeps of the neighborhood as well.

Already, he spotted places that needed cameras. He wanted the entire exterior covered. All the cameras that Zodiac Tactical used transmitted directly back to the security room at headquarters, which was staffed at all times. Pulling out his phone, he sent a text to Mark with some preliminary camera positions as he walked up the driveway. He'd be here soon to help with the evaluation and installation.

An evaluation of the data from the public record about this house had been on Tristan's desk this morning, but he hadn't looked at it yet. He preferred to see new locations with fresh eyes so he could look at them through the lens of the threat. Because of that, he didn't know if Alyse had purchased this house or if she had inherited it from her parents. But if the latter, hopefully Alden had already made sure it was fortified.

It was shocking that people like Alden and Priscilla Peterson, despite all their money and fame, could just vanish in a car accident. Alden had been charming to a fault and made you feel like the only person who had his attention. He made you feel special and important without any of the affectation that so many people in Hollywood had. If Tristan had been a betting man, he'd have guessed that Alden would have cheated death for a long time. He'd only been forty-eight.

But he knew more than anyone that death happened whether you expected it or not. He had his own nightmares regularly to remind him of that.

Tristan set those thoughts aside. He wouldn't let the past derail him in any way. He was too focused on giving Alyse some sense of security and easing that broken look. They were securing her property before she returned to it, and they would have one of the junior members of the team patrolling the neighborhood starting now.

Some of their crew were already in the driveway unloading equipment, ready to install whatever was needed once Tristan did his walk-through. It didn't take him long to realize they'd want to do a complete security overhaul of the grounds and house. Damned near everything about her security needed to be amped up.

Jared opened the door as Tristan walked up to it, ending a call on his cell as he did so. His hand was already out to shake his. "Mr. Zimmerman, good to see you."

"Call me Tristan. I suspect we'll be seeing quite a bit of each other."

"Jared," he said. "And as much as I think you're right, I hope not."

He ushered Tristan into a spacious but understated foyer. Alyse was nowhere in sight. That was the first thing he noticed, followed by the fact that this was a beautiful home. Not glitzy or glamorous, but stylish and well put together.

"I'll give the nickel tour," he said. "If you need something more detailed, I'll leave that to Alyse to decide."

Tristan said nothing, but noted the subtle boundary that Jared was placing. This was Alyse's home, and she got final say over what happened here. Fair enough, but that didn't mean he wouldn't push for what he thought was needed to keep her safe.

Jared took him through the public areas of the house and backyard. Gorgeous pool out back and high fences, but there were more trees overhanging those fences than he liked and several spots for easy cover. Floodlights might be needed out there.

The rest of the house was a reflection of the foyer. Beautiful, tasteful, and subtle. By the time they were finished with the tour, his team was already halfway to completing the security system. They were swift and efficient—Tristan made sure of that.

But there was still no sign of Alyse.

"Is Alyse home?" He used her first name since she'd asked him to—more than once—and he was on his best behavior today. "I need to make sure that my team has access to every window for the system, and to show her how it works."

Jared looked a little chagrined before he sighed. "Alyse isn't exactly thrilled about the idea of seeing you after yesterday."

Tristan kept his face neutral. "I owe her an apology for that."

"Yes, you do," Jared said, though he looked surprised.

"Mr. Zimmerman." A voice came ringing clearly across the foyer. "Good to see you again."

Tristan turned and found Alyse approaching him with a smile that he already knew was not real. She looked impeccable—perfectly tailored jeans and a blue blouse that set off her hair and eyes. Blue heels that matched the shirt enough to complete the look. Subtle makeup aimed to create a glow, and it worked. She was glamorous—just like her media title.

But something made him look harder.

This was her home, a place she should feel comfortable and relaxed, rather than stiff. He suddenly had the urge to reach for her and run his hand through her hair. To muss her.

He wanted to see the *real*, not the perfect.

He shook her hand, trying to get his thoughts in line. "Tristan, please."

She raised an eyebrow, and given how many times he'd reverted to her last name yesterday to get a rise out of her, he couldn't blame her. But she let it go and gestured to the living room where they could gather around the coffee table. "Tristan. Have you finished your assessment?"

"I have," he said, pulling up the schematics of the house

that he had been sent that morning on his tablet. Now that he had seen the place in person, he could more accurately say what was needed. "I want to set up full security coverage on the exterior and gate. The cameras will be running on a live feed directly to Zodiac. Here's where I'd like them."

He placed his tablet on the table and marked where the camera locations should be. "If you'll give me permission, I'll let the crew comb the house for any entries we may have missed. We'll have everything set up today."

Alyse looked cold and stiff, but she nodded.

"Excellent." He sent a text to his crew quickly before he switched the view to the interior schematics. "For interior cameras, I'm recommending all hallways and entrances. Again, on a live feed. And this house is big enough that I feel two guards would be better than one."

"No," Alyse said tightly. "Exterior cameras, I understand, but I don't want cameras inside, and I don't need guards."

Tristan took a breath, not wanting a repeat of his performance from yesterday. Maybe she was being unreasonable because of that. "I assure you, you have nothing to worry about from my team, if that's your concern. They're professionals held to the highest standard, and your safety will be their only priority."

Her fingers flickered for a second in her lap, but that was the only outward sign of any negative emotion. Any emotion at all.

"No in-home guards," she said, her voice clipped. "That's final."

He stared, tamping down the urge to push her. In order for them to do their jobs, she had to take this seriously. She needed to listen and understand that this stalker wasn't just an overzealous fan. This was serious. Her life could be at stake. They locked eyes in a stare.

And fuck if Tristan didn't have the urge to drag her into the kitchen and make sure she ate something again.

He wasn't sure why. She didn't look nearly as fragile or frightened as she had yesterday. The woman in front of him was the very picture of poised glamour princess and would certainly never call him an asshole.

But still, it was taking every bit of focus he had not to ask her if she'd eaten today. She hadn't. Her makeup might have been applied with the skill of an artist and her clothes tailor-made to fit her body perfectly, but every instinct he had told him she'd barely slept a wink last night and hadn't eaten a bit since she'd finished that plate in front of him yesterday.

His gut told him it was true, and it had saved his life too many times for him to start discounting it now.

Although that didn't mean Tristan should act on it in any way.

"Sorry I'm late," Mark said with a smile, stepping into the room. "Got caught up with the guys outside running the initial system."

"I think your timing might be perfect," Jared said, rising to shake his hand.

"Mark Outlawson," he said, shaking both of their hands. Tristan had to hand it to him; he didn't even so much as linger an extra second over Alyse. "Tristan calls me in when he needs the big guns."

Already, Alyse seemed more at ease. Her smile immediately brightened into something more legitimate. "Good to hear."

Outlaw was always so fucking charming. And more of a mediator than Tristan was ever willing to be. "Alyse and I were just discussing her need for interior security," he said as he sat down.

"We were not discussing it," Alyse said. "I refuse to have cameras or strangers in my house."

Mark nodded in understanding. "I get that it could be jarring, but Tristan knows what he's doing. If he recommended it, it's for a good reason."

Tristan saw the ice overtake her again, her whole body going stiff.

"Perhaps there's a compromise that we could find?" Jared asked cautiously.

"Tell me what your concerns are," Mark said. "I'm sure there's a way to properly protect your home while also maintaining your boundaries."

Fuck boundaries. When someone was threatening your life, you didn't need boundaries; you needed protection. Everything in Tristan wanted to demand that she listen, get her fucking head out of the clouds, and do whatever it was they decided was necessary to protect her. Even knowing it was a gross overreaction, he couldn't stop the feeling.

"Can I use your kitchen?" Jesus. What the fuck was he doing?

Tristan barely waited for her nod before he was off the couch and moving, ignoring Mark's furrowed brows. Gritting his teeth, thankful she wasn't following him, he pushed aside the fact that he felt like an idiot. But he was making Alyse Peterson a sandwich. He could not sit there on that couch anymore, knowing that she was hungry and not doing anything about it.

It wasn't a comfortable feeling, not being able to control his actions like this. He prided himself on always being in control, but this woman had gotten under his skin in a way that he couldn't explain.

Thus him in a kitchen that wasn't his.

There was almost nothing in there, but Tristan managed to find enough for peanut butter and jelly. It would be a start. Anything to take the edge off that hunger his gut told him was radiating through her system.

If his gut was failing him now, he was about to look like the biggest jackass on the planet.

Alyse appeared in the doorway of the kitchen as he finished and was cutting the bread. Those blue eyes grew big. "You're making yourself a sandwich?"

Tristan cleared his throat, grabbing the plate and crossing to her. "It's for you."

Her gasp was barely audible. She took the plate and placed it back on the island where he had made it. "Thank you," she said quietly. "I—I haven't been able to eat anything today."

"And yesterday once you got home?"

She shook her head, her eyes dropping to the floor. "Nothing since your office yesterday."

His gut hadn't been wrong. That was at least something. Although he'd hoped, on some level, he had been projecting feelings of hunger onto her. She took a bite of the sandwich, and something inside him eased. He had no idea what exactly that feeling was and wasn't sure he wanted to know.

He didn't want to stand silently and stare at her while she ate. "Did you and Mark reach a compromise?"

She nodded, finishing a bite before speaking. "Exterior cameras, and I'll allow one of your team to be here, provided they're in the separate wing. There's an apartment over the garage they can use."

Tristan held himself back from pushing. The gentle approach seemed to be what worked best. Mark would've laid out the options, and if this is what they'd decided on, he needed to work within those parameters.

He couldn't help himself. "That might not be enough."

She didn't look at him. "It's all I can give right now."

He stepped nearer but stopped before he got too close for his own comfort. "Will you tell me why?"

Her shrug was a beautifully articulated gesture, practiced

to look easy and graceful. Just like the smile she flashed at him now. "No reason. I just value my privacy."

It was perfectly delivered, and it was a lie. He felt it in that same place where he'd known she was hungry. If she valued her privacy, she wouldn't be splashed across magazines and tabloids from every party under the sun.

He had to remember that. Alyse Peterson was a party girl. She was with people constantly, and even the barest shred of privacy wasn't a reality for someone like her. She was hiding something, and he would need to find out what it was. But for now, she had made her choice, and he had to make the best of it.

"I owe you an apology for my behavior yesterday. I was very rude to you."

Alyse paused, looking down at the plate for a moment. She seemed to be considering her words, but she only said a simple, "Thank you."

Once again, Tristan wanted to push. Instead, he pulled one of his business cards out from his jacket pocket. He rarely gave these out, as they had his own personal number on them.

"This will get you me," he said. "My direct number, if there's anything that you want to tell me."

"Thank you," she said softly again.

Something about the way she said it drew him in, and he pulled back. Tristan left the kitchen without another word. It was probably for the best that she refused the guards. If she hadn't, he might have taken Jared's suggestion yesterday and guarded her himself.

Even now, the idea of leaving someone else so close to her grated on him, despite the unparalleled professionalism of his team. She made him lose his objectivity faster than anyone he'd ever met, and if he was going to protect her, that was dangerous.

He needed to stay away from Alyse Peterson.

Chapter 7

Alyse woke up surrounded by blackness. This darkness wasn't normal. Where was she? She blinked away sleep and tried to focus in the dimness. This was her room, but she still felt disoriented.

She blinked again and looked at the clock. Three a.m. Why the hell was she awake right now? The last two days had been a whirlwind of activity in the house, Zodiac Tactical installing all the necessary cameras and turning the apartment over her garage into what looked like a war room. She was exhausted from having so many people around all the time and having to be the person they needed to see when they had questions.

And especially stressful because everywhere she was, Tristan Zimmerman also seemed to be. They hadn't talked since two days ago in the kitchen, but when they were in the same room…she could feel him. She somehow always knew exactly where he was without having to look.

And when he did look at her…it was so much more intense. Like when their eyes locked, he could see the parts of her no one else could.

Which was ridiculous.

But how else could he have known Alyse needed that sandwich? And she had needed it, although she'd gone to great pains not to let it show.

It was like he was some sort of damned mind reader or something. The way her body reacted to him wasn't helping matters either. Even when she was trying not to look at him, her mind had decided to catalog every single one of his attractive details.

Those details had become even more apparent yesterday when he was out of the suit, instead dressed in a T-shirt and jeans, helping with the final installation of the security system. She'd tried not to stare at the muscles straining his black shirt through the shoulders and arms.

And the tattoos—those had taken her by surprise. A sleeve that wound around his arm from under the T-shirt down to his wrist, exactly where his suit would normally cover it. The pattern was intricate—Alyse caught a glimpse of the Navy SEAL trident and some sort of flower, but she had stopped looking after that. The last thing she wanted was to be caught staring at his arms like she wanted to trail her fingers along that ink.

Or wanted those arms wrapped around her.

She certainly didn't spend extra time studying how good he looked in those jeans.

Shaking off the thoughts of Tristan Zimmerman, she blinked again. She shouldn't have been awake, but she was. What woke her up?

Alyse stared at the ceiling, smoothing out her breath and trying to fade back into relaxation when she heard it. The faint ringing of her cell phone from the kitchen where she always left it. She refused to welcome electronics into her bedroom. She had a hard time relaxing enough to sleep as it was—she didn't want a window to the outside world that could occupy her thoughts.

It was strange, though, because she always left her phone on silent for exactly this reason. It was a part of her ritual. Set the phone to charge in the kitchen and flip it to silent. Then she would make sure she had a glass of water before turning off all the lights on the way up to her bedroom.

Now her ritual included stopping to set the house alarm.

The phone rang again, and her entire body went still. She sat straight up, unable to control the chills running over her skin. She had not heard that ringtone in more than a year.

Because it was the ringtone that she only ever used for two people: her parents.

Alyse was out of the bed and running across the house before she realized that's what she was doing. Stupid, impossible hope welled up in her chest as she crashed into the kitchen. She grabbed the phone and swiped across the screen to answer it. "Hello?"

There was nothing. No response.

And then she heard it. Breathing. Deep and steady.

Her irrational hope shattered and left only horror. She ended the call as fast as she could with shaky fingers.

The phone immediately lit up again with the same ring-tone. On the screen, the number was unlisted, but she knew it was the stalker. He had her phone number and knew her parents' ringtone. Panic clawed its way up her throat.

She tried to turn the sound off on the phone, but it kept ringing. She would disconnect the call, and it would start again a moment later. Nothing stopped it.

She tried to power down the phone to get rid of the song, tears flooding her eyes and making the whole device blurry in front of her.

Alyse fought to keep her breath even. She couldn't panic. That wouldn't help anything, and besides, what could she do?

Call the police and tell them someone called her on her phone?

But now, she had other options. Her eyes flickered to the panic button by the sink. It matched the ones that were now in her bedroom and living room. The minute she touched it, the guard from Zodiac Tactical would be there in seconds, along with another whole team that was on standby if there was an emergency.

But she could not make herself touch that button.

Alyse couldn't let anyone see her like this—no makeup, not dressed, mid-breakdown. Not a stranger, even one who was meant to protect her.

Not to mention the sheer number of people she'd been around lately now that the security team was there. The thought of being near someone else right now made her start to itch, panic rippling over her skin.

This very moment was what she hadn't been able to tell Tristan. The big secret he knew she was keeping, but didn't know what.

That America's Glamour Princess suffered from critical anxiety and acute introversion. That being around others, especially strangers, skyrocketed her panic to the point of becoming incapacitated.

That was why she couldn't stand the thought of having anyone else around her at the house. Even if she needed someone, like now.

The phone went silent, and she sagged in relief. But the screen lit up again. Voice mails. Eight of them. She had no idea what was on them, but her mind was spinning theories and imaginary terror around the sound of those breaths she'd heard.

Mom and Dad's ringtone blared through the silence again, and she jumped so hard she dropped the phone onto the counter.

Alyse stared at it. She couldn't do this all night and couldn't figure out how to stop it, short of destroying her phone. She could already feel the edges of her mind starting to unravel.

What could she do? Maybe if she doused the phone in water, it would short out. She could get a new phone.

A patch of white on the counter snagged her attention. It was the business card Tristan had given her. She had shoved it into the corner and tried to forget about it, not wanting to give him the satisfaction of knowing she'd taken it. She'd even gone so far as wanting him to see it on the counter while he was there.

Tristan was safety. He might regularly piss her off, but he would talk her through this. He would help.

She would try calling him. She swiped to answer the stalker's call and immediately ended it, hoping it would give her a second to access the actual phone. It worked, and she frantically typed in the numbers and hit dial before the stalker called back.

Because he would call back.

She sank down onto the floor of the kitchen as it rang. Tristan answered on the second one. "Alyse? What's wrong?"

"Tristan," she breathed. She anchored herself to his voice, even as her hands started to shake from the adrenaline and she felt like she might drop the phone.

She could hear the beep of the other calls coming in. All from him. The monster.

"Alyse," Tristan said again, voice steady and alert despite it being the middle of the night. "Tell me what's going on."

"My phone," she managed. "He got to my phone. He won't stop. I might have to break it."

"Who has your phone?"

"He does. The stalker. He won't stop calling."

There was silence for a moment before Tristan spoke next. "What's your favorite part of acting?"

Alyse blinked, caught off guard. She answered truthfully before she was even aware of it. "Uh, I get to be someone else. Just for a little while."

Her voice was brittle and stiff. Why did he want to know this?

Tristan sounded intrigued. "That's not what I was expecting, but it sounds nice. And about your modeling? Is there something about that you particularly enjoy?"

Still not understanding the line of questioning, she answered honestly again. "It's easy. You basically sit there and look pretty."

"I doubt that. Holding your body certain ways for long periods can't be too easy."

"Yeah, easy isn't the right word. But it doesn't require conscious thought from me. I get to shut my mind off and do what I'm instructed to do."

"Yeah, that makes sense." A low laugh rolled across the phone line, and she relaxed a little, even despite the beep of another call coming through and going to voice mail.

Alyse realized Tristan's questions had nothing to do with security. He was distracting her, and it was working.

"Ask me more questions," she whispered.

He did. Why did she start acting? Was it something she'd always wanted to do? What was her earliest memory on a film set?

All those questions were simple, because they had similar answers. They all had to do with her parents. An ache settled in her chest.

"Do you know what the worst part of the stalker calling me is?" She asked.

"Tell me."

She cleared her throat. "The ringtone he used. It

belonged to my parents. My brain told me it was them. I ran into the kitchen to grab the phone, actually excited." She sighed. "I can't believe I was stupid enough to think that they were calling."

"Patterns that deeply entrenched don't just go away. It takes time. You love them. You wish they were here. That sound was something your mind associated with them."

Alyse didn't respond. It hurt too much to think about.

"I knew your father," Tristan said softly. "He was a good man."

"I remember meeting you." She leaned back against the counter. "On the film set."

She was choosing not to admit how sexy she found him back then. And now. That was something he didn't need to know.

Tristan talked about Dad and how charismatic he'd been, and the security on the show. Even though she'd heard all of it before, she still liked hearing someone talk about her father. Then Tristan talked about Zodiac Tactical and told her how his code name was Pisces, even though that wasn't his birthday.

"I do like to swim, though," he said. "So that part is accurate."

So were some of the Pisces characteristics. Tristan was definitely independent and wise, just like the stars said a Pisces should be.

"How long has it been since you've eaten?" he finally asked.

Intuitive. That was another Pisces characteristic.

"I don't remember." Alyse thought that she might have had dinner. But she couldn't remember what it was, if anything.

There was no judgment in Tristan's voice, only curiosity. "Are you hungry?"

She didn't think she had been until he said something, but as soon as he did, the gnawing appeared in her stomach. How long had she been ignoring it? "Yeah."

"Put me on speaker and make yourself a sandwich."

It was an order, but at the same time, it didn't feel like one. She was hungry, and it was silly to stay that way just to spite Tristan. Not when he was helping her.

Alyse got up and put the phone on speaker, carefully avoiding switching to the most recent call from the stalker. She hadn't had much chance to get more groceries in the past few days, so she stuck to the simple peanut butter and jelly he had made her.

"How did you get into the security business?" She asked.

Alyse could almost see him shrug through the phone. "It was a natural extension of my skills, you could say. I was a Navy SEAL, so security when I got out made sense. A lot of the Zodiac guys are former military."

"Because you're trained in how to use guns and stuff?"

"That, but other things too. Uncle Sam trained me to notice details that an average civilian wouldn't. Not to mention, focus, discipline, threat awareness. And yeah, guns."

Alyse could hear the smile in his voice.

"You like to take care of people," she said. "You're a protector."

He'd done it for her from the moment they'd met.

He laughed. "I wouldn't say that. I'm just a guy who likes his job."

She didn't believe that for a second. "Why did you leave the Navy?" She took a bite out of the sandwich.

"It was time to move on." There was a heaviness in those words that couldn't be denied, and an unspoken wall came with them. This was not something he was going to talk about.

Alyse continued eating the peanut butter and jelly while

thinking of something else to ask him. Tristan didn't say anything, but just knowing he was there helped. There hadn't been any calls in a few minutes, but when she thought about that ringtone going off again, she didn't want to hang up.

"Are you eating?"

She took the last bite. "I just finished. Thank you. Food has always been…hard."

"Yeah?"

Hard was a completely inaccurate description for her complicated relationship with food. With everything else that had happened tonight, Alyse couldn't bear to delve into that part of herself right now. It had already almost destroyed her once. "Hollywood," she said by way of explanation. "Always have to watch yourself."

He didn't respond to that, though she wanted to know what he was thinking. Right now, she could not imagine his expression, and she was dying to see it.

A few moments of silence passed before the panic started to creep in again. She was tired, but she didn't want to wake up to more haunting phone calls. Or worse.

"Tristan," she whispered.

"Don't hang up," he said, knowing where Alyse was going without her having to say it. "Do you feel safe in your bedroom?"

"I think so. The panic button is right there."

"Okay," he said softly. "Go lie down. Leave the call on while you fall asleep. I'll be here."

"Are you sure?"

"Yes." There was no hesitation in his voice.

She made her way back to her bedroom, trying to ignore the way her eyes jumped to the shadows and the darkness loomed large all around her. "I was about to pour water over the phone before I saw your card."

"I don't blame you," he said. "But don't break it yet. Having it might help us find him."

"Do you think it will help?" She asked as she slipped back into her blankets and laid the phone on the table next to her. It was the first time she'd had a phone in her bedroom in as long as she could remember.

"I do," he answered.

They didn't say anything for a while, but the silence wasn't awkward; it was calm. She felt tired more quickly than she'd expected to, and she realized that it was because she felt safe.

Even though he wasn't physically here, Alyse knew Tristan would do whatever it took to help her. That included staying up and listening to her sleep.

A protector. He might argue it wasn't true, but she knew it was.

They were silent for so long that she started to worry if one of them had ended the call by accident. "Tristan?"

"I'm still here."

Her heart relaxed. He was still there. He would keep his word. She liked the feeling of being protected.

Sleep slowly stole over her, all the exhaustion she had set aside crawling back up to claim her. And that was okay, because she knew he was there. "Tristan."

"I'm not going anywhere. Sleep, Alyse."

The way he said her name made her feel safe.

____

Chapter 8

____

Tristan kept the line open with Alyse long after she fell asleep, the first light of dawn painting the sky out his windows. The moment she'd called, he'd pulled up her house security system on his computer so he could monitor it in real time. He'd also immediately contacted the Zodiac agent working in her garage apartment via text and called in for another two as backup.

When Tristan heard the panic in Alyse's voice, every instinct he had screamed at him to jump in his car and get to her as fast as humanly possible. But he knew that keeping her calm was more important. In cases like this, there was a delicate balance between the safety of the body and the safety of the mind. And he fully planned on protecting both for Alyse.

The call line they had open went dead an hour ago, after she was already asleep, probably from her phone running out of battery. He sent her a text message immediately, letting her know that the call had dropped and that she could call him again if needed, but he hadn't received a reply.

Good. He hoped she wouldn't. He hoped she was asleep.

The terror in her voice had tugged at his soul, and he wanted her to rest.

Once Tristan was sure she was safe and calmed down enough that she wouldn't hyperventilate, he'd actually enjoyed their conversation, even though it was only meant as a distraction. He was not the most outgoing person. They had people in their office, like Mark and Isaac, who did the phone calls and generally related to the clients. But with Alyse, it had felt easy. Natural. He was simply talking to a frightened woman and not America's Glamour Princess.

He much preferred her as Alyse.

Tristan still didn't know why she hadn't hit the panic button rather than call him. She had been in the kitchen right next to one, so why not press it? Joshua, the guard currently stationed in her home, was more than capable.

She hadn't opted for the help she knew was within arm's reach. She had called him.

It was hard to push aside the deep, brutal satisfaction he felt that she had turned to him when she felt unsafe. He didn't want to study it too closely, but he couldn't deny the satisfaction was there.

But why had she called him? At the very least, Joshua could've come in and taken the phone so she didn't have to hear it anymore. Calling him didn't make sense.

Tristan was missing something, but he didn't know what. He had to find it, or it was going to drive him mad. For hours, he turned the pieces in his head. As he kept looking through the regular reports from the teams surrounding Alyse. As he showered. As he drove to her home to meet the others and confirm for himself that everything was in order. But nothing clicked.

Tristan had been in contact with Joshua throughout the night, but as soon as he arrived, he had Joshua walk him around the house and show him the security footage to confirm what they already knew: no one had had access to Alyse's house or property last night. That, at least, was a relief.

When they were finished, Tristan exited the garage to find Outlaw and Nathaniel pulling up to the house. Jared's car was now in the driveway, which meant her manager had arrived while he was with Joshua and they could likely now enter the main house.

Outlaw gave him a look as he stepped out of the car. "Long night?"

"I had hoped it wasn't that obvious."

"Only to me," he said, grinning.

Tristan shook his head. "If you can tell how much I've slept just by looking at me, we've known each other too long."

"We'll get you some coffee. It'll make the day less painful," he said with a laugh.

"I'll be better if we catch this bastard."

Jared answered the door like he had the day before, not bothering with pleasantries. He pushed it wide and let them file into the foyer. Tristan wasn't offended. He knew they were there to do a job and didn't need to engage in small talk to be effective. "Here's the phone the calls from the stalker came in on. Alyse will join us momentarily."

He almost wished she wouldn't. After last night, he would rather she rest, and he had no doubt what they were about to find on this phone wasn't going to comfort her.

Tristan handed Nathaniel the phone. He could probably do more with the phone at his nerd station in the office, but they would try here first.

"It's dead," Nathaniel said. "I'll get it charged up so we can take a look."

Jared sighed as he sat on one of the couches. "Any ideas what this is about off the top of your head?"

"Not until I can look at the internal hardware." Nathaniel

plugged the phone into a portable battery. "From the outside, I don't see any blatant tampering. But controlling a device at that level remotely is no joke. He should not have been able to select an individual ringtone or prevent it from being shut off."

Tristan crossed his arms over his chest. "So proximity wasn't a concern?"

Nathaniel shrugged. "Probably not recently. I don't think the perp was anywhere near Alyse last night."

"But…?" He could hear it in his tone.

"But if it wasn't remote access, then our asshole friend has been near her phone long enough to make some changes to it. Then it was just a matter of when he wanted to fuck with her."

"Which would mean that he got close to her. Close enough to take the phone and put it back without her knowing," Jared said.

Tristan nodded. "If that's the case, it could mean that she knows him."

The man looked pale, and he didn't blame him. "Let's hope that it's something remote."

"Good morning," Alyse said from the doorway.

He turned to look at her. They all did.

She was perfect, everything about her pristine and untouchable. If he hadn't experienced her terror with her a few hours ago, he wouldn't have believed it had happened at all.

No one should be perfect after what she'd just been through, but she was. Her hair was in a tidy bun, body dressed in a conservative suit that was tailored to perfection, and heels so sharp they could be used as a weapon. Stunning in every way.

But cold.

She sat next to Jared, posture stiff, the same way it had

been during their first meeting. "Thank you for coming so quickly."

He swallowed his need to muss her. "Of course."

There was no sign of the woman he'd spoken to last night. That woman had a soul and fear and a tender heart that ached with loss. One tiny piece of the puzzle fell into place in his head. The woman sitting in front of him was Alyse, but armored.

Her appearance was one of the few things that she could control in this situation, and she was using it to her advantage. To make others believe that she was strong and unaffected by all this—to make *herself* believe that.

Being untouchable was better than being vulnerable. Tristan didn't like the mask, but he recognized why she thought she needed it. It gave her distance. For now, he wouldn't push it. It wasn't the time.

On the coffee table, the phone chirped, signaling it had enough charge to come alive. "What first?" Nathaniel asked.

"There are voice mails?" he asked.

He typed something on his laptop, the phone already connected to it. "Yeah. Eleven."

Tristan glanced at Alyse, but she showed no sign of being afraid of what they might hear. "Play them."

At first, there was only active silence or the faint white noise of someone being on the line but not speaking. That didn't last long. Soon, there was breathing—long and slow and deep. It lasted for what felt like minutes before there was just one word, moaned. "Alyse."

She didn't move, but Tristan saw her flinch out of the corner of his eye. The voice mail ended. It wasn't long. He'd wanted to call back as soon as possible.

The next one made it clear through the moans and breaths exactly what the fucker was doing. Three more voice mails of just that, the slick sound of movement growing louder and faster as he jerked himself off.

Tristan closed his eyes, fighting the urge to smash the phone so Alyse wouldn't have to hear any more of this violation. And that's what it was. An absolute violation of her. If they caught this man, he would be lucky to make it to the police intact. One look at Outlaw told him he was thinking exactly the same thing.

Alyse's voice made him jump. "I love you."

His eyes snapped to her, and he realized that she hadn't spoken. Her eyes were wide, lips parted, staring at the phone on the table. It was a recording of her being played. The words repeated.

"I love you. I love you. I love you."

The moaning grew louder behind her recorded words, and he looked back at Alyse. This time, her gaze was aimed straight at him.

Tristan could see the sickness there and the panic. The only thing he wanted was to get her out of there so she didn't have to listen to this filth. The voice mail cut off as the loudest groan yet sounded.

Enough. "Skip the—"

The phone jumped to the next voice mail before Nathaniel could stop it.

"Alyse."

The man's voice echoed through the room. He sounded calmer now that his *playtime* was over. He was going to have Nathaniel stop the messages, but this was different. The voice was almost soothing, and he could imagine it being charming under different circumstances.

"Do you see what you do to me?" the voice asked. "Just the sound of your voice is enough."

Alyse shuddered. When Tristan found this man, he was going to put his head through a fucking wall.

"I know you, Alyse. You won't believe me. You won't think that I do, but you're wrong. I understand you. I'm the only one who does. And I will always be here for you, Alyse. You never have to worry about that. There's nothing that could make me leave you, Alyse."

Even Tristan was flinching at him saying her name so possessively over and over.

In her lap, Alyse's hands flickered. They flared outward and curled into fists. He'd seen that movement before—it was a tell. Her face was cool and impassive, only the slightest bit of tension around her lips. But her hands were giving her away.

In that deep, animalistic place where he seemed to sense her needs, he knew that she was about to break. He didn't blame her for it. This would be a lot for anyone.

"I can't even stand to be away from you for a night, you know," the voice continued, amused. "I couldn't bear it. I needed you near me—needed your scent. Do you know how far I had to go? Your salon wasn't easy to find. But they keep good records." A small chuckle that made his gut clench, and a deep, audible inhale. "Your hair is even softer than I imagined it would be. And it smells so good. I keep it right here."

Tristan's instincts snapped. One more word and Alyse was going to crumble. He gestured to Nathaniel, and he shut off the voice mail.

"Alyse." He stood and stepped across the room and stood far, far too close to her knees. Tristan needed to be in her space. "Since I've had a long night of tracking everything regarding your case, would you mind making me something to eat?"

Nobody said anything in the middle of his obnoxious request. Alyse blinked then stood, barely able to rise without brushing against him.

"Yes."

He hated the way her voice sounded small. He'd much rather have her pissed at him than cut so low by what she was experiencing.

As she led the way out of the room, Tristan shot a look at Outlaw. He nodded once, acknowledging that he knew what he was doing. He'd get Alyse out of the room so they could continue working on the phone out of earshot.

When he entered the kitchen, Alyse was robotically pulling a plate from one of the cupboards, and he saw her grab the now nearly empty jar of peanut butter. Tristan sighed. "You don't actually need to make me a sandwich. That wasn't why I asked."

"I know," she said quietly. "It's for me. You said it to get me out of the room."

Her voice was still too stiff, too formal.

"Seems I owe you more than one debt." She spread peanut butter on the bread. "Staying on the line last night, and somehow being able to tell that I wasn't handling that very well."

"You hired me to protect you, Alyse. I was doing my job. Then and now." He wasn't about to explain to her the urgent and nearly feral need that drove that protective instinct. Frankly, he wasn't even sure that he could explain it. But it was there all the same.

Tristan took a step forward so they faced each other across the kitchen island. "This man is escalating quickly. I think it would be a good idea to notify the authorities about the situation so that they know, and they can possibly monitor the neighborhood."

There. Her hands fluttered, and the knife shook. Her hands were a tell he could use. A barely visible chink in that perfect armor. Her breath too. It was coming a little too fast. The thought of the police made her more stressed, not less.

"I can't," she said. "That would mean more people I need

to talk to and interact with, and that is…not an option right now."

He took a slow, deep breath, putting aside the urgency he felt. She seemed to respond to gentle and solid logic, so that was what he would use. "Having more protection around you right now is a good thing. The more people around you with your safety in mind, the harder the stalker will have to work to get to you."

She put down the knife, and Tristan didn't miss the way it clattered against the plate as it shook. "You know who I am. And as you made it abundantly clear when we met, you know my social profile. I am surrounded by people every second of every day that I leave this house—"

She took a breath, cutting herself off, then restarted. "I find the idea of multiple people around me stressful and exhausting. My home is the only place where I can be alone. Please respect that."

He stared at her, barely able to keep his face from showing his surprise.

Alyse Peterson was an introvert.

America's Glamour Princess, the woman splashed on every magazine and who attended every party, was someone who didn't enjoy people. Clearly, he needed to brush up on his skills in reading people, because based on everything he had seen, he wouldn't have predicted that.

Tristan filtered everything he knew about her against this new revelation. He'd made too many assumptions about her based on reports from others. He had taken her press report at face value.

That was a fucking rookie mistake, at best.

She wasn't being difficult about security by insisting no one stay with her in her own house—she'd been trying to protect her sanity.

He opened his mouth to ask her about it when Jared stepped into the kitchen. "Your man found something."

Alyse followed Tristan back into the living room, and every inch of him was aware of her presence. "What'd you get?"

"Malware," Nathaniel said. "It was placed in manually, so he did have physical access to the phone, but it wasn't recent. He only decided to turn it on last night."

Tristan sighed. "That's good and bad."

"Why?" Alyse asked.

"The fact that he had access to you at all is concerning, but it's good that it wasn't recent. It lets us know that none of our security has been breached."

Nathaniel took over for him. "But this kind of software isn't stuff you toy around with. It's serious, and if he can do this, we need to be extremely careful. I might be able to trace it back to him, but it will take time."

"What's the next course of action?" Jared asked.

"Without law enforcement?" Tristan asked, looking at Alyse. She nodded, and his stomach dropped, but he met her eyes steadily. "We stay the course while Nathaniel tracks the software, and we hope that the stalker doesn't realize that we're on his trail."

It was all they could do.

Chapter 9

It had been a week since the phone calls, and things had faded into a new kind of normal. The men from Zodiac most familiar with her case—the guy they called Outlaw, and Nathaniel the tech wizard—had been assigned to Alyse for almost the whole week.

Keeping her anxiety in check was nearly impossible. She could barely sleep, and she probably wouldn't have eaten at all if her mind hadn't imagined Tristan Zimmerman's voice telling her to make food.

And so, she managed to choke down food.

Having a constant guard presence in her house was a painful trade-off. On the one hand, Alyse knew she was safer. She knew if the phone thing happened again—which it wouldn't because Nathaniel had made sure of it—she wouldn't have to freak out. If something happened on the grounds, they'd be there immediately.

But it came at a cost, as she'd known it would. Now, even at home, she felt like she had to be *on*. Like she needed to perform the character of Alyse Peterson—glamour princess— in case the guards needed to be called.

There was no relief from being who everyone else thought she was.

Almost ironically, the time when Alyse felt most herself was when Tristan called her in the evenings to check in. Which he did every night.

She'd grown to expect that call, and her chest eased when she saw his name on the screen. Whenever they talked, she had the urge to ask him if it was a service he provided for all his clients. But she never asked. Zodiac Tactical was a huge firm—there was no way he called every client they protected every night to talk. Asking him about it would just make it weird.

Alyse didn't want it to be weird. And she didn't want it to stop either.

He somehow knew she needed the daily comfort of his presence. Hearing his voice over the phone—and the fact that he made sure that she'd eaten at the end of every day—was soothing in a way she couldn't quite explain. It didn't completely erase her anxiety, but it at least helped reset her levels so she could function the next day.

Her extra security had also followed her on set. Her fellow actors had been curious about it, but no one had asked many questions. Which was good because she didn't want to talk about it.

Alyse could still hear his voice in her head. Those voice messages he'd left still made her sick to her stomach.

A rap on the door to her trailer made her jump, but it was only a production assistant, telling her they were ready for her on the set. Outlaw—Mark—was with her today, and he fell into step behind her. The final scene of the day was simple, just a conversation between her and Kenneth White, the actor playing Alyse's romantic interest.

Mark always drew eyes when he was with her. He was tall and broad and nearly as intimidating as Tristan was. A good shadow to have when you had a stalker, she supposed. She could feel the stares drift toward them as they walked.

They hadn't heard anything more from the stalker. There had been no more phone calls or voice mails. No attempts to get to her at the house. Nothing. Alyse harbored a secret hope that maybe he'd lost interest. Nathaniel had blocked him from accessing her phone, and all the guards and cameras blocked him from getting close to her physically.

Alyse certainly didn't want anyone else to have to deal with this monster, but it would be a huge sigh of relief if he decided that she'd become too difficult a target to pursue.

Kenneth waved as he stepped out of his own trailer. A new and rising star, he had a burly security guy of his own. He smiled as he fell into step beside Alyse. Unlike her, Kenneth was exactly who everybody thought he was. Absolutely genuine and bursting at the seams with energy and smiles that could charm the devil himself.

"Still have Batman at your back?" he whispered, gesturing to Mark.

She tried to laugh and fell short. "Yeah. Trying to discourage any stalkers."

His grimace was almost comedic. "Stalkers suck."

"You've had one?"

He shoved his hands into the pockets of his costume jeans. "No, but I've heard the stories. I just don't get it. Can't quite wrap my head around how those people's minds work."

"And we're actors," She said, forcing a smile. "It's our job to do that very thing."

Kenneth laughed. A big belly laugh like she had just landed the world's most perfect joke. "Exactly. Of all people, we should be able to at least try to get into their heads, right? But I don't think I'll ever understand that level of weird."

Another production assistant pulled him away, and she took a breath. She'd fully poured herself into filming this last week. Partially because the first week on a new film was inherently stressful, and partially because she desperately needed the distraction.

The first week was so important. You were trying to meld with a brand-new crew, and for her, she had to uphold the Alyse Peterson brand. That meant being even more over the top and shiny than she normally needed to be. Jared helped when he could, but there were so many new faces every day that he couldn't be everywhere all at once.

And all of them were expecting her to smile and be perfectly poised. All of them would be disappointed if she didn't live up to her image. Now more than ever, everything had to be perfect. She couldn't let the situation affect anything about her life.

She could imagine the news stories swirled together. *America's Glamour Princess is not who we thought she was! We have an exclusive interview with someone who knows details of her stalker. But not only that, her secret life! If Alyse Peterson prefers sweats to heels, what's next, will the sun stop rising? Come inside and read about the real Alyse and help us decide if she's really worth the attention of this stalker. Or anyone, for that matter!*

The way her mind twisted it was dramatic, but Alyse had firsthand knowledge of the way others' careers had suffered when their image shattered over something small.

Her image and the Peterson name were the biggest things her parents had left her, and she would protect them at all costs. Stalker or not.

She pushed the stalker out of her mind as they started the scene. It went smoothly but took longer and involved a lot more physical exertion than she'd expected. By the time it was finished, she was exhausted.

Alyse was glad they were on set in LA and she had the benefit of sleeping in her own bed after long days like this. In fact, the idea of a bath sounded nice. She'd enjoy a soak until she heard the phone ring and got to talk to Tristan before relaxing into a deep sleep.

She quickly changed her clothes, and Mark escorted her to today's car. It was one of the rotating circuit of cars that she'd been driven in since they'd hired Zodiac.

A different Zodiac Tactical employee pulled up, driving the vehicle they'd be riding in. Zodiac never left the car that she was driven in unaccompanied. The driver got out while Mark got in, and then she opened the door for Alyse.

While Mark drove her home, the woman left behind would sweep the perimeter of the set for any new signs of forced entry or indication the stalker had tried to get to her today. And tomorrow, they would do it again with a different car, driving a different route, so that no one could spot their pattern and catch them off guard.

It was a lot of work, but Zodiac Tactical was the best because they paid attention to that sort of detail. And because Tristan Zimmerman demanded excellence from everyone on his team.

"How was filming today?" Mark asked from the front seat.

She liked Mark. He seemed very easygoing. Especially when compared to Tristan, who somehow managed to have a stern and brooding expression at all times. But Mark was charming, and even though Alyse didn't like having people around, he'd managed to make her feel at ease enough that he was growing on her.

"Long," she said. "As usual."

He chuckled softly. "Do you have plans for dinner?"

Alyse met his eyes in the rearview mirror. Mark had never crossed any lines that she found inappropriate.

Still, worry knotted in her stomach. "No. Why?"

His eyes crinkled with a smile she couldn't see in the small mirror. "Because you know Tristan is going to ask you about it. I imagine he's getting bored with the same answer every night."

"Oh," she breathed, relief flowing over her like water. Alyse had been eating the same thing every night, but there was no way Mark could know that. "How did you know?"

"He and I were both at the office last night when he made the call. I heard him ask." He glanced out the windows and back to her again. "You should have some fun with him. Tell him you're having chocolate-covered crickets or something equally ridiculous and see if he can keep his cool without scolding you. Or showing up at your house with something better."

In spite of herself, she smiled. The image of Tristan arriving at her house with bags of food, absolutely exasperated at her meal, was a sight that she would enjoy. "Why would I do that?"

"Why not?" he asked. "He's fun to toy with when you get the chance, and you've got plenty of those."

"I don't want to distract him."

Mark laughed again. "Trust me, Tristan is rarely distracted."

"Still," she said. "I don't think he'd welcome that kind of teasing from me."

"I think we both know that he'd welcome a lot from you, Alyse."

Heat crept up her cheeks in a blush. Alyse couldn't deny she was attracted to Tristan, but she thought she had done everything in her power to disguise that fact. No words came to her mind in response, so she just stared out the window, trying to think of anything to say that could make this less embarrassing. She should be used to someone wanting a quick one-night stand with her.

"It's just—" Mark cut himself off and blew out a breath. "I've never seen him like this. He's usually detached from our cases. But with your case, he's all in, and honestly, I think it's good for him. I didn't mean to imply anything else."

Oh. Alyse stretched her hands against her legs. Amazing how a little context changed everything. One bit of insight and what was embarrassing was now…endearing. If it was good for him, for the sake of his friend, she could play along. That was the only reason.

Or at least, that was what she was going to tell herself.

"What's his least favorite food?" She asked Mark.

"He'll eat anything," he said. "The only time I've seen him not— Fuck. Jesus."

The car stopped abruptly, and she jerked against the seat belt. "What's happening?"

Mark already had his phone to his ear. "We have a situation at Alyse's gate. You need to get here. *Now.*"

Alyse focused out the window, and suddenly, the world was falling out from underneath her. Her neighborhood was circled with ten-foot walls, and just outside the gate, two banners were now hanging on either side. Each one was at least six feet, lit up with shining spotlights from below. And the images were her.

The pictures were obscured with enough pixelation to make the average person question, but she knew they were her. Alyse recognized her face. And her body. One image was from yesterday. The clothes she wore as a costume during a party scene on the set.

And the other… Nausea swam in her gut. In the other, she was naked. In a bathtub. The water and pixels didn't obscure much, if anything. The last time she had taken a bath was in Paris. And she had just thought about taking another one.

People were standing in front of the banners, gawking at them. Flashes let her know that they were taking pictures, and in minutes, these would be all over the internet.

Her. Like that.

Alyse was going to be sick.

"Mark," she said.

"I'm on it," he said, his phone still to his ear.

The horn blared, and people moved as he drove. The man at the gate waved them through with barely a glance, not knowing which car it was. She felt faint.

The stalker had seen her—*filmed* her—in a moment when she'd thought she was alone and safe. Had he been thinking about these pictures when he'd touched himself on those horrible voice mails?

Alyse threw up right there in the car.

Mark drove faster than he had any right to through her neighborhood toward her house, and he spoke the only words that could make her feel any better right now.

"Hang in there, Alyse. Tristan is on his way."

Chapter 10

Mark's call came in while he was on a conference chat regarding security for a tech firm. The second Tristan saw Mark's number, he knew something was wrong. That deep, animal instinct suddenly went sharp—something bad had happened.

Something with Alyse.

Over the last few days that he hadn't seen her, he'd convinced himself this connection he had with her was all a fluke. That it was him being overworked and weakness was seeping through. Rule #1 in this business: you didn't catch feelings for a client. Any client.

Even clients as beautiful and as vulnerable as Alyse Peterson.

But as hard as he'd tried, she wouldn't get out of his head. He'd stayed at the office after hours, working his brain into exhaustion on other cases to try to distract himself. And when that didn't seem to work, he'd hit the gym twice as long and hard as he normally did to try to exhaust his body.

Tristan still found his attention wandering to her case. To

her. Wondering if she was doing all right in between their nightly phone calls.

Calls he knew he shouldn't make. But every night, he found himself dialing her number, eager to hear the sound of her voice and know she felt safe before she went to sleep. If she felt safe, he felt better.

There wasn't a chance that he wasn't going to take this call. He turned the meeting over to another Zodiac employee and stepped away, sliding his finger across the screen of his cell. "Outlaw."

His voice was tense. "We have a situation at Alyse's gate. You need to get here. *Now.*"

"I'll be right there." Tristan hung up and turned back to the table where Nathaniel and a few others were still on the video chat. "I apologize. There is an emergency situation that I need to address with another client. Can we continue this tomorrow?"

"Of course." He didn't wait to disconnect the call.

"Let's go," he said to Nathaniel. "Grab your gear."

Within minutes, they were in Tristan's car and racing toward Alyse's house. Mark texted updates to Nathaniel as they drove toward the house.

"Jesus," he said under his breath.

"What?"

"He put up giant posters of Alyse outside the gates to her community. One is scandalous and barely covered, the other is from the set yesterday."

Fury burned through his gut. This was an attempt to humiliate and frighten Alyse. It was a well-aimed blow that would cause her to retreat inside herself more.

They hadn't heard from the stalker in over a week, and although Tristan hadn't held out much hope that he was gone, he'd hoped it meant the escalation was slowing.

Nathaniel showed him footage of what the stalker had

done as they got closer to Alyse's neighborhood. Definitely an escalation.

"How did he manage to do that without the guard seeing?"

He heard Nate typing. "Mark is interviewing the guard now. And—" His voice cut off as they rounded the corner. Oh shit.

A huge crowd of people was outside the gate, all gawking at the pictures Mark and a couple of the neighborhood gate guards were trying to take down. But it didn't matter. Too many people had already seen them, and the media had been called.

It wasn't every day that a nearly nude picture of America's Glamour Princess showed up larger-than-life and available for anyone to see.

Flashing lights painted the scene, and the cops were trying to disperse the crowd. But Tristan still saw people recording on their phones and taking pictures. This would be all over television and internet soon, if it wasn't already. Their protection of Alyse was about to get much more public.

Mark waved them past and nodded at him as Nathaniel ducked out of the car to help with crowd control. They would handle the situation here while he checked on Alyse. Tristan was just glad he had called him right away and wasn't judging him for whatever weird thing Alyse and he had going on between them.

Tristan didn't stop until he was in the driveway. He was the only Zodiac employee who had the code to Alyse's front door. She hadn't wanted his men coming in and out of the house without her knowledge. But he used it now, rushing in without knocking.

"Alyse?"

She didn't answer, but he found her in the living room. She was sitting stiffly on the sofa, still dressed to the nines from arriving home after work, and it didn't look like she had a hair out of place. Only a couple of lights were on, lending a dim glow to the room.

Tristan watched her for a moment. She was wearing high heels, and her hair was back in a sleek ponytail. Skinny jeans that had been meticulously tailored for her long legs and a flowing shirt that emphasized how slight her frame was. Her armor had been perfect even before she had left the set, and it was still perfect now.

Her phone was in her hand, and even from across the room, he could hear it buzzing with alert after alert. Tristan was sure it was postings on social media and phone calls from people both kind and predatory. People offering condolences and asking for interviews and reactions.

He knew she had to be upset, but she didn't look it. Instead, she looked cold almost. Like nothing could touch her.

"Are you all right?" He asked.

He wanted to reach out and touch her—to offer her some kind of comfort. But the stiffness of her posture and the blankness of her face didn't allow for that. She didn't want comfort, and she would not accept it.

She kept looking at her phone, simply scrolling through whatever was on the screen. "I'm fine. It's just photos. No one was hurt. It could have been so much worse."

Her voice was empty.

Tristan sat on the coffee table directly across from her. He wasn't touching her but was too close for her to ignore. "Just because it was photos doesn't mean that no one was hurt."

More buzzing from her phone, and she looked down at it again. "I called Jared. He'll be here soon."

"Good. We're taking care of the situation at the gate, and there's nothing else to do before he gets here. Why don't you change into something more comfortable and try to relax a little? We'll take care of this."

Her hand flared slightly at his suggestion of changing clothes. If he hadn't been watching her, he would have missed the tension. "I'll be all right as I am. Thank you for your concern."

Her voice was thick with tension. She obviously wasn't all right as she was, but pointing that out would just stress her out further.

Slowly, Tristan shifted himself onto the couch next to her. She didn't react in any way. No tension to tell him to back off, but also no encouragement to move any closer.

"I'm sorry to have to tell you this," he said, "but we no longer have an option regarding law enforcement."

She sighed, her head hanging slightly, though her eyes were still locked to the damn phone. "I was afraid of that."

"The nude picture is a sex crime. But it's not only that, it's the fact that the other picture was taken yesterday. That means the stalker was closer than acceptable."

She nodded.

"I have a friend named Callum Webb. He works with a special task force in law enforcement called Omega Sector. This isn't his normal area, but he owes me a favor, and there's no one I would trust more with this kind of case."

Her fingers fluttered again. "Okay."

This time, her voice betrayed her. She couldn't pretend this wasn't devastating for her, and he could no longer stop himself from acting on his instinct.

Just like with the voice mails, she was at the point of fracturing. Tristan reached out and drew her to him gently, and to his unending relief, she didn't pull away.

Another small gasp of breath was the only sound she made as he wrapped his arms around her. Tristan knew this wasn't professional, but he didn't care. It was like he'd had sand in his shoes, a friction that he couldn't explain, and caring for Alyse soothed it.

She held herself stiff, then she exhaled and leaned into him just a fraction. The smallest concession, but it felt like a victory worthy of shouting from the fucking rooftops. That she trusted him enough to relax even an inch was enough.

But at the sound of the front door opening, she pulled away, all of her tension back.

Jared strode into the room, face tight. "Are you all right?"

Alyse smiled wanly. "I'm fine."

Her phone buzzed in her hand, and her eyes immediately shot back to it. Before Tristan could even blink, Jared was across the room and pulling it from her hand.

"Let me take care of that," he said, voice gentle. "Now isn't the time to fall back into old patterns."

Old patterns?

Alyse didn't protest, though he saw her move her hands absently, like she was itching to hold the phone again.

"And for the love of God, Alyse, you're still in high heels? Get out of those and relax."

"I can't." Her voice was calm but firm.

"Alyse," Jared said, and he could tell immediately that it was an argument they'd had before.

She shook her head. "I just… I can't, Jared."

The man looked tired, and he didn't blame him. Handling this for her had to be exhausting, and Tristan could tell he cared deeply about Alyse. "Will you at least try to rest? It's been a hell of a week."

She hesitated. "You'll wake me up if something happens? If you…find anything?" Her eyes flicked to his.

"Of course."

She headed out of the room before stopping at the door and looking back at him. For the first time since he entered, he saw some kind of feeling on her face. "Thank you, Tristan."

"Any time, Alyse." He had never meant any words more.

Her footsteps faded into the rest of the house, and Jared sighed. He was working on the phone, and the buzzing eventually went silent. "Notifications?" Tristan asked.

"Only about a hundred thousand," he said. "I wish I were kidding."

"I'm sure you're not."

He shook his head. "It took her years to be able to let go of all this and not check in every second to see what people were saying about her, and she's been doing so much better. I'm not going to let this fucker undo all the work she's done."

There was that grinding reminder that Alyse was a famous person who loved attention, even if she was an introvert or shy. Clearly, she loved it if it had taken her so long to give up something as superficial as media about herself.

It left a bad taste in his mouth, and Tristan found himself once again questioning his pull toward her.

He couldn't stop the words. "Is she so vain that she needs that kind of validation all the time?"

Jared's eyes narrowed until they were slits. "Maybe you shouldn't believe things just because you read them in the media. I'd thought you'd gotten to know Alyse a little better than that."

Tristan didn't say anything. He couldn't. The words he'd let slip were out of line, and they both knew it. They were a product of his own frustration and his inability to understand this thing that was springing to life between he and Alyse. Tristan wished he could take them back.

"You're right," he said. "I'm sorry."

A knock at the front door interrupted them, and Tristan let both Mark and Nathaniel inside. They didn't wait to start giving him the report.

"The cops have taken care of the crowds, and the posters are being taken back to the office. We were careful," Mark said.

By that, he meant they had done their best to preserve any DNA data the stalker may have left behind. "Anything else?"

"Yeah," Nathaniel says. "I'll show you on the footage."

On the screens in the over-garage apartment they'd customized, Nathaniel pulled up the footage from the remote cameras they'd placed at the edge of the community. They'd only installed a couple there. They'd been more concerned with direct threats to Alyse's person and home than the neighborhood in general.

On the footage, a dark figure crept along the wall. At no point did he expose his face to the camera. He was so stealthy, so smooth, the guard at the gate didn't even turn around. He never had a reason to. Tristan could tell from the man's movement that he was making little to no sound.

He hung the posters in the slimmest of blind spots and planted the battery-operated lights before sneaking away again. The lights came on after he was already long gone.

Nathaniel was glaring at the footage. "There were no strange cars, according to the guard, and I checked every camera angle I could find. Nothing."

Fuck. "Does that mean—"

"Yes." He didn't let Tristan finish.

The stalker walked. He didn't bother to use a car. He evaded every one of their cameras, which he had no reason to know were there.

The stalker had hacked their system.

Chapter 11

A couple hours later, Tristan opened the door of Alyse's home and shook hands with Callum Webb. He'd known the federal agent for a lot of years. Had worked closely with him about a year ago on a case involving undercover work to take down some terrorists.

Zodiac Tactical had helped Omega Sector, the special task force Callum worked in, on more than one occasion. Now it was time for him to help them.

Callum had been courted by the FBI early for his brilliant mind. He was unparalleled at reading people and getting into the heads of criminals. It made him an incredibly valuable asset for profiling the kinds of people he needed to track down.

Which made him Tristan's new best friend. He wanted his insight on how he could better protect Alyse. This stalker seemed to be several steps ahead of them at all times, and that needed to end.

He was grateful Callum had come so soon. "Good to see you."

He smiled. "You too, man. I wish it were under better circumstances."

"Considering we live in the same city, you'd think we would see each other more," Tristan said.

"We'll have to work on that when the case is over."

I sighed. "Right. Want the breakdown?"

"Go ahead."

Tristan led him into the living room as he summarized the details of Alyse's case, noting the way his eyebrows rose when he told him exactly whose house he was standing in. It had seemed better to leave that detail out before he arrived, just in case. The media getting a hold of a story that Alyse was talking to the FBI would only make things blow up bigger—and tip off the stalker to their actions.

"If we'd known you were calling me in for Alyse Peterson, I would've had to fight off my coworkers to keep them from taking over the case."

Tristan gritted his teeth. "Trust me, there's been no shortage of Zodiac employees volunteering to take bodyguarding shifts."

Callum chuckled. "According to everything I know about her, she's very much the social butterfly. That's tough. Has to make your job harder."

Maybe you shouldn't believe things just because you read them in the media.

"She's not so bad."

Mark stepped into the room and shook Callum's hand. "Not bad? Honestly, compared to some of the clients we've protected, Miss Peterson is a dream. Kind and thoughtful. Goes out of her way to be helpful."

Callum tilted his head in interest. He was going to analyze Alyse when he met her—he did it to everyone. But he liked to get an idea of what he might see. And Tristan tried to pretend he wasn't hanging on Outlaw's every word, but he was—he knew Mark hadn't complained about Alyse, but Tristan didn't know he thought so highly of her.

"So, not a party girl?" Callum asked.

Mark chuckled. "I can't imagine Alyse being comfortable at a party of any kind. She shuts down when she's around people, like going on autopilot."

That was almost exactly what Jared had laid into him about a couple of hours ago, and what he'd seen glimpses of over the past week. There seemed to be two versions of Alyse, but only one of them was real.

And it wasn't the party girl glamour princess.

He'd wanted that to be the real her. That version was so much easier to categorize and ignore. To mark as a client and keep his distance.

Even when they'd been talking each night on the phone, Tristan had refused to accept her as more than the glamour princess. Because the quiet, vulnerable woman he spoke to daily—the one Mark, not surprisingly, called thoughtful and kind—was on his mind way too much. He was drawn to her in a way he didn't understand and couldn't ignore.

And if that was the real her, Tristan was in fucking trouble.

Nathaniel came in with his laptop and got right down to business after a quick greeting with Callum. "This guy is good," he said. "Really good. He hasn't left any traces we can follow, knows his way around encryption and security systems."

Callum nodded. "He was also smart enough to plant a microcamera and get nude photos of her in Paris without getting caught."

"He did," Tristan confirmed.

"As bad as that is," Nathaniel said, "that's not my main concern. The fact that he managed to get a picture of her from the set yesterday is. This guy seems to have ports into all the different pockets of Alyse's life—bad news for her and us."

He heard the telltale click of high heels a few seconds before the woman in question entered the room. She was wearing the same clothes he'd seen her in earlier, but her makeup had been refreshed and she once again looked perfect. She smiled charmingly at Callum.

Her armor was intact.

For the first time, Tristan recognized it for what it was. The more perfect the image, the further unraveled she was. And looking at her, the glossy surface stiff and static, Alyse was hiding everything she was feeling.

Callum stood, and she shook his hand. "Very nice to meet you, Miss Peterson."

She smiled a dazzling smile—the one cameras loved. "Call me Alyse. I'm sure you'll know me well enough to be on a first-name basis after all of this."

Callum smiled too. "Very well. I'm Callum."

"Tristan told me about you," she said. "I hope you'll be able to help."

"I'll do my best." Callum took his seat once more.

Tristan knew him well enough to know that even though he would be the consummate professional, he was more than impressed by Alyse. Who wouldn't be? Even in the midst of this crisis, she was coming across as the epitome of shimmering charm.

Once again, Tristan wished this were the real version of her because that would mean she wasn't terrified and barely holding it together.

He'd rather her be pouty and cranky and messy and less careful with her words. He wished she'd lay down her armor and let him take care of her.

She took a seat in one of the armchairs where she could see all of them and also control the way they saw her while

Nathaniel ran Callum through the evidence they'd found. She kept her cool as Nathaniel played the surveillance footage from both Paris and earlier tonight. She kept her composure even when those sick voice mails were played.

"Paris was the first time you had any idea he was watching you?" Callum asked.

"Yes. I had no idea before that. Do you think it's been longer?"

Callum looked grim. "I do. I think he's been watching you for a long time. The depth of his obsession is not something that can be developed over merely a couple of weeks."

"Oh," Alyse said, her face going pale. "I guess that makes sense."

"Do you recognize the voice? Maybe it's a fan or somebody you've met before?"

"I suppose it's possible I've met him at an autograph signing, but I can't be sure." She shrugged one shoulder. "I meet hundreds of people at signings, but no one stood out to me as someone who would do this."

"I understand," Callum said. "But I encourage you to memorize the voice now, so if you hear it again, you can tell us."

She nodded.

"I'll be digging further into the evidence. Zodiac Tactical is giving me everything they have on him, and my team and I will be working up a full profile on him, which should help. But this is a very specific kind of escalation."

"How so?" she asked.

Tristan watched her hands. They were steady for the moment.

"He's illustrating his reach. He wants to show you that he can get to you in multiple times and places. The pictures he chose to display weren't random. One from a moment that should have been yours alone, and one from work where you have no choice but to be. He's leaving voice mails to show you he can infiltrate your space. All of this, he's doing from a distance, and he wants you to know that he can do it whenever he wants."

Her fingers weren't steady anymore, but she wrapped them together to stop them from flaring. "What happens now?"

"Now, he tries to show you that he can access your space physically. We might have some time since this stunt with the posters is big enough that he knows he'll have to lie low. Plus, this pandemonium will satisfy his urge to insert himself into the center of your life, but it won't last. The next step will be getting close to you, because each thing he tries isn't enough to scratch the itch."

They were all quiet for a moment, taking in the ramifications.

"Okay," she finally whispered.

Callum stood up. His gaze met Tristan's as he did, and he looked at Alyse again. "I'll be in touch tomorrow with a more thorough profile."

Tristan stood also, nodding. "Thank you. Meanwhile, we'll be revamping Alyse's protection protocols."

He already knew what needed to be done.

He inclined his head toward Mark and Nathaniel. "Will you both make sure that Callum has everything that he needs to finish the profile? He could use your insight since you both have been here for the whole case."

"Sure thing," Mark said.

"It was wonderful to meet you, Alyse," Callum said, extending his hand.

She shook it delicately. "You too, Callum. Thank you very much for your help."

"No thanks are needed," he said before shaking her hand and leaving the room.

Now that everyone was gone, Alyse was looking much more fragile. She was struggling to keep her armor around her. "Why me?"

"What?"

"That's the question I keep asking myself. Why me? What did I do to draw this man's attention?"

He sat across from her on the coffee table again, mimicking the positions that they'd held a few hours ago. "You didn't do anything."

"You don't know that."

"I do. The people who do these things are not logical. Their obsessions are not based in reality. It's entirely to do with some connection they're making in their mind. A fixed point that's somehow been tangled up with you. You didn't do anything to bring this on yourself, I promise. And Callum would tell you the same thing."

She was quiet, fingers flaring. He wasn't sure if she believed him or not, but his words were true.

The silence around them was comfortable. Not strained and filled with tension the way it might have been a week ago.

Finally, she took a long, slow breath. "He's going to come after me."

"We're not going to let him get close."

"How?" she asked. "You saw the same things everyone else did. Heard what he said. He's proving that he can get to me, and it worked because he did get to me."

He hesitated a moment, weighing the words that needed to be said. "I want to thank you for meeting with Callum. I know you didn't want to do that."

Alyse looked at him now, suspicion clouding those stunning blue eyes. No matter how he might want to see her undone and messy, there was no denying that Alyse Peterson was beautiful. Eyes, skin, lips…all of her was gorgeous.

"Just hit me with the bad news, Tristan. I know there's

something."

She wasn't going to like what he was about to say, but after Callum's revelation, there was nothing she could do. He could rely on his team to do everything they could to end this situation quickly, but for now, it was becoming too dangerous, and he knew in his gut that he couldn't leave her protection up to anyone else. Not anymore.

"I'm moving in here."

Her eyes flared wide. "What?"

"And not in the apartment above your garage," he said. "It's too far away, and if the stalker made a move, by the time I got to you, it would be too late."

"I—" She paused, looking visibly panicked. "Tristan, I can't."

In a split-second decision, he decided to push her boundaries. He reached out and took her hand in his. She didn't let go. "I don't want to scare you, Alyse. But he is going to escalate. He will try. I—*we*—are going to take every fucking precaution we can to make sure that he doesn't get anywhere near you. But if he did…" Tristan swallowed, uncomfortable with the thoughts currently plaguing his mind. "I don't know what his plans would be, but I doubt you'd have a chance to press the panic button. You need someone close. Someone inside the house. I don't want to take a chance on anyone else. I want to be close enough to take him down."

Alyse stared at him, emotions flickering in her eyes faster than he could determine what they were. Fear was present— and panic. And maybe, just maybe, trust.

Softly, he squeezed her hand. "Please, Alyse. Let me help keep you alive."

More slowly than Tristan thought possible, she squeezed back. He could feel the effort it took for her to speak. Just one word.

"Okay."

Chapter 12

Alyse asked Jared to be there when Tristan brought his stuff over. She wasn't afraid of him—of course she wasn't. But this wasn't something she wanted to face alone. Having someone in her house like this was basically unthinkable.

"You're making the right decision, Alyse. I promise," Jared reassured her.

For about the hundredth time.

Tristan had just brought in a suitcase and had gone out to get some other equipment of some sort. She wasn't sure what. "I know that, Jared. It's just…difficult."

She'd only had a few boyfriends in her life, and outside of her parents, she had never lived with anyone.

Alyse liked her privacy. She liked knowing she had a haven where no one would judge her. Where no one would be given the *chance* to judge her.

She'd learned with her last boyfriend, an up-and-coming Italian model named Salvatore Marino, just because you were intimate with someone didn't mean they wouldn't judge you.

People wanted the fantasy, not the real.

"What will Tristan think of me, Jared? Remember Salvatore?"

"That's what you're worried about?"

She took a deep breath. "Partially."

"Salvatore Marino is as pretentious as his fucking name. I'm glad you're rid of him. Tristan Zimmerman might be a lot of things, but he's not pretentious. And he's here to keep you safe—not to reflect on your personal choices in any way. This is the best course of action."

Alyse knew that. All of it was true. Tristan was overbearing and even an asshole at times, but also steady, caring, and calm. She knew in her gut that having him close was the best thing for her safety-wise.

But that didn't keep the anxiety from bubbling in her gut and making her jumpy.

Tristan returned from his car with another bag—perhaps containing a computer—and another, smaller box of something. "Where would you like me to stay?"

Her house wasn't big by the standards of some people in her profession, but it was big enough for her. No matter what, Tristan would be too close for comfort. Her only hope was to try to maintain a little distance.

"You've seen the layout," she said. "There are two wings. I was hoping that you might agree to stay in that one?" She pointed in the direction of the wing where she didn't sleep.

Because the thought of having Tristan near her while they were sleeping had a different kind of nervousness plowing through her system. One that had nothing to do with anxiety and everything to do with this attraction she had for him.

"You sleep in that one?" He pointed to her wing.

"Yes," she sighed.

"Then you know I need to be there with you."

Be there with her. Alyse clenched her hands to keep them from fluttering. "It was worth a shot."

The corner of his mouth tipped up into a small smile. "I promise you'll barely notice I'm there."

She highly doubted that.

"But I'd also like a room that I could use as an office during the day, and I'm more than happy to use the opposite wing for that. The boys will get it set up if you show us where."

"Jared," she said. "Do you mind picking a room for the office? I'll show Tristan his room."

Alyse wanted to show him personally, so she knew he was fine with it. She needed to see him agree to it. She didn't think he would change rooms without her permission, but she had to make sure. She needed to know exactly where he would be.

"We're putting up more cameras around the exterior on a different system." Tristan carried his suitcase up the stairs behind her as if it weighed nothing. "If the stalker decides to get that close to the house again, I want to make sure there's no chance we miss his face. And once we get the computers set up in the office, Nathaniel will go through everything. He's been busy making sure that bastard can't get into our network again."

"Thank you."

A couple weeks ago, Alyse would've argued against having more cameras, but it would be foolish to fight it, given what had happened. And besides, all her energy was being taken up by the fact that Tristan was moving into her house.

The room she'd chosen for him was closest to the stairs and the farthest from her room. She stepped inside the door. "Will this be okay?"

Tristan glanced down the hall to where he knew her room was, then looked back at her. For a moment, she thought he was going to argue, but he didn't. "This will be fine, thank you."

"Okay."

She turned to leave, and he stopped her with an outstretched hand. "Thank you, Alyse. I know this isn't something you wanted. I'm going to do my best to make sure my presence doesn't disturb you. And thank you for letting me be close. I want to be able to make a difference in an emergency."

He sounded so sincere that she couldn't be upset with him in any way, but she couldn't meet his eyes either. "You're welcome. I'll leave you to get settled."

Alyse disappeared into her own room before he had the chance to be nice to her again. He was going to be around constantly, and she knew she would have to monitor her energy for their interactions. He couldn't get too close. He wouldn't understand her reality.

She would have to be careful to dole herself out in small pieces so she could get through it. She'd lost her house as her sanctuary, but she still had her room where she could be alone and let go of the glamour princess role.

Starting right now. Tristan and his team had work to do and didn't need her.

Alyse texted Jared on the temporary phone they had given her and told him to make her apologies and smooth over the fact that she wouldn't be around for installation and details, then she sealed herself in her room. She fully intended to stay there until there were fewer people in the house.

For the rest of the afternoon, she read and took a nap. She reviewed her lines for next week's shoot and looked through new offers for movies in her email—ones that Jared had forwarded. It was finally early evening by the time she got a text from Jared saying that everyone had left but Tristan, and he was leaving too.

Usually around this time, Alyse would be chilled out in her living room. Ratty sweatpants that she'd had for years and soft T-shirts. No makeup or hair product. She'd watch trash TV or read another book. She'd just…enjoy being herself, by herself.

But Tristan was still there, and that meant the mask stayed on. But she would at least venture out of her room to see how things were going and show him she wasn't entirely a recluse.

Alyse found him in the office they had chosen and set up in one of her guest rooms in the opposite wing. She barely recognized it. There was tech equipment everywhere, with so many monitors, it looked like the security room at a casino. And on all those monitors was every possible angle of her house that she could think of. And some she would never have thought of.

"What do you think?"

She jumped when he spoke, glancing toward him once. "It's overwhelming."

"And hopefully effective."

Alyse just nodded.

"Everyone is gone," Tristan said, hesitating.

"Jared told me."

He cleared his throat. "I meant that you could be more comfortable if you wanted."

His eyes were on her shoes. She hadn't realized she was still wearing heels, but she had never taken them off. That was okay—they completed the image. "I'm fine. This is comfortable to me."

That wasn't even close to the truth.

Tristan studied her. "There's no need to dress a certain way on my behalf—"

She stiffened. "This is how I prefer to be clothed. Thank you for your concern."

That did the trick. He turned back toward the screens without pushing it any further.

That was what she wanted, right? For him to ignore her as

much as possible? For them to keep their distance? So why did she feel sad that that was exactly what was happening?

They both stared at the monitors in silence.

"I usually work out around this time in the evening. Monitoring will be staffed by someone at the office. Would it bother you if I used your gym?"

Alyse locked her arms around herself, feeling dizzy. She hadn't set foot in the gym in her house in years. Just thinking about the room practically made her break out in hives. The familiar feeling of wanting to throw up rose, but she shoved it down.

She'd worked through this. It had taken many years of therapy, but she had worked through it. She was okay.

She wasn't here, and Alyse didn't have to do anything she didn't want to do. She repeated that to herself over and over.

Just mentioning the gym should not affect her this deeply after so long, but it did. She hated it.

The memories swam before her eyes before she could stop them. Hours upon hours upon hours on the treadmill and the bike.

Remember, Alyse. You asked for this. You wanted it. Be perfect.

Alyse shuddered at the memory of her voice. Thirteen years and she could still hear the exact inflection of the way she'd said those words. Every fucking day for two years.

Be perfect. Be perfect. Be perfect.

Tristan was still looking at her, and she realized she hadn't answered him. She swallowed against the dryness in her mouth. "Sure. I'll show you where it is."

"I'll change," he said, "and meet you in the foyer."

Alyse wished she could just tell him where it was and be done with it, but he was already slipping past her into the hall.

How was it she could still be traumatized by a woman she hadn't seen in over a decade? Deborah McDowell was the source of a lot of awful things in her life, and if Alyse could, she would tear her out of her memories entirely.

How she would revel in knowing she still controlled so much of her life, though Alyse hadn't seen her since her father threw Deborah out of their house all those years ago.

She made her way back to the foyer slowly and walked down one set of stairs as Tristan walked down the other. Seeing him in his workout gear—gym shorts and a tight-fitting black T-shirt—had her doing a double take despite her anxiety.

He obviously wasn't kidding when he said he worked out daily. There was no way someone was in the shape he was in without it. Even if Alyse hated to exercise, she could appreciate the fruits of that labor. For a moment, Tristan didn't notice that she was staring at him, and she took full use of that moment to soak it all in.

Attraction punched her in the gut. She wasn't used to it. She especially wasn't used to it with someone living in her house with her.

He caught her eye and smiled. "All ready."

And just like that, her stomach turned again. The gym was on this side of the house, as far away from her as she could physically make it. She wasn't even sure why she still kept the room as a gym. She never set foot inside it.

Alyse was sure Dr. Elliot would have some opinions on why she was holding on to it, and she didn't want to dig deeper into that subject. She didn't want to think about it at all.

She had to hold her breath as she pushed open the gym door, the floor seeming to move as her eyes fell on the silhouetted form of that stupid exercise bike. The lights flipped on automatically, and Tristan strode in, taking in the room in one glance like he was assessing the whole place for threats. She supposed since he was there for that reason, he wasn't going to take chances even in her own house.

"This stuff looks brand-new," he said, looking around at the equipment. "Not used much?"

Never, actually. Alyse hadn't done a real workout since the day everything came out and her parents finally realized what Deborah had been doing for years—nothing short of physical and emotional abuse. She had wielded exercise as a weapon and cut her heart out on a daily basis. And she'd allowed it.

"I don't particularly like to, no," she said.

Alyse's abusive past and complicated relationship with her body and this equipment were not things she needed to tell Tristan. It wasn't any of his business, and she had shown him where the gym was. Her job was done.

"I could help you," he said. "Show you a few things. I'm sure someone in your industry always needs new workouts. America's Glamour Princess has to be perfect to keep the job, right?"

His voice was light and teasing, and rationally, she knew he was joking. But all she could hear were those words in her head.

Be perfect. Be perfect. Be perfect. You asked for this.

"Come on." He grinned. "Take off some of that armor and get sweaty. It could be good for all the stress. And I know you're not afraid of a little hard work."

If I didn't know any better, I would say that you didn't want this.

You need to work harder. Longer. No one will ever take you seriously if you don't put the work in now.

Alyse stared at the exercise bike, then the treadmill. How many hours had she put on those? One after another. Then switch.

Her breath came in shallow gasps, her feet glued to the floor. She couldn't move nor stop the voice in her head.

Alyse needed to get out of there. Away from Tristan. Away from this room. Away from everything.

"Goodnight," she managed to gasp out before she ran. She didn't stop until she was once again locked behind her bedroom door.

The one place she could be safe. The one place she could be the Alyse she'd finally come to terms with.

These walls were her only safe place now.

Chapter 13

Tristan watched Alyse run out the door. What the hell just happened?

He'd hoped getting her to show him her gym might get her out of those thousand-dollar heels. Nothing would've made him happier than for her to have arrived in workout attire to show him the gym. Something comfortable.

But if anything, every step they'd taken toward this room had made her stiffer.

He went over to the treadmill and started to warm up, looking around more closely. The equipment wasn't dusty; everything was obviously cleaned regularly. But there was no sign any of it had ever been used at all.

He walked around, looking at the treadmill then the stationary bike. Both still had the sticker tags and clear plastic film over the electronic panels. That seemed...strange. From what he knew of Hollywood, most stars spent hours working on the state of their bodies since that was what they were judged on.

If Alyse was working out, it certainly wasn't in this room.

Could she really have the career she did without any exercise? Possibly, but it seemed unlikely.

Something wasn't adding up, but he couldn't put his finger on what.

Maybe it was just the type of exercise. Perhaps she preferred swimming or something outdoors. Though none of the data about her schedule indicated any of those things.

Tristan had no idea what was happening, but he knew he never wanted to see that look on her face again. He found himself wanting to apologize even if it wasn't his fault.

He started a brisk run on the treadmill. There were obviously still things she wasn't telling him. Big things. Her reaction to this gym had been deep and instinctual, like some sort of wound. Something that ate at her.

He pushed himself faster. If it didn't have to do with protecting her, then why did he want to know about the root issues at all? He shouldn't want to.

He did.

Tristan wanted to know what made Alyse Peterson tick, and he had a feeling that he had just discovered a piece of it in the worst way possible. He wanted to know the rest of the pieces too—not just what caused that look on her face, but what she did to get through it. Did she have someone to turn to? Some sort of coping mechanism?

Did she drink? Smoke? Take prescription drugs to get her through the hard times? Or something less destructive—read, binge a TV show, gossip with friends?

He knew what it was like to have wounds. Nightmares that woke you up in a cold sweat. He knew what it was like to have to find coping mechanisms and to change them up when they stopped working.

But somehow, Tristan didn't think Alyse's wounds were caused by being responsible for someone else's death.

He ran faster. After five miles, he hit the weights. By the

time he was done an hour later, he was covered in sweat but at least clearer in his head.

Exercise was one of his own coping mechanisms. He was never not going to see Cliff Johnson's face in his nightmares, but he had learned how to function around it. Pushing himself hard helped.

He could almost convince himself that he'd read too much into Alyse's reaction too. She struggled with change and with people in her space. Today had been a large, jarring step for her, and so it was possible that was what was upsetting her. He needed to cut her some slack and not read too much into it.

Tristan made his way to the kitchen for something to eat, only to realize they hadn't discussed food arrangements. Were they roommates now? Buying their own food, but not sharing? Would she mind if he helped himself to what she had? The next time he saw her, he would ask, and in the meantime, he would make do with what was available.

But there wasn't much available. The cupboards were nearly bare, and the fridge as well. A little lunch meat, some bread, a few pieces of fruit. Once again, Tristan was left trying to put together pieces of the Alyse puzzle.

She made literally millions of dollars a year, not to mention what she'd inherited from her parents. Why did she not have a chef? Or have fresh meals delivered multiple times a day? One look at the activity logs for the house had already let him know neither of those was true.

She'd arranged groceries to be delivered twice in the last two weeks since they'd taken over her security. And he already knew no deliveries were scheduled for today or tomorrow or the next day.

What did Alyse eat?

And, once again, why did he care so much?

Tristan managed to find enough fixings to make a turkey

sandwich, and he took it to his room. The room was a bit more feminine than his natural taste. But it was still stylish, well-appointed, and comfortable.

Down the hall, Alyse's door was shut, although light poured from underneath. At the very least, he knew where she was.

His room had a small desk, and he sat there with the sandwich and pulled out his tablet, double-checking out of curiosity. There was no chef on Alyse's personal schedule. He knew that she struggled with food, but he thought at the very least someone would come in to help.

He grabbed his phone and dialed Mark. He answered on the first ring. "Did she hang you out a window by your balls yet?"

"Not yet," he laughed. "It's on the schedule for tomorrow."

"Good. It's been a while since you've had a good ball-hanging."

"I'm confirming there's no chef or meal delivery on Alyse's schedule? Anyone that's been here in the last week?"

Tristan heard typing. "No chef, and groceries delivered sporadically. Alyse confirmed for us that she prefers to cook for herself."

She barely did that. Making peanut butter and jelly sandwiches did not count as cooking. He was starting to understand why she didn't need to exercise and why he'd been having the inexplicable urge to feed her. Alyse was already on the edge of too thin, and Tristan could almost guarantee she hadn't eaten anything today since she'd spent almost the entire day in her bedroom.

The low-calorie content combined with stress wasn't good for her. "We still have some secure grocery services?"

Mark hummed his confirmation. "Yeah, we have a couple we work with that are good about security concerns."

"Send them to me, will you?"

"Sure thing," he said, and then he hesitated. "For real, though, everything okay over there?"

Tristan gritted his teeth. "Yeah. Fine."

Mark chuckled. "Sounds like it's fine."

He told him about Alyse's reaction to the gym. "I may have hit some sort of nerve by accident. The look on her face, Mark…it was bad."

He was quiet for a moment. "You'll figure it out. I know you're not a big people person, but that's by choice, not because you're not able to read them. And I know you're motivated to understand Alyse."

"What is that supposed to mean?"

Tristan could almost hear his eye roll. "You know exactly what it means, you closed-off bastard. You like her. She likes you. Get over yourself and talk to her."

"I don't date clients, Mark."

He snorted softly. "I think we both know she's more than a client to you."

Tristan didn't want to admit that he was right, but he was. There was something spinning in the air between him and Alyse. It had started early, and he couldn't seem to get a hold of it.

Wasn't sure if he *wanted* to get a hold of it.

Was sure that it fucking terrified him.

"Send me those delivery services," he said finally. "I'll check in tomorrow."

"You got it, boss."

Mark made everything seem so simple. *Just talk to her.* But talking to Alyse wasn't like talking to other people, and it had nothing to do with her wealth or celebrity status. Those meant nothing to him.

What tied Tristan in knots were these instincts he couldn't curb when it came to her. This compulsion to protect her, to see to her needs. To figure out what it was she was hiding.

He was used to putting himself between danger and his clients—that was his profession. He'd even done a couple of live-in jobs before.

But he wasn't even going to lie to himself that this was the same as with those. The need he had to protect Alyse went way beyond what was required for his employment.

And now it was just the two of them in this house.

Tristan wasn't going to ignore what was between them, if only because it could put her in further danger if he refused to acknowledge it. He might not know what the hell to do about these instincts, but he wasn't going to pretend they weren't there.

His phone chimed with the names of the grocery services, and he settled in with his sandwich and a screen full of delivery options. Tomorrow, at least, Alyse Peterson's kitchen was going to be stocked.

Chapter 14

Chicken Parmesan wasn't the fanciest dish in the world, but it was one of the few solid meals that Tristan could make from scratch and memory. He made a damned good chicken parm.

It was Saturday evening, and he hadn't seen Alyse all day since she didn't have to be on set. Like yesterday, she hadn't emerged from her room.

He was hoping the smell of his cooking would entice her out.

The food delivery service was prompt and brought everything he'd needed this morning, just an hour after his order. The kitchen was now full of food. No excuses for Alyse not to eat.

Tristan specifically ordered a plethora of premade healthy snacks and things she could grab quickly without much preparation. It was part of his battle plan: steering around the points of major friction. If preparation of food was a barrier, then they would remove that barrier.

And he wasn't even going to fight this excessive need he had to feed her. Combating his deep instincts had never served him well, so he wasn't going to start now.

The chicken sizzled in the pan in front of him, but even through the sound, he suddenly heard the click of heels in the foyer. His plan was working.

When Alyse's head peeked around the corner and into the kitchen, Tristan pretended not to notice, despite his near visceral reaction to her presence.

"You're cooking?"

"I am cooking," he confirmed.

She stayed in the doorway, looking around as if she'd never seen the room before. "I didn't know I had the ingredients to cook a real meal."

"You didn't." Tristan shot her a smile. "I had groceries delivered by a service we use for high-priority clients. They're very security-conscious, and they didn't enter the house. But now we are fully stocked."

"Wow." She seemed a little stunned. He studied her out of the corner of his eye as she watched him cook.

Once again, she looked tired in that brittle way that he had come to know—like she hadn't gotten much sleep, if any at all. He froze for a second, realizing they hadn't had their nightly phone call. He hadn't even considered it since they were both in the same physical location.

But now, Tristan realized that had been a mistake. She'd needed it, especially after whatever had happened in the home gym.

Not that you could tell from looking at her if you didn't know to dig deeper than the surface. On the surface, Alyse was still perfect. Crisp blouse with pale-blue skinny jeans that emphasized her long legs. Her hair fell in waves around her shoulders, and her pristine makeup looked like she could be on the red carpet.

Beautiful, but armored. And that armor skillfully hid what was going on inside. She had it down to an art form.

He flipped the chicken in the pan. "I realized last night

that we hadn't talked about how we would handle food. There wasn't much here, so I took the liberty of ordering groceries. I hope that's all right."

"Yeah, that's fine," she said. "Were you planning on eating alone?"

"Actually, I had hoped that the smell would lure you out and I could talk you into eating with me. Would you like to help?" Getting her invested in the meal was the best way to make sure she ate.

She smiled a little. "Sure."

Tristan intentionally glanced at her outfit. "It's all right if you change. I wouldn't want you to get anything on your nice clothes." His own clothes were jeans and a T-shirt. Casual, like he hoped she would become with him.

Alyse stepped to the side and picked an apron off a rack that held several. "I'll use this. What do you need me to do?"

He gestured to the island where he'd laid out vegetables. "Start on the salad, and we'll go from there."

She did, and he stepped to the side, turning to lean against the counter so he could see her. "Have you eaten today?"

She glanced at him before quickly looking back down at her work. "No."

"And yesterday? You were in your room almost the whole day."

"I had a little something for breakfast before you arrived, but other than that, no." He could barely see the blush that stained her cheeks.

He needed to be gentle here. "I know I keep pushing you to eat. Am I triggering something by doing that? Some sort of eating issue?"

He should've thought of this long before now.

She turned to him for a minute and smiled. A real smile. "I don't have an eating disorder, Tristan. I promise. Though, thank you for asking. I swear it's not that I'm trying not to eat. It's just that…most of the time, I don't want food. It's like my body forgets how to be hungry. But this smelled so good."

"Have you thought about bringing in a cook?" he asked, flipping another couple of pieces of the chicken.

She shrugged one shoulder. "Despite the publicity events we plan, I don't really like to be around people much. And definitely don't like having anyone in the house. I prefer to be alone."

He'd questioned that more than once, but he wasn't questioning it anymore.

"Well, while I'm here, we can cook together if you want. Maybe not every day, but a couple times a week."

She paused. "I would like that, thank you."

He opened a nearby cupboard, showing her the prepackaged snacks. "I got a bunch of things that you don't have to cook. All you have to do is grab them and eat."

She blinked those big blue eyes. "You did that specifically for me?"

"For us both. Being hungry makes me distracted and cranky. So now, it will be easier for both of us to grab something when we need it."

"Thank you," she murmured, going back to cutting up the tomato in front of her.

A few minutes of easy silence passed before she spoke again. "You know everything about me, Tristan."

"I hardly think that's true." He knew for a fact there was a lot she was not telling him.

She shrugged. "You know what I mean. You have files on me, and I know almost nothing about you."

The chicken was almost done. "What do you want to know?"

"Anything." She divided the salad into bowls. "What about your family?"

"I'm one of four siblings. My older brother Gavin, baby sister Lyn, and then I have a twin, Andrew."

He loved the smile that lit up her face. "Identical?"

"No, although we look pretty similar. He works for a different branch of Zodiac Tactical and has twin daughters. Toddlers."

She shook her head. "Oh man, I guess that keeps him and his wife busy."

Andrew didn't have a wife, but that situation was too complicated to get into right now. "It does. But Caroline and Olivia are adorable. My sister Lyn got her doctorate in linguistics and got married not long ago. She and Heath have been living in Egypt for her work, but they'll be back in Wyoming soon."

"You grew up in Wyoming?"

Tristan nodded as he once again stepped away from the chicken and took down a wineglass from the cupboard. He poured her a glass of white wine and pushed it across the island to her. She was sitting on one of the barstools and already looked more comfortable. He guessed this was what Mark meant when he told him just to talk to her.

"Yes. Lived there until I went into the Navy. My family is entrenched there."

"Wait. Zimmerman. As in Ronald Zimmerman, the governor of Wyoming?"

"That's Dad. He isn't too thrilled that Andrew and I aren't residing in the most beautiful state in the country with him. But Gavin is firmly planted in Oak Creek, which is a small town in the mountains. And Lyn will be home soon too."

"I've never been to Wyoming."

"It's difficult to describe how beautiful it can be, although the harsh conditions are nothing to be scoffed at. But if you're looking for somewhere to get away from people and just enjoy nature around you, Wyoming can't be beat."

Her face relaxed into a dreamy pose. "Maybe I'll visit."

Maybe he would take her.

It was all he could do not to say the words out loud. He would love to take her to some of his favorite places in his home state. Love to experience them for the first time through her eyes.

But first, they needed to catch this stalker.

He finished cooking the chicken and put it on two plates. He slid her food across the island to her too but didn't sit on the stool next to her. He wanted to be able to see her, and this was the best vantage point.

"You made a good salad," he said.

She rolled her eyes. "Anyone can make a salad."

"Doesn't mean that it's not good."

She blushed lightly but dodged the compliment. "What about your mom?"

A pulse of sadness moved through him. "She passed when I was in college. Cancer."

"I'm sorry."

"It happens," he said. "She went peacefully."

She pushed her empty salad bowl to the side. "Do you still miss her?"

"Of course," he said. "Absolutely."

"I miss my parents," she said softly, looking down at her plate.

"I never met your mother," he said, "but I really liked your dad."

Alyse's smile was laced with pain. "He was the best. They were the only ones who…" She trailed off and didn't finish the thought, but he knew not to push it. This was still an open wound for her. "They were my parents. They loved me, and I just…I miss them every day."

"They would be really proud of you."

He saw the struggle in her face not to shoot down the comment, but she didn't. "Thanks." She took a bite of the chicken and groaned. "Holy shit, that's good."

"I think anything would taste good to you after almost two days of not eating."

"You're not wrong, but even though I don't eat much, I know good food. And this is great."

Primal satisfaction welled in his chest as she continued to eat. That urge to protect and to care for her was satisfied, and his ego was stroked too. She liked his food.

Around the corner of the island, Tristan saw she'd kicked off her shoes and tucked one of her feet into the bars of her stool. The blouse she was wearing had come untucked from her jeans, and she was sparkling. This was the most relaxed he'd seen her, and she didn't even realize it.

This was the real Alyse Peterson. The one beneath the armor. Not all of her, but more than he'd seen.

"You haven't drunk much wine," he said. "And I didn't see any other alcohol in the house. Do you not drink?"

She took a tiny sip. "No, I don't drink much. You're not drinking anything either."

"I'm on the job," he said simply. "I need to be fully alert at all times. I can't afford to be slowed down at all." He'd learned that fucking lesson the hard way. There was every chance that if he hadn't had that beer, Cliff would still be alive.

"It's kind of the same for me." She took another bite. "I like to be alert."

A new piece of information clicked into place. Her clothes were part of her armor; not drinking—wanting control—was too. And to a degree, that made sense, especially when she was in public and near the press.

But this was her home, and he was the only person there.

The fact that she didn't want to let her guard down in this situation spoke volumes. Yet another knot in the tangled mystery that was Alyse. But he didn't want to press her on it right now.

Just talk to her.

They both finished their meals, and Tristan reached across the island to take her dishes. "You cooked. I can do the dishes," she said, hopping off the stool. A tiny piece of him rejoiced when he saw that she didn't put her shoes back on.

"We can both do the dishes," he said with a chuckle.

"I'll rinse. You put them in the dishwasher."

He smiled. "Deal."

They made a good team, and since there weren't that many dishes to begin with, it only took a couple of minutes for them all to be put away. He gestured to the machine. "Want to do the honors?"

Alyse leaned in and pressed the button, beaming. "Thank you for dinner," she said. "It was what I needed."

She was so close and so beautiful; Tristan didn't realize what he was doing until his lips met hers.

And the world changed.

There was a small gasp from Alyse, but she didn't pull away. And suddenly, she kissed him back.

Kissing Alyse was like falling into comfort and pleasure all at once. Her lips were softer than he'd imagined, and the way her body pressed into his felt like the answers to questions he hadn't known to ask.

More. Tristan wanted more. He brought his arms around her, holding her to him, and he needed to feel all of her. She was so much smaller than him, and they needed to move so he could get as close as his body was demanding.

Lifting her slight frame, he placed her on the counter where she was suddenly perfectly matched in height, and the world changed again. Their kiss turned hungry. He slipped his hand around her neck and pulled her closer.

Her legs curled around his hips, pulling him in, and he locked his arms around her so he could feel every inch of her sweet curves. She wasn't just a client. On some level, she never had been. Something deep and raw had existed between them since the first moment she'd walked into that conference room, and it would not be denied.

He traced his tongue along her lips, and she opened for him, accepting him, letting him taste her and take her lips until they were both gasping for air.

And he still didn't want to let her go.

When they broke apart, they were so wrapped up in each other there was no longer any space between them. His hand was tangled in that perfect hair, and her lipstick was smudged from his kiss. Those gorgeous sapphire eyes that he could drown in were dazed with the pleasure that spun between them.

Then suddenly, they weren't.

Clarity snapped back into her gaze along with terror. She didn't have to tell him to let her go. He stepped away immediately, even though every nerve in his body wanted to keep her close.

She hopped down from the counter and didn't look back as she ran from the kitchen. He didn't follow her. If she needed space, he would give her the space.

She would need a chance to process that kiss. Hell, he would too.

Whatever had just happened between them, everything was now going to be different.

Chapter 15

The next few days slipped by quickly, without any more kisses, but also without another event or contact from the stalker. But he wasn't gone. He was simply hovering in the background, waiting for another moment.

Alyse and Tristan fell into a routine within her security protocols. He accompanied her to the set in the mornings, driven by a Zodiac employee. Different route and different car. Not taking the same routes also varied the times that they needed to leave the house, which was a good thing as well.

There was one thing that he couldn't deny—that anyone with eyes couldn't deny—Alyse Peterson was a hard worker. The days on the set ran over twelve hours regularly, sometimes well beyond what was scheduled. He watched her rehearse and redo scenes as many times as needed until everything was perfect, and she did it without complaint.

She always had a smile for everyone around her, and not once did she show that she was under any major kind of strain. The studio was cooperating and allowed Tristan to be near with a laptop so he could continue to do work for Zodiac while also watching Alyse.

He wasn't particularly concerned about the stalker trying to attack her while she was at work. They'd made it extremely difficult for anybody to get in and out. Not to mention they had an employee at the gate and at the door of the studio itself. But that didn't mean he was going to let her out of his sight.

Keeping his eyes off her was damned near impossible anyway.

Every day, she continued to prove she was the antithesis of what he had originally believed. She wasn't spoiled or shallow. In fact, her behavior put Victoria Thorpe and their previous celebrity clients to shame. She hadn't demanded anything of them besides the security that they offered, and she took every new development in stride.

The meetings they'd had with Callum to look over security footage and discuss specifics of the stalker, she'd handled with grace. She'd been charming and well-spoken, with a smile plastered on her face. Even when there had been no new leads.

Glamour princess. There was a real reason she had the nickname. The press and social media had had a field day with the stalker's posters, but she'd addressed it by offering a brief statement, then ignoring the entire situation as if it didn't bother her at all.

As a matter of fact, according to her social media, she'd been out partying just two nights later—pictures of Alyse, drink in hand at a club, laughing out loud like she didn't have a care in the world, included.

Tristan knew for a fact that event hadn't occurred. She hadn't left her house once since he'd moved in. Barely left her room except to come to work or when he could coax her out for a meal.

Looking back through her social media, he realized her entire public life was staged—some parts more of an elaborate lie than others. But all of it, at least what the public knew, was a lie.

And she was always smiling in it.

As he was around her continuously, he became more able to read her. Her tells were subtle, but they were there. She was stressed but refused to show it.

She never relaxed.

Not when she was on set, not when she was in her trailer between scenes, and not when they were at home. They had dinner together as often as her schedule allowed. But even then, she remained stiff and uncomfortable with that armor of clothing and makeup firmly in place.

But why?

Tristan understood having to keep up a public image she'd created. On the set, he understood keeping her armor in place. But why at home? Even there, she was always in full makeup, nice outfits, and heels.

He would've said it was just her normal MO, remaining perfectly coiffed until she went to sleep each night, if it weren't for the fact that she sometimes forgot to remain so stiff while she was eating and kicked off her shoes.

He never drew attention to the practice and could tell she was a little embarrassed each time she realized what she'd done. Immediately, she'd re-stiffen, and they were back to uber-formal Alyse.

He wanted her to kick off those shoes and get comfortable even more than he wanted to kiss her again.

That was a lie.

He wanted to kiss her again almost more than he wanted his next breath. But he wanted to kiss the no-armor Alyse, the barefoot Alyse. The *real* Alyse she didn't show anyone else.

But mostly, he just wanted her to feel safe and comfortable.

Tristan swore sometimes he caught her looking at him

when she thought he wouldn't notice, and he wondered if she was thinking about their kiss too.

He woke up in the mornings with the memories of her lips on his, hard to the point of aching. He wanted to kiss her again. He wanted to take his time showing her exactly how beautiful it could be to come utterly undone and be less than perfect.

To set the armor to the side. It was too heavy to wear all the time, especially when it wasn't needed.

Today on the set, Alyse was filming a romantic scene with her costar Kenneth White. They'd done a thorough background check on him, as they'd done on literally every person who had access to Alyse, and Tristan was as sure as he could be that he wasn't the stalker. Not only did he have alibis for more than one of the incidents, but he didn't fit the physical description. He wasn't quite tall enough and was blond, unlike the man in the Paris footage.

In the scene, the two of them were in a kitchen setting, with lighting set to indicate it was late at night. They had rehearsed the scene in detail, getting the movement sequence down, from the way Kenneth would cross to her to the way he would cup her cheek before he kissed her so that it would look the same in every shot.

It was hard to ignore the way the scene reflected their own kiss in the kitchen, and he knew that Alyse felt the same. She kept stealing glances at him, and most of the time, he managed to resist meeting them. But the times he couldn't... he savored the blush that colored her cheeks.

He didn't like watching him kiss her—that deep protective, and *possessive*, instinct rearing its head again. But satisfaction rose too because their kiss had been real, and he could see the difference.

She had come apart in his arms for a moment, and with this kiss, he saw calculated passion. When the director called cut, she was wearing the same polite smile that she always did with Kenneth.

But Tristan still didn't like seeing them kiss over and over again.

When the director announced a wrap for the night, he walked Alyse to her trailer. She didn't speak, so he didn't either. Despite having one of their agents outside her trailer door, he still went in and did a thorough search before allowing her to enter.

He waited outside for her to change. It was early enough that if they held to their current pattern, they could make dinner together.

She smiled at him when she came out of the trailer, and it was a real smile, but tired. Her work today had drained her more than she would admit. Her makeup was still on, but she was in her own clothes: a flowing violet dress that was striking against her pale skin.

And high heels. Of course, high heels.

It was becoming his mission in life to get her to kick them off.

They didn't speak as they walked to the car—another part of their routine. It wasn't something they had expressly discussed, but he knew it was important to her that he was seen as her bodyguard while on the set. Not her friend. Definitely not more than that.

Aaron, today's driver, pulled up in a large SUV. Tristan opened the door and helped Alyse inside the car before climbing inside himself. The route home today was fairly direct, so there wouldn't be too much car time. That was good. In the car, he could feel the tension stretch between them. That invisible pull that seemed to be drawing them together. A pull they were both resisting.

As they passed through the gate into her neighborhood, his phone rang. It was Mark. "Outlaw."

"Hey, boss. We need you to come into the office."

"What's going on?"

Mark sounded grim. "Isaac's mission in the Middle East has been blown all to hell. The client is MIA. We have to formulate a new plan and need your eyes on it."

Shit. Isaac's mission had been volatile from the beginning, which was why Tristan had sent him. Isaac was highly skilled in languages and cultural nuances, not to mention one of their top negotiators. But if Mark was calling him in, things had gone even worse than they'd contended.

Tristan was hesitant to leave Alyse, even for a night. Their stalker could strike in a window that small. Not to mention this client was halfway across the world. With time differences, if it was as bad as Mark suspected, he could be gone till morning.

"I'm already sending two more guards as backup to replace you," he said.

"Roger that." Mark wouldn't have done that if it weren't an emergency. But he still needed to talk to Alyse, and they were pulling into the driveway. "I'll call you back."

He walked around the car and helped Alyse out. "Is everything all right?" she asked as they walked to the house.

"There's an incident with an overseas client. I need to go into the office to consult." He keyed in the code and started the standard procedure of checking the house before Alyse entered. She stayed with the other agent as he did his sweep. He wasn't taking any chances, even though they had secondary security measures that would notify them if someone entered the house while they were gone.

The house was as empty as they had left it. When he returned to the foyer, she nodded at him.

"You can go, Tristan. I'll be fine for one night." He hesitated, and she smiled softly. "I solemnly swear that I will not leave the house and will maintain total lockdown. It must be hard enough for you to run a business while living here. You don't have to put everything aside for me."

Tristan studied her face, torn. She was right; he'd been trying to keep up with his supervisory duties of the office while also guarding her.

"It's an emergency, or I wouldn't go. I'll be back in the morning or by noon at the latest. Eric will be in the garage apartment, and we're stationing two more people outside the fence. The panic buttons still work, and you can still call me."

"Okay." She nodded.

"And please eat something," he said. "I'm sorry we can't have dinner."

A light blush crept up her cheeks. "I promise I will."

They stood looking at each other in silence for a moment. He wanted to say more. He didn't want to leave.

He wanted to kiss her again.

"Lock the door behind me."

He turned and walked out the door, listening for the click of the locks behind him. Tristan put his phone to his ear as he walked to the car to let Mark know that he was on his way and to double-check everything was in place there.

And pushed all thoughts of kisses aside.

Chapter 16

Four hours later, Tristan was pulling back into Alyse's driveway, frustrated and tired. The complications around Isaac's mission in the Middle East had settled themselves much more quickly than expected, but not in a good way. The client had refused to take the threat seriously and had gotten himself killed.

Death happened sometimes. It was a shitty part of their job, but sometimes unavoidable. Especially in a situation like this one, where their client—the entitled son of a British businessman—had refused to cooperate.

Their contract with someone like him was ironclad; Zodiac Tactical would not be held liable for decisions he made that put himself in more danger. So they weren't responsible for his death.

But the kid was still dead.

Isaac would be there covering paperwork and tying up loose ends for at least the rest of the week. They'd need to have a full team debrief when he got back. But there hadn't been any more they could do right now, so he'd come back to Alyse's house.

He knew everything was all clear there. He'd had an access channel open on a separate monitor the entire time he was at the office. He'd kept an eye on the guards' updates each time they'd been made. They were outside; Alyse was inside. They hadn't seen her or had any issues concerning her safety.

Alyse was probably holed up in her bedroom. No big surprise there.

Tristan checked in with the guys then unlocked the main house, keying in the alarm code as he went in. As he stepped into the foyer, he froze. He could hear the sound of the television in the living room.

Not once in the four days that he'd been staying there had Alyse turned on the TV in the living room. He walked closer, listening to the canned laughter from a familiar sitcom rerun.

The sight in the living room made Tristan pause once again, because it was everything that he'd ever wanted to see.

Alyse was sitting on the couch, cross-legged with a bowl of popcorn in her lap. She was wearing an old pair of black sweatpants—complete with a small rip at the left knee—and a camisole with one strap falling off her shoulder. Barefoot. She had no makeup on her face, her hair was hastily thrown up into a bun, and for the first time, there was no tension in her body as she laughed at the friends sitting in the coffee house on television.

Her armor was gone, and she was absolutely fucking breathtaking.

This was what his instincts had been searching for: the real Alyse. The woman beneath the armor. Who she was when no one was around.

His body reacted instantly. Heat and arousal called out from where he'd been pushing them away for the past week. Now that he'd seen her like this, he wouldn't be able to push them away anymore.

At that moment, she looked over and froze. The blood drained out of her face, and her eyes filled with horror. "Tristan. You said you wouldn't be back until tomorrow."

"I didn't mean to scare you. The situation at the office got wrapped up sooner than expected."

All that tension came screaming back into her frame. She stood, pulling up the strap of her camisole and releasing her hair from its bun, rapidly attempting to smooth it. She touched her face, as if she'd just remembered she wasn't wearing makeup. If anything, she got paler.

"Alyse," he started, unsure of how to start this statement. "This is how you relax?"

She grabbed a blanket from the couch and wrapped it around herself. "Sometimes."

"If relaxing in sweats and watching TV is what you enjoy, why haven't you done it every night?"

She still looked far too pale and wouldn't meet his eyes. "I didn't want you to see me like this."

"Like what?" Tristan was completely out of his element. This was the human Alyse Peterson. The real her. He could not imagine that anyone wouldn't want to see her this way.

"I'm *America's Glamour Princess*," she said, tightening the blanket. "And this…isn't glamorous."

He took one step toward her and then another. That magnetic force dragging them together was overwhelming now. And he was done resisting. He wanted to rip that blanket away.

"I don't care about that. You have to know that you're beautiful even without makeup." And especially without dressy clothes and heels.

She didn't move as he crossed the space to her. And she still didn't look at him. "It's just that—" She cut herself off. Hesitated. "People have a specific image of me. And they don't always…" She took a breath. "They don't always react well when they see that it's not real."

Tristan didn't say anything, because she wasn't finished, and any words he said would break this moment for her. She needed to get this out.

When the words came, they were a whisper. "I didn't want to disappoint you," she said. "I didn't—I didn't want to see you realize that how I am is just an illusion."

Someone had done a number on her. Hell, maybe multiple people had done a number on her.

He closed the remaining gap between them, so close that they were almost touching. "Alyse, look at me."

She stared at his chest, unmoving, hands still clutching that blanket to her like a shield.

"Please look at me." He kept his voice gentle. He wanted to touch her, but she looked like she might shatter.

Slowly, *finally*, she lifted her gaze to his. There was fear in her eyes, and such vulnerability, his heart ached. But he wasn't going to do anything but tell her the truth.

"Since the moment I met you, all I ever wanted to see was the real you. The Alyse behind the armor of custom-fit clothes, perfect hair, and impeccable makeup. You look wonderful."

Doubt clouded her eyes, and Tristan wanted to kill whoever put it there. "I know that's not true."

"It is true. Someone made you think otherwise, and that's on them. How you dress and act here, in your own house, should be only to please yourself."

"I know."

"I think you're even more beautiful without your glamorous clothes and makeup, but what I think shouldn't matter, especially here at home."

She looked down at her feet. "Believe me, I know. My therapist and I have been over all of this."

He was glad to hear she'd been talking to someone about it but hated that she needed to at all. "Then why?"

She shrugged, still not meeting his eyes. "My image is important to me. I need to be professional in front of the public."

"You're not in front of the public here. Here, it's just you and me." He slowly moved his hands up to hers clutching the blanket and gently stroked his fingers against them. "And while I'm willing to do whatever I need to in order to keep you safe, after all our conversations and meals and that kiss a few days ago, I hope I'm more than just the hired help."

Now her eyes met his. "You are."

Tristan pulled the blanket gently from her fingers and looked down at her body. "Then please allow me to say that of all the gorgeous versions of you, this is the one I like the best. I've never seen you look sexier."

Her pupils dilated, beautiful blue eyes going dark with need. He couldn't ignore the fact that her defensive pose was gone, and her nipples were suddenly visible through that damned thin camisole.

Everything in his body ached to close those final inches— to show her exactly how sexy he found her and taste those soft lips again. But he wasn't going to take more than he was given, and so he waited. He didn't look away.

He didn't think she realized that she licked her lips, keeping them parted as her eyes dropped to his own before looking back at him. "Really?"

"Yes. Seeing you relaxed and comfortable is sexier than—"

It was she who closed the final distance between them, lips pressing against his and stopping his words. He could taste the salt of the popcorn and that deeper sweetness that was her alone.

The blanket fell to the floor, and for the first time, Tristan didn't hold back anything. Every desire he'd kept at arm's length, every want and need, he let pour out into that single kiss. When they broke apart, they were both gasping, and he had Alyse pressed against his body so that he could feel all of her.

And she could feel all of him.

He was still wearing his suit, and he shrugged out of the jacket, it joining the discarded blanket. He was about to step back, slow things down, but she reached for him, unbuttoning his shirt and running her hands along his chest. He let out a groan.

"Are you sure this is what you want? We don't have to—"

Her lips stopped his words again. "Yes. This is what I want," she said against his mouth.

It seemed strange to have denied this. The energy between them was so natural; the fact that they had waited this long was a miracle.

They weren't going to make it to either bedroom.

He picked her up in one movement and laid her out on the couch so she was beneath him. She was flushed pink and breathless, eyes roving over his bare chest as he got the rest of his shirt off. She looked at him like he was everything and she could never get enough.

She made him feel the same. Her hair was spread out across the couch, and everything about her was so real like this. He was hard to the point of pain, and he'd barely touched her. He kissed her again, tugging the camisole up over her head, and she arched to help him take it off.

For a fraction of a second, he saw that fear and doubt cross her face again, and he wouldn't let it stay. He leaned down, capturing one dusky nipple between his lips. He savored her gasp, letting his mouth drift over her skin. She was so soft, and he wanted more.

He wanted everything.

He moved down her body, never letting his mouth leave her skin as he pushed those sexy sweatpants off her hips along with her panties. He was going to taste her. And Alyse realized it when he guided her legs apart.

"You don't have—" Her voice was breathy. "You don't have to do that."

"I disagree," he said with a smile, licking into her. She was already wet, further evidence of this connection between them, and, damn, he didn't think he had ever tasted anything better.

Tristan wanted to devour her whole, and he did just that. Sealing his mouth over her, he used his tongue in long, sure strokes until she was shaking underneath him and her hands fell into his hair and urged him closer.

Her orgasm came fast, and he almost missed it. One restrained moan, and he realized that it had happened. When he looked up to her face, she was biting her lip to keep quiet, that same hesitation painting her features.

Being quiet now was just as much armor as her clothes and makeup. She was afraid of showing her true self, afraid she would be mocked for letting go.

If he ever encountered whoever had built such doubt into her, he would ruin them. The fucking beautiful, kind, special woman in front of him didn't need to hide anything. She deserved someone who valued her for exactly who she was, and he was determined to show her that.

He stood, stripping out of the rest of his clothes and donning the condom he kept in his wallet—a habit to always be prepared—before lying with her again. This time, he kept their faces close, and he kissed her again.

He kissed her until he felt her body go pliant beneath his, even just this skin-to-skin contact glorious. When he kissed her, she relaxed. When he kissed her, she felt that she could let go. He wanted that for everything between them.

"You came?"

Her blush was pure fire. "Yes."

"Don't hide that from me."

"I wasn't." But her eyes slid away from his.

Tristan moved so that they were nearly connected but not quite. One rock of his hips to show her exactly what she did to him before he spoke against her lips. "In case it wasn't already clear, I want you, Alyse. I want *you*. Not what you think people want to see. Don't ever feel like you need to hide from me. When you come again, don't hold back."

Her smile was small but genuine. "*When?*"

"That's right. *When.*"

He didn't wait any longer, pressing slowly inside her. Sinking into her heat was heaven and a homecoming all at once. It was what he had been waiting for, that deep, animal instinct suddenly sated as he pushed farther, sheathing himself to the hilt.

This time, she was the one who kissed him. She wrapped her arms around his neck to keep him close and her legs around his waist to take him deeper. It was all he could do to hold himself still, to give her a chance to get used to him. But that didn't stop Alyse from arching her hips into his wantonly.

When she squeezed down on his cock, Tristan went blind for a second. He sucked a breath through his teeth, trying to keep this from becoming embarrassingly short. Slowly, he pulled back to thrust in again, setting up a smooth rhythm that kept getting faster.

Every movement brought pleasure rolling down his spine, but it was so much more than that. It was the barriers falling between them. It was the way Alyse's fingers curled around his neck, holding on. It was the way she stopped biting her lip and let herself moan as he ground his hips against her with each thrust. It was the way she kept her eyes open, locked on his, gaze drowning in pleasure.

There was no more fear. No more doubt. No more hesitation. He swallowed her moans with his kiss, thrusting into her harder and moving his hips until he found the spot that made her dig her nails into his back. There. That was what he had needed.

Tristan focused all his attention on that one spot, driving her higher and higher until he felt her start to shake. And even then, he didn't stop. Her orgasm couldn't be missed this time. She shouted, her spine arching off the couch as her core gripped his cock in spasms that nearly made him lose control.

Her body fluttered under his in tiny aftershocks, and it wasn't until she was finished entirely that he gave in, letting that pleasure rise up and take over completely. Pure, perfect pleasure. It sizzled down his spine, crashing through him with the force of a storm before leaving him spent and panting.

Alyse's open gaze met his. No matter what happened now, there was no going back to the way it was before. They had catapulted over that line in the sand, and he had no regrets. He kissed her again, because he couldn't hold himself back anymore.

He didn't think he would ever get enough.

Chapter 17

Alyse woke up slowly, swimming in a haze of happiness. As she rose to the surface, she realized that she was warmer than usual—in a good way. She had her own personal heater in bed with her. Tristan's arm was wrapped around her waist, and her back rested against his chest.

That sculpted, perfect chest that she hadn't been able to take her eyes off last night.

Everything about him was…fascinating. Cut muscles that proved he was definitely not someone who sat behind a desk for a living. And the tattoos that covered the skin of his chest and shoulders were just as interesting as the muscles themselves. The SEAL crest, Stars and Stripes, and other military signs woven into a framework of birch trees and leaves. A name she didn't know—Cliff Johnson—marked onto his shoulder in script along with a date.

It was a beautiful piece, and she knew just by looking at it that it was steeped in personal history and pain. She wanted to ask about it, but even after the intimacy they'd just shared, she wasn't sure she should.

She trailed her fingers along the bicep under her neck,

marveling at the muscle. He'd carried her into her room when they'd finished on the couch like she'd weighed nothing. Then carried her once more, over his shoulder this time with her laughing like an idiot, to the shower for more mind-blowing sex.

She was still smiling thinking about it. About *all* of it. He'd definitely been telling the truth when he said he found her sexy without makeup or dressy clothes.

Either that or he needed to give up his job protecting others and get one as an actor. Because he'd had her completely convinced.

Over and over last night, every doubt had been shoved away, and then every thought completely, until the only choice she was left with was to *feel*.

To nearly drown in all the physical pleasure he gave her.

But that was last night. They'd both been carried away, and now as the dawn was pouring through the windows, those thoughts and doubts came creeping back.

She could feel the stiffness of her hair, which meant it was sticking up in every direction. She could smell her own morning breath. She had zero makeup on, which had been fine last night in the relative darkness of the house. Now in harsh daylight, it might have Tristan whistling a different tune that had nothing to do with *sexy*.

Behind her, he was still breathing steadily. Maybe she could escape and get herself at least somewhat presentable before he had a chance to figure out he'd made a huge mistake.

Alyse eased herself toward the edge of the bed, trying to be as smooth as possible. But the moment she moved, Tristan's arm tightened around her waist, holding her to him, and she was reminded how very, very naked they both were.

"Where do you think you're going?" he asked with the rasp of sleep in his voice.

She was glad he couldn't see her face. "To brush my teeth. And hair."

He moved with perfect grace, rolling her onto her back so that he could see her and let his weight sink down on to her side. It effectively trapped her with him. She was torn. Even though she didn't like him to be able to see her this way, she liked the feeling of his weight—it made her feel more solid. Somehow more real.

"Why were you sneaking away?" he asked.

"I wasn't sneaking." She'd been totally sneaking. "I didn't want you to see me in the morning light and think you'd made a mistake. Or…you know…morning breath."

He shook his head, intentionally leaning down to kiss her softly. Then he pulled back, studying her face. Her real face, not the one she put on for the world.

It was all she could do not to bolt.

But he didn't look turned off; he looked hungry for her. The hand he dragged down her ribs said the same thing, as did the fact that he was hard, pressing against her leg.

But he made no move to take things further. He ran that hand back up her body, leaving goose bumps in its wake, until he could tuck it behind her neck and tangle his fingers in her hair. She already knew he liked his hand there because he could keep her looking at him. She couldn't look away.

Right now, she didn't want to anyway.

"I have morning breath," he whispered. "My hair is crazy. I'm pretty sure I have some drool dried at the corner of my mouth. You offended by any of those things?"

"No. Of course not." As soon as she said the words, she knew she'd walked herself into a trap.

"Alyse," he said. "Tell me who it was that made you afraid to be human."

Anxiety crept into her gut. He thought he wanted to hear about it, but she didn't think he'd want to know the truth.

Even if she could manage to get it out. It was all so tangled and made her seem like an idiot.

"Looking good is just what people expect from me," she said. "Part of the brand."

He shook his head. "I don't want the brand. I want the real Alyse Peterson. And I want to know why you go to such lengths to keep her hidden."

She let out a little sigh. "It's not a very interesting story."

"I don't care about interesting. I care that it made you feel like you can't be yourself." He tightened his fingers in her hair, that little movement sending tingles through her scalp. "Your secrets are safe with me. *You* are safe with me."

Alyse knew that. She felt it deep in her gut, in a place that only the truth reached. If she hadn't felt safe with him, then last night never could have happened.

Clearing her throat, she moved her gaze down to Tristan's chest, and he let her. She wasn't sure that she could say this while looking him in the eyes.

"You knew who my parents were. I grew up on movie sets and photo shoots, and I loved it. I thought every part of that world was glamorous, and I wanted to be a part of it, just like Mom and Dad. They told me I should wait and see if there was something else I might want to do for a living, but I knew I wanted to be in front of the cameras."

How many times later had she wished she'd listened to them as a child?

Alyse forced the words out. "I held my ground, and when I was eleven, my parents agreed to hire me a coach for acting and modeling so I could give it a fair shot. And they hired the best in the business. Her name was Deborah McDowell."

Tristan frowned. "I've never heard of her."

"Not surprising. It's not something you're famous for outside of our industry, and she's not in the industry anymore."

She slid a little bit away from him. If she was going to say these words out loud—and she'd never done that except to her parents and her therapist—she was going to need a little distance. He let her get the space she needed but kept a hand hooked on her hip, drawing tiny circles on her skin with his thumb.

"She *coached* me for years. But really, she was abusing me." She focused on the pattern his thumb was making. "I've been through a lot of therapy to be able to say that sentence."

She probably needed to make another appointment with Dr. Elliot soon. Given everything with the stalker, it wouldn't be a bad idea.

"This McDowell woman hurt you?"

"Not physically, not in the way most people think of when you say abuse. That was why it was able to go on for so long."

"Abuse is still abuse, even if it's not typical."

Alyse relaxed just slightly. One of the reasons she'd always had difficulty talking about this was because of her fear, not that someone wouldn't believe her, but that they would think she was making a bigger deal out of what happened than she should.

"Deborah would tell me it was my fault when my father's movies didn't do well or when my mother's campaigns faltered. She told me it was because people looked at me, saw that I wasn't perfect, and decided not to support my family because of me."

Tristan muttered a foul word under his breath.

"She convinced me it was my job to be perfect. That if I didn't want to embarrass my parents or ruin their careers, I would be willing to do whatever I had to."

"You were an adolescent."

"I know." She blew out a breath. "Nobody was looking at me, I know that now. As a matter of fact, Mom and Dad kept me relatively sheltered from the press. But Deborah was sick—and, worse—smart. She knew I had demanded a coach."

She sucked in a breath and concentrated on his thumb on her skin. "She never did anything to me. She convinced me to do it to myself. Work harder. Work longer. Be better. Be perfect. If you're not perfect, you're useless."

It was all she could do not to cover her ears with her hands. She could hear Deborah's voice so clearly. Could remember believing her words as absolute truth.

"What did she have you do?" he whispered.

"Constant exercise. Hours switching between the bike and the treadmill. Holding planks until I collapsed, and being locked in a closet for a while if I didn't hold it long enough or if I added five extra calories to my diet. That wasn't perfection, that was selfishness, and I should be ashamed."

"Alyse—"

She had to get this out. "It went on for over three years. I guess I was a better actress than anyone knew, because I convinced my parents I wanted Deborah around. Hell, I even believed I wanted Deborah around. I would get hysterical when my parents would suggest taking a break from her."

He tightened his hand on her hip. "That's not unheard of in situations like this. Like you said, she was smart. She manipulated you into believing what she said."

"Eventually, my parents caught on to what was happening, with a hidden baby monitor, no less. They fired her, made sure she'd never be able to work in the business again. I think they wanted to press charges but eventually let it go when it all came out. Like I said, Deborah never actually *did* anything to me. Even when she locked me in the closet as punishment, the door wasn't really locked."

"Just because she didn't physically hurt you didn't mean she didn't abuse you."

She shrugged. "She told them I wanted it. Had video of

me crying when she threatened to leave, begging her to stay. Begging her to make me work harder."

She'd done it to herself. She glanced up at Tristan, half expecting to find disgust in his eyes, but all she found was anger, and not at her.

"You were a child, and she was sick."

"Yes." It had taken her a long time working with her psychiatrist Dr. Elliot in order for her to be able to say that word and believe it.

"That's why you never use your gym." He began moving his thumb on her skin again. "I'm so sorry I pushed for you to work out with me."

"It's okay. You didn't know."

"I know the look on your face is one I don't ever want to see again." He kissed her hard, and she found herself wrapped up in him, even closer than they had been moments before. "And I plan on taking every opportunity to show you how much I like you like this. No makeup, messy hair, and preferably naked."

Alyse blushed. "You don't just have to say that, you know."

"Why would I just say it?"

"To make me feel better," she said. "I know that no man really wants to see a woman in sweatpants. Maybe I don't have to be perfect, but I can at least make an effort."

In a second, Tristan shifted himself fully over her body. The way that they lined up, and just the overwhelming presence of him, made her lose her breath. His lips were on her neck, and he dragged them up to her ear. "Did Deborah tell you that?"

"No. My last boyfriend, Salvatore." She knew Tristan would know the name. Zodiac had done a full background check on all the people in her life, including her exes. There weren't many of those. "He saw me the way you did last night, and that was that. I didn't match up to the vision he'd had of me, and he made it clear that no man would want me without the glamour."

Tristan pulled back far enough for her to see him roll his eyes. "That man is a fucking idiot. I would have the real you any day of the week, and anyone who doesn't want you to be yourself isn't worth your time."

"Even if that means that I'm far more boring than my press and social media team makes me seem?"

"I'd already figured out your appearances are staged."

Alyse nodded, not surprised. Zodiac had studied everything about her life. "Partially because of the image I want to keep up—and believe me, I'm well aware of the fine line between Deborah's brainwashing me to desire to be perfect and the fact that I've been dubbed *Glamour Princess* by the press."

He trailed a finger down her cheek, his big body still hovering over hers. "Both put pressure on you to look and act a certain way."

"I don't like being around people. I don't like cameras and publicity. It's why, when I do go out, my press team helps get multiple shots of me in what appears to be different clothes so the images can be used more than once."

He kissed her softly. "But you'd just rather be home."

She nipped at his lip gently. "I do wish I could go out more, but going out means people and cameras. So, it's easier to just not go. Keeps my anxiety in check."

He grinned. "It sounds like you need something normal. Something like a date. Maybe with me."

Alyse sighed. "If you want, I can coordinate it with my team."

"What do you mean?" he asked.

"All my dates are photo ops. To make sure that we get the benefit of the press."

Tristan looked stunned. "You've never been on just a date?"

She tried to smile, but she didn't think it quite worked. "I'm America's Glamour Princess, Tristan. Even if I wanted to be—and I really do—I don't get to be normal. The Peterson legacy is all I have left, and I need to protect it."

He looked at her for a moment, considering. "What if I told you I could give you normal for a night?"

Alyse wanted to believe him. "That's not possible."

"What if it was?" He didn't look like he was joking. "Let me take you on a date. A real one. I promise there won't be any cameras. No coordinating with the press and no running from paparazzi. Just you and me."

That sounded…wonderful. She didn't see how it could be real, but if anyone could make it happen, it was Tristan. "Okay. Where are we going?"

"That will be a surprise," he said. "But I do have one thing I want."

She raised an eyebrow. "What's that?"

"I want to choose what you wear."

He said it like she might be surprised, but that request was normal for Alyse. Her closet was regularly curated by her publicity team, and she had lists of approved outfits weeks in advance. "That's fine."

"Really?"

"Really. I'm used to having my outfits picked out for me."

Would he want a certain type of dress? Formal? That didn't bother her either way. Not knowing where they were going or what was going to happen was more stressful.

But Tristan wouldn't do anything to hurt her. That was something Alyse knew for sure.

"This is going to be great." The smile on his face was blinding, and she couldn't help but smile back. "I can't wait to take you out."

"Me too." She was surprised how much she meant it.

"You hungry?" he asked.

She shook her head. "Not right now, no. Why?"

He kissed her slowly before whispering in her ear, barely audible. "If you're not hungry, I'm not letting you leave this bed any time soon."

Heat rose through her body as he captured her lips again, and she had no arguments there. She had no plans, except to let this man drown her in this brand-new pleasure.

Chapter 18

Tristan flipped through the cameras surrounding Alyse's house while he waited for her to appear. She was getting ready for the date he had promised her a few days ago.

If he'd had it his way, they would have gone right away, but as much as he wanted this to be a memorable occasion for her, her safety was the utmost priority. He wasn't taking any chances.

And it hadn't been as if either of them had much interest in leaving the house over the last couple of days.

Hell, all weekend, they hadn't left her bed until almost noon, and then after lunch, they fell back into each other, wherever they were—back on the couch, in the kitchen, in the shower.

He couldn't seem to keep his hands off her.

The good news was that the feeling seemed mutual.

This morning when he woke up in Alyse's bed again, the beast that had been riding him to care for her finally felt sated. She was in his arms, well-fed and well-loved, resting comfortably.

He was smug, he'd admit it. But mostly because right at

that moment, he felt like things were fitting together in exactly the way they were supposed to.

Alyse blushed when she woke up and saw him studying her. She didn't have to be on the set today, so they had more time to themselves.

She smoothed a strand of hair behind her ear three times. He knew that meant she had something she wanted to say or ask but was finding the words. He was becoming a connoisseur of Alyse's reactions. She held so much of herself back that he had to look for the tiny tells that helped him read her.

"Go ahead and ask me." Tristan stroked a hand down her back.

"Ask you what?"

"Whatever question is floating around in your head."

She leaned up on her elbow. "How did you know I was about to ask you something?"

He wasn't about to draw attention to her tell. "Were you?"

She narrowed those gorgeous eyes at him. "Maybe. Maybe not."

"Was it about our date?"

Now those eyes got bigger. "I wasn't sure if you'd forgotten."

He hooked a hand behind her neck and pulled her down so he could kiss her forehead. "Didn't forget at all. Just wanted to make sure we had the security we needed. We're going tonight."

She froze completely still. "Really? Where?"

"Not going to tell you. I want it to be a surprise."

Her little pout was adorable. "Okay. But what type of place?"

"A restaurant." He could barely keep from grinning.

"You're not going to give me more than that?"

"Not yet." Tristan pulled her closer to him, thoroughly enjoying the feel of her and the fact that her hair was tangled and flying across the pillow. Her lips were still a little swollen from his kisses the night before.

He couldn't help but be thankful for the situation having gone so bad in Qatar. If not for that, he might never have seen Alyse messy, and she might never have let him in.

But even as he pulled her to him, he could see her mind working. "How dressed up do I have to be? I know you said you want to pick what I wear, but you don't know my closet."

She was nervous. He was asking her to stretch beyond her comfort zone in multiple ways. She wasn't familiar with normal dates; she wasn't familiar with going out without an entourage.

Hell, she wasn't even familiar with *him*.

Tristan knew she was constantly waiting for the other shoe to drop. She still had to battle the need to slip out of bed to fix her hair or put on makeup.

To be perfect.

He fucking hated the thought of what she'd been through as a teenager and how much it still affected her. But at least he knew about it now and could try to help offset the continual damage.

Like not letting her overthink tonight's date and what she would wear. So, he kissed her.

He was enamored with her lips. Their softness and the way they opened against his sent his feral instincts roaring. He wanted that softness close to him, surrounding him. He liked the way she melted underneath him, and he kissed her until her anxiety was gone, at least for the moment.

Tristan didn't need to know what was in Alyse's closet in order to know what to tell her to wear. He'd known from the minute he'd asked her to let him pick what his choice would be.

Jeans and a T-shirt.

No makeup. No fancy hair. No high heels.

He'd kept her in bed all afternoon, distracting her with his body every time he could feel the tension building back up. Giving her too much time to think would be a mistake.

She'd find a way to turn it into armor.

With less than an hour to go, he finally let her into the shower and told her the attire for the evening. You would've thought he'd asked her to wear a trash bag.

"You. Me. No cameras." He turned on the water and backed out, leaving her in the spray. "I don't say these words lightly, and I know they're not easy for you either—I need you to trust me."

He thought she might fight him about the clothing choice, and if she did, he would find a way to compromise. What she wore didn't matter, and if jeans and a T-shirt threw her into a panic, then this wasn't a hill he was prepared to die on.

But finally, she nodded. "Okay."

They were supposed to leave soon, and he was waiting to hear her steps on the stairs. If she didn't come down soon, he wasn't opposed to going up there and finding her and carrying her to the restaurant in his arms if that's what it took to get her out of the house.

But she would come down. He knew it. In spite of her nervousness, her curiosity about where he was taking her and what a real date was like would win out at some point.

Tristan's phone chimed, and he checked the message. Everything was in place. Three Zodiac guards were in the restaurant he was taking her to, making sure that there was no threat. He hadn't sent the address electronically, only said it verbally to Mark in case the hacker still had access to their network.

He had asked Alyse to trust him, and she'd agreed. He

would take no chances with her. Not with the stalker, not with the press.

Her trust was precious, and he'd treat it that way.

She'd never know that his men were at the restaurant, but he was more comfortable having backup. Because in this instance, he wasn't just her bodyguard. He was her *date*.

And he planned on letting his focus be on Alyse the woman, not Alyse the client.

Finally, Tristan heard soft footsteps from the stairs, and he smiled. That was not the sound of high heels. He shut the laptop and went to meet her.

Anyone used to Alyse's normal level of glamour might barely have recognized her, and he loved it. The clothes she wore were still perfectly tailored—he doubted her team let anything into her closet that wasn't—but more casual than he'd ever seen. A soft purple T-shirt that clung to her curves in a way that he found very distracting, and dark jeans that emphasized her long legs.

She was smaller without the heels she constantly wore, her flats making her have to look up to meet his eyes. Tristan didn't mind. Her face was fresh and free of makeup. Her dark hair hung simply around her shoulders.

She smiled, but it didn't reach her eyes. She was terrified.

He reached for her gently, pulling her to his body. "You look beautiful."

"But not perfect," she whispered.

Winding the fingers of one hand into her hair, he brought her gaze to his. "You look real. Real is better than perfect. I'll take the real you any day."

She rose up on her toes and kissed him. It wasn't a timid kiss—it was passionate and full and open. It was easy to kiss her back. It didn't matter that they had done this so many times over the past few days that they should be sick of it.

Her hands slid up his chest and pulled him closer. It was

only a moment before the kiss turned into something even more fiery. He was hard, and the idea of being inside her again was so fucking tempting. Even if it was just here against the wall.

"Tell me again," she said against his mouth.

It was the voice that tipped him off. He'd heard that voice before on the set, when she was performing that scene with Kenneth. Tristan smiled, laughing under his breath. "You're clever, Miss Peterson."

"What?"

"Trying to seduce me so that we don't go out?"

Her cheeks turned pink. "Would it be so bad?"

Tristan hauled her into his arms so her feet left the floor and he could kiss her again. They were both breathless by the time they pulled apart.

"We both know it would be amazing. But you told me you wished you could go out more, and I want to show you that you can. You can be safe and happy and anonymous outside this house. You can have a life, Alyse."

She searched his eyes, like she was checking to see if he was telling the truth.

He was.

Finally, though the nerves were still visible, she nodded. "Okay then, Pisces. Lead the way."

Chapter 19

The date was nothing like what Alyse thought it would be.

Even when she was a child, her parents were famous. She'd never stepped out of the house without planning or knowing that she'd be recognized. She'd never just gone out to dinner and been able to relax.

But with every passing minute, her anxiety was easing. Because everything was…normal. Or at least what she thought normal was supposed to be. She hoped so because it was nice.

Tristan had driven them to a barbecue place on the outskirts of Los Angeles. It took them a while to get here, but she didn't mind. She enjoyed just sitting and holding Tristan's hand as they chatted.

But even with his hand holding hers and the sincerity with which he called her beautiful, discomfort had slithered in her gut. Alyse never left the house without doing her makeup and hair. She'd had to take the tags off the T-shirt and jeans when she put them on because she'd never worn them.

Knowing how far she was from the image people pictured

of America's Glamour Princess was enough to throw her into a panic.

But Alyse didn't let it. Not because she was avoiding the feelings and shoving them down.

But because she was choosing to trust Tristan.

The restaurant he'd chosen surprised her. From the outside, it looked like a building in serious need of repair, barely on the plus side of seedy. Her acting skills had come in handy as she plastered a smile on her face.

At least Alyse didn't need to worry about anybody recognizing her.

Tristan grinned as he walked around and opened the door for her. She hadn't fooled him. He kissed her on the top of the head and led her inside with a hand at the small of her back.

And with that tiny touch, it hadn't mattered. What it looked like, who was here, even if the food was terrible.

Because his fingers at the small of her back reminded her of everything she needed to know: Alyse was there with Tristan, he wasn't going to let her down, and there was nowhere else she'd rather be. Her smile turned real.

As Tristan opened the door for Alyse, her smile grew even wider. Inside didn't look anything like the outside. Inside was as homey and warm as the outside was sketchy. The lighting made the tables and booths, filled with people not paying any attention to them, seem cozy and intimate.

But that all took a back seat to the most mouthwatering smells she'd ever experienced.

"Tristan Zimmerman," a voice boomed as soon as they walked in the door. People glanced at them, but then went back to what they were doing. "Been way too long."

"Maddox." Tristan walked them over to the handsome man who stepped out from the entrance to the kitchen. "Good to see you. Thank you for being accommodating."

The man—Maddox—laughed. "You finally getting a

woman to agree to date you? I had to be on board." His light-green eyes, exotic-looking against his dark skin, found her. "And I assume this is the beautiful woman you've tricked into coming here with you?"

Tristan grinned. "This is Alyse. Alyse, Maddox Holmes."

Alyse shook his outstretched hand. "It's nice to meet you."

"On the contrary." He winked at her. "It's nice to meet anyone who gets Tristan out of his shell."

Tristan laughed softly. "You make it sound like I'm some cranky old bastard all the time."

Maddox simply gave him a pointed look. Tristan scowled in jest and snatched her hand away from his friend.

And that was obviously what these two were. Friends.

If Maddox recognized her, he didn't give any hint of it. No one did. Or if they did, they didn't care.

That had never happened before.

"Let me take you to your table." He led them toward the back. Theirs was against the back wall but wasn't private. She could feel her spine tightening, waiting for someone to realize who she was and for the chaos that would follow.

"What are you guys having?" Maddox asked.

Tristan held out her chair for her. "The works. Thought I'd let you show Alyse what you can really do."

Maddox grinned and winked at her. "You got it."

Tristan sat and took her hand from across the table. "How does it feel to be anonymous?"

"Weird." She fought the urge to look over her shoulder to see if anyone was watching them. "I'm not convinced it's going to last."

"If it doesn't, we'll handle it. But I think for now, you're safe."

Alyse was safe. If she was with Tristan, she was safe. And while she was tense waiting for someone to recognize her, she wasn't frightened.

Like he said, they would handle it, whatever happened. Alyse relaxed a little and squeezed his hand. "How do you know Maddox? Does he own this place?"

"Yep. It was his lifelong dream. We were in the SEALs together. I offered him a position at Zodiac when he got out, but he turned me down." He looked around the restaurant, smiling. "The man has always loved food, and this place is amazing."

The restaurant was packed, especially for a Monday. "Looks like it's doing well."

"It is. Maddox constantly has people knocking on his door to franchise or do features on the restaurant. As far as I know, he's said no every time."

"Why?"

Tristan shrugged. "He prefers to keep it small. He has a lot of dedicated customers. And Maddox's food is really personal to him. He loves connecting with people over it. He wouldn't be able to do that if he were the owner of a bunch of restaurants."

"That makes sense," Alyse said. "So, you guys have known each other for a long time?"

A look passed over Tristan's face. A moment of darkness and sadness before it disappeared. "Yeah, we have."

Clearly, there was more to this story than he was telling. But she couldn't exactly argue with that, given how much of herself she had hidden until this weekend.

It wasn't long before Maddox came back to the table, bearing a giant platter of food. Ribs and mashed potatoes and cornbread and steak. It had smelled good when they first came in, but close up, it was even more amazing.

"Thanks, brother," Tristan said.

"Any time." He offered them both smiles before leaving again, stopping at a table to chat with some other customers.

"Okay," Tristan said. "Here we are."

Alyse stared down at the table. "There is so much food."

Tristan took a plate and started piling food on it from the platter. "Maddox doesn't do anything by halves. And believe me, you'll be glad there's a lot."

She was hungry. But her hesitation, born from years of knowing that the wrong camera shot of a mouth full of food could ruin her image in seconds, couldn't be ignored. It was always there when she ate in public, no matter if she was being watched or not.

Tristan took his first bite and closed his eyes in bliss. Evidently, her hesitation wasn't going to stop him from enjoying himself. Alyse picked up a plate and took a little of everything on the platter. Somehow knowing he wasn't going to try to talk her into eating made it easier to do so.

It didn't take her long to figure out why he hadn't waited for her. The meat fell apart and melted in her mouth, and the potatoes were just about the best thing she'd eaten in her life. "Holy shit."

He laughed. "I know."

"Eating this won't be a problem," Alyse said.

Screw her hesitation. If anyone caught a picture of her chewing orgasmically, she would demand they come there and try not to do the same.

They'd both cleared half their plates before they spoke again.

"Your coach, that Deborah lady. She's the reason why eating is hard sometimes?"

She nodded. "Yeah. Anything I ate she didn't like would add on time to the workouts. Or end up with me locked in a closet for a while to think about what I'd done. So, it was… easier to not eat sometimes. I guess the habit became ingrained."

Alyse had good genes. She was lucky. She didn't really have to worry too much about dieting because she'd always been naturally thin. But she'd convinced her it wouldn't matter.

She took another bite, enjoying it despite talk about Deborah. "She did a lot of damage. But..." Her cheeks turned pink. "It's easier with you."

He stopped eating. "Really?"

She blushed harder. "Even before you knew about any of my past, you tried to feed me. It was like you understood somehow."

He shook his head. "Yeah, believe me, I know trying to feed you must have come across as weird, but...I couldn't seem to help myself."

He almost looked befuddled.

"You protect people. You're always the one to take care of the people around you, aren't you?"

Now he looked a little uncomfortable. Good. Turnabout was fair play.

"It's habit," he finally said. "I was the leader of my SEAL team, and you do whatever you can to protect your men. And once you're used to doing that, you don't stop. But sometimes it's not enough."

There was near-tangible pain in those words. She wanted to know what was buried there. She wanted to know *him*. This dark, mysterious man who had swept into her life and somehow managed to make the real Alyse feel safe and beautiful and calm all at once. Something no one had been able to do for her, ever.

Tristan was staring down at his food, and she took the moment to really study him. He was gorgeous. Chiseled features that might have been too harsh on anyone else. But on him...the sharpness worked.

He looked up at Alyse then, caught her staring. The shadows fell away from his eyes, and he smiled. "Eat, beautiful."

They did. They ate all the amazing food Maddox had brought until there was nothing left but the bones from the ribs. She felt stuffed and full and happy and normal.

Maddox came and took the platter away and dropped off a bottle of wine and two glasses. Her date didn't hesitate, grabbing the bottle in one hand and handing her the glasses before catching her free hand in his. She followed, wide-eyed, as he guided her back through the kitchen. But no one spared them a second glance or yelled that they weren't supposed to be there. At the back of the kitchen, they came to a set of stairs that led up onto the roof.

Alyse looked around at the view. The restaurant was settled in the hills around Los Angeles, and from the roof, they could see all the way across the valley and the lights starting to flicker across the massive city.

Tristan sat down in the single lounge chair and pulled a bottle opener from his pocket. She laughed. "Always prepared?"

"Always."

"I thought you didn't drink when you were on the job."

He shook his head. "I don't. But tonight, I'm not on the job. Tonight, I'm on a date."

Alyse instinctively looked behind her, suddenly aware that she was exposed on the roof. Tristan caught her hand and pulled her closer so she was standing between his legs. "I have people here. You're still safe."

Of course he had people there. Her safety was a priority to him.

He guided her down to sit with him, resting against his chest while they looked over the spectacular view.

"There were three men in the restaurant while we were inside," he said against her ear. "And now that we're up here, they're on the perimeter. No one is getting close to you, except me."

She leaned back against him while he poured the wine. "I don't drink very much, Tristan."

"I'm not trying to get you drunk," he said with a low chuckle. "But while we're here, and you're safe, you can let yourself relax."

His lips brushed the tip of her ear, and she shivered in spite of the warmth of his body.

"This is beautiful." She took a sip of wine, looking out. The sun had just set, painting the sky deep purples. The bottom of the valley sparkled like a field of stars.

It was a part of Los Angeles she'd never witnessed, even after living here her whole life.

Alyse took another sip of wine and let the warmth of it flow down into her stomach. She could already feel the effects after barely a glass. But right now, she didn't mind the comforting, floating feeling. Not when she could lean against Tristan's hard chest and close her eyes and listen to the breeze.

He wrapped his arm around her waist, and she could feel him harden behind her. She knew what he could do with that, and suddenly she wished that they were somewhere more private.

Nobody had ever made her feel this way.

"Can I ask you a question?" She said, turning to the side so she was leaning her head on his chest.

"Of course."

Alyse took another sip of wine and let it give her courage. "You like me…messy. But I don't know why. I believe you when you say it, but it doesn't make sense to me."

Tristan ran his fingers through her hair, and Alyse closed her eyes. She loved that feeling. Simple, absent affection. "It might sound strange, but it has to do with battle. Being in the field."

That wasn't what she'd been expecting him to say. "How so?"

She could feel his lips against her hair. "Everyone has walls in normal life. But in a battle situation where it's life or death and you don't have a choice but to trust the people that you're with, you can't have any walls. You're just…you."

He paused and took a sip of his own wine. "Being without walls bonds you in a way that doesn't let go. Take Maddox, for example. I haven't been able to get out here as much as I would like, but no matter what, we'll always have that bond. We'll always know each other in a way that is completely honest because we didn't have the walls."

She finished the wine in her glass and set it down beside the lounge chair. She turned to face him, sliding her legs over his so she was straddling his lap in a way that was so inappropriate but felt so right. Watching his eyes go dark as she slid closer put a smile on her face.

This was something she never would have done if it hadn't been for him. She would've been too afraid of being seen or caught in photos, like the ones that had been plastered on her gate. But here in the middle of the hills with nothing but the sunset, she wanted to be a little bit reckless with him. "So, you like seeing people…stripped back?"

He reached out and wrapped his hand around her neck so he could pull her lips to his. "I like to see people for who they really are, especially you," he said with his mouth against hers. "No walls and no boundaries. Not a fake face presented to the world. That's why I like you messy and casual."

"But—"

Tristan cut her off with another firm kiss and a grin. "You are beautiful no matter what. But when you were by yourself, in nothing but sweats and eating popcorn, that's something you chose because you enjoyed it. Because it made you feel comfortable and happy, not because you were afraid of the press. Or afraid of your past. Or because you're upholding an image that's been created for you."

His teeth nipped gently at her bottom lip. "It was the real you—messy and all. And that's who I want to be with."

Warmth filled her chest, and it wasn't the wine. Once again, this man proved that he had the ability to see through her. Alyse didn't mind maintaining her public image, but he was right; it wasn't her.

When everything was said and done, sweatpants and no makeup was who she was.

Alyse thought when he moved into the house that she wouldn't have any room to be herself. Little did she know that Tristan Zimmerman would be the man to give her enough space to truly be herself alongside someone else for the first time.

"I like being myself with you," she said.

"Even out of the house?"

She couldn't stop the smile that crept across her face. "Yes, even out of the house."

"You can have a life, Alyse. It doesn't all have to be photo ops. It can be like this."

She laughed softly. "I don't know that I can always have three bodyguards making sure no one acknowledges who I am."

"They didn't." His grin was so bright and genuine it matched the shining view. "I brought guards in case the stalker found out where we were going, even though we were careful. No one but me knew they were there. Not even Maddox."

"Really?"

He nodded. "Really. There's a lot of this world you'll miss out on if you never venture into it."

No one recognized her. Hope bloomed in her gut, even though that same anxiety was still hovering. "It won't be easy for me," she said. "The way I feel around people…I can't turn it off. I don't want to just give in to my fears and anxiety, but I know that I won't be able to do things like this all the time."

"I would never force you. I just wanted to show you that you can have a bigger life than the one you've settled for."

Alyse smiled and leaned into him. "Like I said, it's easier with you."

He pulled her down to him, wrapping his arms around her and locking her body to his. The energy between them shifted as she felt how hard he was. The wine in her stomach made her warm and comfortable. As much as she'd enjoyed this, she needed them to be home so she could take advantage of the state of him. Take another small step forward. Asking for what she wanted. "Take me home?"

"Will you let me take you on more dates?"

Alyse nodded. "It might take me time, but yes."

Tristan smiled before he kissed her. "We can take small steps together."

The kiss between them deepened until she was almost moaning into his mouth. Wanton. She wanted him, and she couldn't have him there. Even trying new things, she couldn't let herself do that. Not yet. "Take me home, Tristan," she breathed.

"I'll have someone drive us back," he said, voice low and rough. "I'm not taking my hands off you."

When he stood, he lifted her into his arms, and he kept his promise.

Chapter 20

The next two weeks slipped by quietly, but not uneventfully. Every day that she had to be there, Tristan went with Alyse to the set. It was a routine they settled into easily, in the same way they'd slipped into the routine of sleeping in the same bed.

And waking with their limbs tangled together. And indulging in each other without any worry or embarrassment.

And sweatpants and no makeup while at home.

Tristan was still handling other Zodiac business when he could while on the set, but he was also watching Alyse more closely. Especially now that he knew what to look for to know how she was handling things.

She'd been telling the truth—people made her stressed. Now that he was looking for it, he could see the strain behind her constant smiles and her kindness. Her actions came from a genuine place. Alyse was truly grateful for what she had and enjoyed her job, but it still caused her anxiety. He could now easily see the tension behind the smiles.

When they left the house in the morning, she was fully polished. Armored. And throughout the day, she never let that go. It was only when they went home that she was able to drop her guard and, depending on the day, even that wasn't always easy for her.

But she was trying.

They'd met with Callum twice over the past two weeks, and the meetings had gone as well as they could have. He'd been combing through the security footage from Paris and the flight records around when Alyse had taken her trip, but he hadn't found anything productive on that front.

But the stalker hadn't been quiet. Nearly every single day, he'd left multiple voice mails and texts on Alyse's phone.

But she never saw them. Since that first night with the voice mails, she hadn't been carrying her phone. There was no way he was going to allow her near the filth this asshole was spewing.

Because he was escalating. The further they kept Alyse out of his reach, the more determined he was to get to her.

Not going to fucking happen.

They'd given Alyse an emergency brick burner with no smartphone capabilities. Just enough for calls and the most basic of texts. So many people were on their phones so often, he'd worried she might feel isolated. But if anything, she seemed relieved not to have constant access to social media and the rest of the world. She assured him that the only person she really called was Jared, and now, Tristan. Everyone else could wait.

They'd left her real phone in service, and he'd been carrying it around on silent. The stalker still had access to it and thought she was ignoring him.

When he couldn't get in touch with her digitally, he'd changed tactics—going old-school, with letters. They'd started as typed, but this week, the letters they'd received were hand-written. Callum agreed that was another sign of escalation. The asshole was getting more desperate to get close to her.

They arrived by multiple means: delivered by hand at her mailbox, mailed, and delivered to her by messenger on the set. Although they hadn't been able to pinpoint him yet, every time he used that method of contacting her, it gave them more intel.

They would catch the bastard.

And Tristan hoped soon because these letters weren't pretty. At first, they had been similar to the content of the voice mail messages. He told her that he knew her better than anyone else, that it was impossible anyone could understand her the way he did.

But more recently, the tone had shifted to aggressive and angry. Why was she ignoring him? Did she think she was too good for him? Didn't she know what they could have together?

Don't worry, he would show her. Soon.

Over his fucking dead body.

Keeping Alyse safe was much more than merely a professional endeavor to him now.

There was no way he was going to allow anyone to hurt her. Not now that Tristan knew her and saw when she gave him those small, real smiles. Not now that he'd seen how hard she worked not only to be the best actress she could be but to overcome her fears and anxieties.

Alyse Peterson was unlike any woman he had ever met, and Tristan would do anything in his power to keep her safe. Her protection was the most important thing in his world.

If that bastard wanted to get to her, he was going to have to go through him.

Today was different on the set, which had all of them on high alert. Alyse and the cast had done a couple hours of filming but now were holding a press junket.

This was one of the first times the public would be receiving any information about the new film. A long line of journalists would be asking Alyse and Kenneth questions, followed by a public autograph session.

Tristan had argued against the autograph session, but the studio knew the star power Alyse had with fans and it was deemed nonnegotiable. So they had made it work.

The place was secured at every entrance with their people, and Nathaniel had been scouring all the networks in the buildings for days, trying to make sure there weren't any digital security leaks. Even Callum was on-site today to help out. No one wanted to take any chances.

Especially since another letter had arrived this morning.

One of the neighborhood guards brought it to the house. A woman had delivered it. They'd already tracked her down, and like all other letters that had been hand-delivered, she'd been paid to give it to the gate attendant.

The stalker chose his delivery personnel wisely. Most of them were obviously on drugs, didn't pay much attention to any details about him, and were from all over town.

Dead ends.

Tristan glanced at the letter when it came in, but it was more of the same intensifying threats against Alyse. He handed it off to the Zodiac agent who'd be staying at the house while they were at the studio. He would get it to Mark and Callum for further evaluation.

Alyse saw the letter. "That's from him?"

He nodded.

Tristan hadn't liked the way her breath shook. "Do you think that I need to see it?"

"No." His answer was instant and firm. She was already nervous for today and the number of people she was going to have to interact with. Showing her the letters—and their increasing violence—wouldn't do anything but upset her.

If she'd insisted, he would've shown her. Tristan didn't believe in hiding info from clients about their own safety. But she hadn't insisted, and, moreover, providing her with the info wouldn't help. It would only make her more worried.

So when those blue eyes met his, seeking confirmation about whether he was telling her the truth, Tristan gave her a reassuring nod. She trusted him not only to keep her safe, but to know what info about the stalker would be more damaging than helpful to her.

He wouldn't let her down.

Chapter 21

After today's junket, Alyse had four days off, and he was glad. All they had to do was get through it, then she could have a break.

She needed it.

They may not have shown her all the details of the stalker's escalation, but she still knew it was happening. And she had been throwing herself into work in reaction.

Tristan could understand the coping mechanism—hell, he'd been guilty of it himself—but watching her work herself into exhaustion the last two weeks had been difficult. By the time they got home each night, the most he could do was feed her and put her to bed.

And hold her all night.

Without it needing to be spoken, they'd been careful about their relationship in public. Alyse being romantically tied with someone had ramifications beyond just the two of them, and he wanted to honor that.

Not to mention what effect it might have on the man who was hunting her.

Neither of them had broached the subject of where they

were going. It had been too easy to just fall into each other at the end of the day without asking the hard questions or diving into that conversation. But Tristan knew what he wanted. Even if the stalker revealed himself today at the junket and they caught him, he had no plans to leave her life.

She'd swept through his like a hurricane, and he wasn't ever going to be the same.

The director called a wrap on the day, and Alyse retreated to her trailer to change for the junket. There would be a catered lunch for the cast and crew at the hotel before the actual interviews started.

She was quiet and withdrawn on the way to the hotel, but she still held his hand. Tristan didn't like the way she was retreating, but he let it go. He wished he could make her feel as safe in the world as she seemed to feel when she was in his arms. As they got out of the car, they didn't touch, and he felt the absence of her warmth.

Once they were at the junket, Tristan would be entirely focused on her safety from any threat. But before he put in that earbud, he wanted to take a moment that was just for them. Give her something she could emotionally lean on. The corridor behind the ballroom was empty, so he pulled her to the side and pressed her against the wall.

He lined up his body with hers so that she could feel him —all of him—and it worked. For the first time in what felt like hours, she looked him in the eyes and took a breath. "What are you doing?"

"Distracting you," he said before he leaned down and kissed her. Her tiny gasp made his body react so fast he hissed out a breath himself. He was hard to aching, and he kissed her deeper, suddenly wishing they were home alone instead of in this damn hallway.

"I don't need to be distracted," she said against his lips.

But Tristan felt the way her body had entirely relaxed between his and the wall.

"You sure about that?"

Alyse's eyes were closed, but he felt her lips curve into a smile. "No."

He curled his hand around the back of her neck and brought her mouth to his once again, reveling in the feeling of her melting under his kiss. It took everything in his power to pull himself away from her.

She now had pink in her cheeks, and those sapphire eyes weren't heavy with dread. What he liked most was the slightly dazed smile on her face. "I would distract you longer if I could."

"I would let you," she said softly, that anxiety creeping back in as she glanced toward the doors they were about to walk through. "You're going to stay with me all afternoon?"

"Every second," he said, pressing his lips against her cheek. "I'll never be out of your sight, closer if I can be." It was a promise he wasn't going to break.

"Okay." She nodded.

Tristan wanted to hold her hand as they walked through those doors and lend her his strength. But he knew that wasn't what she wanted. Maybe at some point, but not right now. He watched her straighten her body and square her shoulders, putting her armor back in place. "Let's go."

The room was set for lunch for the cast and crew of the film—no journalists yet. But there were several photographers and video cameras wandering about for bonus behind-the-scenes material. They didn't have much time, and immediately, he saw the problem. With so many people in the room, including cameras, Alyse wasn't going to eat.

But she was hungry. He no longer questioned why he knew it—he just did. She wouldn't make it through the rest of the day without eating.

Tristan put his earbud in and immediately heard Mark's voice instructing Zodiac personnel they had on-site. They had protocols in place: watching every person who came into Alyse's proximity, double-checking every ID that walked into the building, and making regular sweeps of every public entrance.

"I'm online, Outlaw," Tristan said softly.

Immediately, the rest of the voices cut off.

"Roger that," Mark responded. "I'm going to keep the chatter out of your ear unless there's something you absolutely need to know. Keep your focus where you need it."

"Thanks." He was right; Tristan would prefer to keep his focus completely on Alyse.

He glanced at her. She had settled at a table near the edge of the room, a bottle of water in front of her, talking to Jared. It was good that he was there. He had Alyse's best interests at heart and would be another set of eyes for potential threats.

While they were talking, Tristan moved to the buffet table and ran his gaze over it. He needed food that she could eat in between the journalists. Nothing messy, nothing heavy. Simple finger foods. Things she could stomach even at her most anxious. He grabbed what he thought would work. It wasn't as much as he'd like to feed her, but it was better than nothing.

Alyse gave him a small smile when he approached, and it got deeper when she saw the plate. "Feeding me again, Zimmerman?"

Since no one could see his face, he winked at her. "Maybe. Easy bites for in between interviews."

She reached out with her hand like she was about to take his before she realized where they were and pulled back.

But her eyes told Tristan how much she appreciated the gesture, and that was enough. "Thank you."

Jared looked in between them for a moment before

checking his watch. "Speaking of, we need to get up to the press room."

He'd been security for press junkets before. But the way they transformed the hotel rooms never ceased to surprise him: curtains, lights, and cameras made it a mini set.

And people. People everywhere. Assistants, makeup, film, sound, press.

As soon as they stepped inside, Alyse was swept into the chair where she would sit for the next several hours. They perfected the lights for her skin and touched up her makeup, and just like he promised, he never left her sight.

Tristan made sure the plate of food was available, and she did eat a little before she started. He wanted to touch and comfort her when he saw she was tightening up, but he didn't. This wasn't the place. Instead, he directed his own tension into focusing on potential threats.

Soon, the stream of strangers started to parade through. Tristan watched every person for any hint they might mean Alyse harm. Given the protocols they had in place, no one without perfect credentials should be able to make it through to this point, but he wasn't going to underestimate this guy.

He wasn't rational but was very smart. That was a dangerous combination.

The reason for Alyse's moniker as America's Glamour Princess was evident in these interviews. She met every journalist with a smile and answered the same questions about the film over and over again with the same genuine inflection she'd used the first twenty times.

Even when the camera wasn't rolling between takes, she was polite and gracious. If Tristan didn't know what doing things like this cost her, he would never know she was anxious. But he saw the way her fingers were flaring on the arm of her chair—the only tell that she allowed herself—and he couldn't wait to get her away from there and home where she could relax and breathe normally again.

When the last reporter finally left the suite, everyone was exhausted. Especially Alyse, though she would never show it. He moved by her side, and he couldn't stop himself from placing his hand on the small of her back as they headed toward the autograph room.

"Are you all right?" he asked softly.

"I'm fine."

"Are you lying?"

She leaned back slightly into his hand. "Yes."

"Not much longer," he whispered.

"Yeah, but this is the worst part. Reporters are generally pretty consistent. But you never know what you'll get with the general public."

Like the press, everyone in the ballroom for autographs had been vetted to the degree they'd been able. The bulk of their security would be focused there.

But the stalker could easily create a fake ID, and they had no idea what he looked like. There were unknowns to the situation, and when it came to her safety, he didn't like that.

All cell phones were being checked at the door, and each person could only bring one item with them to be signed. The studio was controlling the photography, no personal cameras or phones allowed—something Tristan had insisted on, given the attack on Alyse through her photos.

"You ready, Alyse?" Jared asked.

"Sure." The brightness in her voice rang false.

The group that moved from the hotel room to the ballroom included Jared and a couple of the studio executives. They were speaking to Alyse about the presentation of the film.

"The interviews were really good," one of them said. "Keep up that same perky energy. We really need to draw in a wide range of women on this film, and that energy tested really well in the early interviews and clips."

"I can do that," Alyse said, voice tight. This was what terrified her. The expectations of others in this role that was her life. She was afraid of what people would think if she didn't meet those expectations.

So much more of her armor made sense to him now.

The other executive barely looked at Alyse as he spoke. "This is very important, Alyse. This isn't really a public event. There are a few people we picked from public applicants, but most of the attendees of the meet and greet are influencers, and we're really going to be relying on them to spread word-of-mouth about the film. So, every person you take a photo with, every person you sign an autograph for, they're your favorite person, got it?"

"Yeah," Alyse said, but she sounded like a robot on autopilot. "I got it."

She was shutting down; Tristan knew it. He could sense it.

"Don't worry," Jared said with a laugh. "When has America's Glamour Princess ever not delivered?"

It was his attempt at defusing the tension, but it was the wrong thing to say. Tristan caught the tiny slump in Alyse's shoulders, her fingers flaring wide before clawing into fists. The door to the ballroom was coming up fast, and he knew that if Alyse walked through those doors right now, she would crack.

"Excuse me," he said, just before they reached the doors. "I need to review the final security details with Miss Peterson before we enter the ballroom. We will meet you there."

"Of course," the first executive said.

Jared gave the two of them a knowing look before disappearing through the doors, but he didn't say anything. Alyse barely glanced at him.

"Hey." Now that we were alone, Tristan tilted her chin so

that she was looking directly into his eyes, but she wasn't seeing him. "You can do this."

She shook her head. "I can't. All those people, they want me to be perfect, and he could be out there."

"You can do this. You're one of the strongest people I've ever known."

"That's not true," she said softly.

"I promised I would never lie to you. That's still true. You are so strong."

She sighed. It was almost a sob before she leaned her forehead against his chest. "I'm not a Navy SEAL."

He let himself pull her tighter now. "You can be an honorary SEAL."

One burst of laughter that didn't sound remotely funny shot out of her. "How would that even work?"

"Bravery comes in all forms, sweetheart. SEALs know that. And what you do…I don't know a lot of people who could handle it. Today, you're an honorary SEAL, and you have all the strength that you'll ever need. And if that isn't enough, I'll still be right beside you."

"Okay." Her voice was muffled by his shirt, but she pulled herself back and dug deep. A moment later, a charming smile took over her features. It might not be real, but it was close.

"Last thing." Tristan kissed her on the forehead. "Then we can go home."

Alyse took a deep breath and pulled open the door to the ballroom.

Screams erupted the second they walked in. A sheer wall of sound that felt like it could knock a person back a step. Mostly young women peppered the crowd, but there were enough men to be wary.

Two hours passed in a blink. Alyse took photos with every person and signed what they presented to her. Some had posters or memorabilia from her other films. A few people had perfume bottles. A woman around Alyse's age gleefully handed over a Gucci purse for Alyse to autograph and was nearly passing out with excitement.

Those people weren't his focus. His focus was on the crowd for anything out of place. He couldn't see anything, but something was off. Nothing looked wrong, but he couldn't shake the feeling.

"Tristan." Mark's voice echoed in his ear. He hadn't broken radio silence to this point, and they were close enough to the end of the day that if he was doing it now, it had to be important.

"I'm here, over."

"Stalker made a move, but it wasn't what we expected. He sent out an email to every email Zodiac has. Set it up as an urgent alert so everyone looked at it immediately."

Tristan had felt the buzzing in his pocket and had ignored it in favor of keeping his attention on the situation at hand.

"Is it a threat?" he asked. "Do I need to get her out of here?"

"No. But you need to see it as soon as things are wrapped up. This guy just changed the game."

Chapter 22

Tristan rubbed his hand over his face. It had been hours, and he was exhausted.

Alyse was safely home and asleep. She'd been so tired, she'd almost passed out by the time they made it home in the car. He'd made sure that she was in the house and felt comfortable before he left.

He didn't mention what the stalker had done. She'd been through enough today.

Despite the late hour, they were in the Zodiac Tactical conference room, the email the stalker had sent blown up on the screens in front of each of them. Mark, Callum, Nathaniel, and a few others were present, and now all of them knew about him and Alyse.

In fact, every person in his company knew, thanks to the email the stalker had sent.

Tristan guessed he was going to have to bring Michael back from his assignment in Alaska, where he'd been stationed in direct response for sleeping with Victoria Thorpe.

The image was blurry, but it was clear enough to see exactly who was in it and what was happening. Alyse and him, locked in an embrace today as they kissed right before they went into the lunchroom. It was the last few seconds they would be alone, and he'd wanted to comfort her.

Their kiss looked intimate and passionate, and if it had been a picture only seen by the two of them, it would have been something he cherished. As it was, it made him nauseous. If Tristan had known that kissing her in that moment would expose her to further danger, he wouldn't have done it.

"If the stalker leaks this, that's one thing," he said. "But if this is leaked by someone in our office, that person will be immediately fired."

"No one will do that," Mark said softly.

"And to be clear, I don't give a shit about myself in this image."

Nathaniel cleared his throat. "We know that too."

Tristan sighed, rubbing his hands over his face again. "I guess I owe Michael an apology."

Mark snorted. "The kid made the wrong call, and he knows it. Besides, being seduced by a movie star and falling in love with someone are two very different things."

The entire room went deadly silent, and Tristan's heart stilled in his chest. Was that what was happening here? Love? He looked at the picture again. He didn't have the time to unpack any of that, because the words on the screen were more urgent.

The email that had gone to everyone wasn't just the image. It was a threat against his life. According to the stalker, Tristan had touched what belonged to him.

And he would pay for it.

After that was just more of the same bullshit about how he was the only one who knew or understood Alyse. How he was the only one allowed inside her head. Inside her body.

He then went into a description of how he planned to kill

Tristan. Long and slow, removing the skin from his body an inch at a time. He would slit his throat while Alyse watched. Then she would be his forever, as it was meant to be.

Tristan could ignore the death threat against himself. When he was a SEAL, plenty of people had tried to kill him. Same for being a bodyguard.

But the possessive way he spoke about Alyse made rage boil under Tristan's skin. Even if she were just another client, he would feel ill, but this was *Alyse*.

There was no fucking way Tristan was allowing that to happen.

He'd already spent nearly an hour on the phone with Ian DeRose, his boss and owner of Zodiac Tactical overall. The fact that he hadn't said a thing about Tristan's obvious involvement with a client spoke to the trust he had in him.

Instead, he'd offered to send more core team members out to help. Tristan knew Landon Black was itching to help with the situation, and it was only a matter of time before his brother Andrew showed up if they didn't get this under control.

The people at Zodiac might not be family by blood, but they were family in every way that mattered. And a death threat against him wasn't anything anyone was taking lightly.

He pushed the tablet away so he wasn't staring at it. "Let's go around the table. What do we have? How did he get this picture? How did he get it out to every single Zodiac Tactical employee? And how much time do we think we have until he makes an actual move?"

"The picture itself is from the security footage from the hotel." Nathaniel's face was grim. "He probably remotely accessed all of it."

"They have cameras in that hallway?" Tristan asked. "That's surprising. That hallway leading to the kitchen isn't a high-traffic area."

"There isn't a camera there. That's why the picture is of such poor quality. This is a reflection off a glass panel taken from the *kitchen* security camera." Nathaniel pulled up a second image, a map marking the security cameras in the kitchen and the window from which the stalker got his image.

Mark shook his head. "Him pulling this suggests he knew the route she would take. Combing through all the security footage so quickly and finding this shot is improbable. He knew where to look."

"He's obsessed," Callum said. "There were about five hours between when the security camera caught Tristan and Alyse and when the stalker sent the email. He might have used a program to search and identify Alyse, but I wouldn't put it past him to be poring over the footage himself."

That made a sick sort of sense. "We cut off digital access to her, so he's making it up by digging through anything he can find on the security footage."

Callum nodded. "He's getting desperate to find a way to be near her."

Tristan turned to Nathaniel. "How did he get into the Zodiac system to send the email?"

The younger man grimaced. "He got around all the firewalls I set up by ping-ponging off neighboring networks. To be honest, I wasn't expecting him to try to break in to our outgoing internal network, so I hadn't been focusing my efforts there."

"So he doesn't have access to all our emails?"

"No. I had defenses in place to keep that from happening. But I didn't expect him to spam us. I'm working with Jenna Franklin to make sure it doesn't happen again."

Mark sat up a little straighter in his seat at the mention of Jenna's name. "Do we know Jenna's current location?"

"I thought she never left her house in Denver," Callum said. Jenna had helped him on more than one mission.

Mark shook his head. "One of your guys infiltrated her house a few months ago, and she didn't feel safe there anymore."

Callum's teeth ground together. "Theodore Wilson. Yeah, that bastard is the poster child for *end justifies the means*. I didn't realize what he did had affected Jenna so much."

Mark ran a hand through his short-cropped hair. "Tends to happen with agoraphobes."

Jenna Franklin had her reasons for not wanting to step outside her house.

"She's in some Podunk town in Wyoming," Nathaniel said. "Although I guess they're all sort of Podunk towns in Wyoming." He caught Tristan's raised eyebrow and grimaced. "Sorry, boss."

"She's in Oak Creek?" Mark sat up even straighter in his chair.

"Yeah, Oak Creek. You've heard of it?" Nathaniel asked.

Mark looked over at Tristan and nodded. "Yeah, I did a job there a few years ago."

Mark had been in-house security for country music superstar Cade Conner. Cade was from Oak Creek.

Tristan's brother Gavin and his wife Lexi lived there too.

"Okay," he said. "Work with Jenna and make sure something like this doesn't happen again."

Nathaniel nodded. Mark looked like he was forcing himself to stay in his seat. The man had it bad for Jenna Franklin and, until now, hadn't known where she was.

"I'm concerned about the content of this email." Callum got them back on track. "It's all been pretty fucked up, but these aren't idle threats in his mind. This email is his way of showing you he knows who you are and he knows you've touched what's his."

Callum saw him bristle and held up a hand. "To someone with this level of obsession, Alyse isn't a person. She's an object. More importantly, *his* object. She's a doll he's projecting his desires on to—not someone he sees as real and complex."

Tristan's hands closed into fists. "Then it's our job to make sure he never gets to play with his *doll*."

Callum pressed his lips together. "This death threat is real, Tristan. You need to take it seriously."

"I'm just glad that he's focused on me and not her for the moment."

Mark leaned across the table toward him. "This doesn't give you license to do anything stupid. Alyse doesn't benefit at all if this fucker kills you."

Tristan knew they were right, but he would much rather be standing between this man and Alyse than the other way around. Let him focus on him. He could take it.

He turned to Callum. "What sort of timeline are we talking about here, in your opinion?"

"The footage he found will continue to get him worked up. I'd say he'll make a move within a week."

It was silent around the table for a few moments.

"I'll be careful," he finally said.

"Good," Mark said, grinning. "Now, are you going to add lessons on how to kiss like that to the Zodiac training or…?"

Tristan chuckled in spite of himself. "No. Get out of here. It's been a long day."

Everyone started gathering their things. He didn't need to tell everyone to keep doing what they were doing to find this guy. They would.

He wanted to get out of there too. Back to Alyse. Two of his best men were guarding her, and with the stalker's current fixation on him, Tristan knew that she was safe, but it wasn't the same as being there with her.

That wasn't the only reason he wanted to get back to her. He wanted to hold her—feel her body against his and know that she was safe. That sensation when she relaxed and melted against him, assured he was close to her.

Tristan was glad Alyse had a few days off so she could rest, and he could rest with her. Right now, he felt as if he could sleep for a week. But a few hours and he would be just fine.

It was late enough that the roads were fairly clear. Alyse's house was on the far side of LA from the Zodiac offices in a less populated area—on the other side of the valley. He'd driven this so many times, the way to Alyse's house was almost as familiar as the route to his own.

He hadn't been to his own house in weeks.

Tristan didn't want to go back to his own house now if it meant being parted from Alyse. She'd first walked into his life a month ago, and he couldn't believe how things had completely changed.

Was Mark right? Was he falling in love with Alyse Peterson?

When he thought of how opposed he'd been to taking on the case in the first place… How he'd almost insisted—

The screech registered first in his senses, but not a half second later, his body was thrown toward the passenger side as a vehicle hit his from the back corner.

Instinct took over. Tristan jerked the wheel to the left, keeping his car on the road—barely. They were in the hills, and the guardrails there were no protection against the steep drop-off on the other side.

He let out a low curse as the other vehicle rammed him again. It was trying to force him over the edge.

And Tristan wouldn't survive the fall.

He looked over to see who was driving, but the windows were dark and he couldn't see inside. But he knew it was the stalker.

Callum had said the bastard would strike within a week. Looked like he'd jumped the gun.

His vehicle was bigger than Tristan's. It had more weight, and he was pushing him closer to that deadly edge.

Motherfucker. This was *not* the way he would go out.

Gritting his teeth, Tristan jerked his wheel farther to the left to get just a little more traction.

It didn't work.

There was too much force coming off the guy's car, and Tristan knew he was going to go over the edge. He'd waited until the perfect time to ram him—right as they were at the steepest part of the hill with the most slope.

Tristan jerked as the stalker rammed him again, gritting his teeth against his seat belt's attempt to keep him in place. He barely managed to stay on the road.

He hit the gas harder. Tristan's car wasn't big enough to stop the guy from powering him off the road, but if he could at least get a little farther down the road, the slope wasn't so bad. His knuckles were white on the wheel, foot jammed against the pedal, trying to hold on.

All he could do was be thankful Alyse wasn't with him.

There. Tristan saw the curve that was his best chance. It was still steep, but not a sheer drop.

Maybe he would survive.

Once he made it to the curve, he stopped trying to counter his rams. He took the opening, pushing harder and accelerating.

The plunge over the edge was brutal. The guardrail shattered against the hood, and Tristan slammed against the seat belt. He was going way, way too fast. He prayed the car wouldn't flip.

As soon as he was off the road, he grabbed the wheel and turned it hard, steering into the skid. It was enough. Barely. The change in direction slowed the car sufficiently that the tree it hit didn't destroy it, but the collision wasn't gentle. His head cracked against the window, and his vision went fuzzy.

But Tristan had to get to him. This might be the only chance he got. He grabbed the gun from the glove compartment and flung himself from the car, trying to clear his vision.

He was there. Tristan could finally get a look at this bastard. Adrenaline rolled through his veins, and he didn't stop climbing until he was pulling himself back onto the edge of the road. The SUV sat there where it had forced him off the road, but as soon as Tristan pulled himself over the edge, the guy spun back in the direction from which he'd come.

Tristan aimed his Glock at the shape racing away from him, but his head was still blurry. He didn't fire. He wouldn't hit him from there even if he could see straight.

Sinking to his knees, he pulled his phone from his jacket and dialed.

"Outlaw." His voice was raspy. "I need help."

Chapter 23

Alyse

Alyse woke up warm and calm. That wasn't her normal state of mind after an event like yesterday—it usually took her days to recover completely physically and emotionally. But this morning, she felt…clear.

She reached across the bed for Tristan, waiting for him to slip his arms around her and pull her closer, the way he did the second Alyse knew that he was awake. Funny how quickly she'd gotten used to having him beside her. She slept better knowing he was in bed beside her.

But he wasn't there.

Rolling over, Alyse looked at the bedside clock. It was almost noon. She was surprised she had slept so long, although she knew her body needed it. Everything about yesterday had left her drained. Toward the end, it was only knowing Tristan was there, and that he would not hesitate to get her out if she needed him to, that had kept her going.

Alyse wouldn't even have had to say a word. He would've known it with just a look. Because he really *saw* her.

And it meant everything.

Tristan's side of the bed didn't look slept in. She tried to fight her disappointment that he hadn't come back at all. Alyse knew he'd gone to the Zodiac office after he'd put her to bed—something had happened to the email server at the office. She'd been so exhausted she'd fallen asleep immediately, but she'd assumed he'd be back.

She knew she should be grateful he was there with her as much as he was. Zodiac was a prominent company, and Alyse wasn't their only client. It made her wonder how long this arrangement could possibly last. Tristan must have other things to do than merely being her personal bodyguard.

The thought of anyone else being in her personal space made her stomach twist, but Alyse had to acknowledge the possibility. Tristan couldn't live there forever.

And once they caught the stalker…would he still want to be with her? Did she want to be with him?

Following that line of thought made her heart pound harder than she wanted. Until that moment, Alyse hadn't realized how strongly she'd come to feel about him. And that was terrifying. And exhilarating.

She put the thoughts aside. Delving into what-ifs wouldn't be helpful, especially when she had a day of relaxation in front of her. She had nowhere to go, and she could wear and do whatever she wanted.

Whenever they got home from the studio, Tristan was the one who insisted that she relax and get comfortable. And if Alyse showed any doubt, he took it upon himself to kiss her senseless and strip her out of her clothes himself. She usually didn't end up with any clothes at all for several hours when he did that—a state of things that she didn't mind in the slightest.

She missed him. It was amazing how easily she'd adapted to his being around all the time. But Alyse knew what they'd be doing if he were there: eating. She wandered into the kitchen and made herself some food.

While he was gone, she should probably call Dr. Elliot. It had been a couple weeks since she'd talked to her. She could use an update on everything that had been happening, and Alyse needed to talk through it all—the stalker, Tristan, everything.

Her mental health did better when she checked in regularly and had some accountability. They'd learned that the hard way over the years. So now she called every couple of weeks, even when nothing seemed to be going on.

Alyse didn't want to have their conversation in front of Tristan. He wouldn't judge her for it, but it still felt like she was admitting to some kind of weakness. He was so in control and so capable that she doubted he'd ever had reason to talk to a psychiatrist. Ever.

She grabbed the emergency burner phone he'd given her and called Dr. Elliot's private line. She'd been with Alyse for so long, she had the number memorized. She input her code to her mailbox and entered the callback number. Her system was designed for ultimate privacy, given that she catered to public figures.

The phone rang only a few minutes later, and Alyse answered on the first ring. "Hey, Doc."

Her voice was as smooth and calm as always. "Hello, Alyse. Are you doing okay?"

"Pretty good today, actually."

She could hear her smile. "That's good to hear. Glad to know that it's not an emergency call."

"No. Just a check-in."

"How's the stalker situation?"

One of the best things about Dr. Elliot was that she was

direct. It helped when she had a hard time verbalizing things. She'd known Alyse long enough to be able to press.

"Still going," she said. "I know he's been escalating, but I haven't really asked for any details because they make me more anxious."

"As long as you're informed enough to keep yourself safe, I think that's a smart choice."

Alyse nodded as if she could see her. "I think it's working. I feel better than I have in a while. Tristan seems happy to take charge, and he's been working with the FBI. I know he's keeping Jared informed too."

They'd talked about Tristan before. "It's good to lean on people. Especially if that person has earned your trust. It's healthy."

Alyse knew that, but it was still terrifying in some ways.

"How is it going between you?" she continued. "Romantically."

The last time she'd talked to Dr. Elliot was right after the first time Tristan and she had slept together, and Alyse had told her about it. She'd been caught up in her happiness and her wariness.

"It's going well, I think," she said. "Not like I'm any relationship expert, but it's been pretty seamless so far, and I've gotten used to having him close by. I think he cares about me, and I know that I'm…starting to care about him. But who knows what will happen."

That last statement was a bit of a lie. Alyse knew full well that she was already way past only *caring* for Tristan. But it seemed like too fast and too much, and she wasn't sure she could say it out loud yet.

Saying it out loud would make it real.

"None of us ever knows what will happen. But sometimes the risk is worth it."

They spent the next half hour talking more about Tristan, her life, and the stalker.

"What's a scary thing you're willing to do today, Alyse?"

This was the way that they had ended sessions for many years. A way for Alyse to push boundaries within certain lines. She hadn't really considered anything for today, so she thought for a moment.

A few nights ago, Tristan had tempted her to come to the gym with him. Not to work out, just to stay near him. He worked out nearly every night after they arrived home, or sometimes in the morning before she woke up.

Alyse hadn't wanted to—just setting foot in the gym was enough to make her nauseous. But knowing he wouldn't force the issue had made her decide to try.

It hadn't been too bad. She watched him work out, and he rewarded her by removing his shirt.

She knew he did it on purpose and didn't care in the slightest. He showed her some simple, easy weight-lifting moves he thought she might like, even though Alyse couldn't bring herself to touch the weights that night. It had been too much.

But maybe she could try.

"Tristan showed me some exercises the other night. I could go into the gym and do some of those for a little while."

Dr. Elliot knew all about her past. "I think that's a great idea. Remember, you don't have to push yourself harder than you feel you should go. But this is an excellent step. I would love for you to be able to use your gym in a way that fulfills you rather than frightens you."

"Me too," she said softly.

That was kind of a shock. Alyse hadn't realized until then that she missed exercise. Not the kind of stuff that Deborah would make her do, or the terrifying, sickening dread that went with it. But she liked moving her body, and she liked the nice feeling of "good tired" after a decent workout.

"Before we go," Dr. Elliot surprised her by continuing. "I know you're nervous about Tristan. It would be natural to wonder if it's been too short a time to develop any real feelings. But I've known you for a long time, and I think he's been good for you so far. I wish you hadn't met under the current circumstances, because these kinds of things can intensify emotions. But don't be afraid of this, or him."

Her voice came out in a whisper. "I think I might be falling in love with him."

"Trust your feelings," she said. "We've done a lot of work on that, and you deserve to be happy. Even if you're not together in the end, being with someone like Tristan could be good for you. Trust yourself."

That was hard.

"Thank you," she said.

"As always, call me any time."

Alyse disconnected the call and rolled her neck. Talking to Dr. Elliot did make her feel better, but it also meant she had to follow through on the scary thing she said she would do. Might as well do that now. Her stomach turned as she put on some lighter clothes and headed to the gym.

That familiar, sick feeling only came over her when she saw the bike and treadmill, even though she wouldn't be touching them. Those were her main two triggers.

Alyse almost turned and left. Maybe she could try this later when Tristan was with her. But she forced herself to keep walking forward toward the weights.

She should get rid of the treadmill and the bike. Why was she keeping them? So what if they were staples in most home gyms? Alyse didn't have anything to prove to anyone, especially when all those pieces did was remind her of the time she was too weak to stand up for herself.

Deborah McDowell could kiss her ass. She would ask Jared to get someone to cart this stuff away.

Tristan would be proud. He wouldn't see it as weakness to admit she would probably never use a treadmill or exercise bike again. He would see her strength that she was moving forward.

Alyse picked up the weights—lighter than Tristan's—and mimicked the movements he'd shown her. She had far less motivation than when he was there with her, shirtless and sweaty, and she still felt a bit queasy, but she pushed herself through a few sets. When the other equipment was out of there, it would be better.

For the first time in years, Alyse felt hopeful about the prospect of exercise. She definitely wasn't in shape—she was fortunate her metabolism helped her keep her slim figure—and she could only do a little, but it felt good all the same.

She was putting down the weights when she heard something near the door, and she nearly jumped out of her skin before she saw Tristan in the doorway, tired smile on his face.

"You scared me. When did you get back?"

He stayed where he was. "Just now."

Something was wrong. Alyse didn't know what, but it was something. He looked almost gaunt. And the way he was leaning in the doorway, the way he had many times before, should've been casual but somehow wasn't.

"Is everything okay?"

A shallow smile. He moved stiffly across the room to her and pulled her into his arms in one movement. Alyse had no time to breathe as he kissed her, gentle and firm at once. Touching him felt natural and easy and right, even though she was covered in sweat and no makeup.

She really was falling in love with this man.

"I'm glad to see you in here," he said against her lips.

"Me too. Though I'm getting rid of the bike and the treadmill. They need to be gone."

He leaned back and nodded. "Good idea."

Alyse lifted her arms and hooked them behind her neck. "I could use a shower, if you'd like to join me."

Another barely there smile. "As amazing as that sounds, I need to eat something and probably sleep. I didn't get any. We were…working on the case."

"Did something more happen?"

"More escalation. But no direct threat to you, so we're okay. I just had some stuff I had to handle at the office."

Alyse still felt like she was missing something, but she didn't press. If he'd been up all night, it warranted him acting a little off.

"Okay. I'll go take a shower then see if you're still awake."

Tristan nodded again, but she already felt like he was gone, absorbed in other thoughts.

Alyse showered quickly, and somehow she managed to avoid panic. A couple of months ago, she would've been wondering if Tristan's distance meant he was about to break up with her. But this was Tristan. There were a lot of things she could trust about him, first and foremost being that he wouldn't play games with her. If there was a problem with them, he would talk to her about it.

Maybe she could help. Alyse wanted to do whatever she could to lighten his load. Maybe she could just listen if he wanted to talk about it.

After she got out of the shower, she pulled on shorts and a baggy T-shirt and went to find him, but he wasn't in the kitchen. Nothing looked touched, and there were no dishes, as if he hadn't even come in. The door to "his" room had been open when she'd passed, and she hadn't seen him. Where had he gone?

A light was on in the living room that hadn't been on

earlier. Tristan was lying on the couch, his arm thrown over his eyes. Even from across the room, Alyse could tell he was asleep. She'd grown used to the rhythm of his breathing while he was next to her. He really was exhausted.

There was only one thing for this: a peanut butter and jelly sandwich. Quick, easy, and he'd understand immediately why she'd made him that. It took only minutes to make, and she had to take a second to think about how far they'd come from him forcing her to make him a sandwich just so she wouldn't have a panic attack.

Tristan was always the one caring for people. For her. At some point, something had to give. Alyse felt bad waking him up, but his eyes were open the second she placed the plate on the coffee table. Slowly, he sat up.

"You fell asleep," she said, sitting down next to him.

"Did you make me a PB and J?" he asked, his voice rough.

"Yes."

There was that ghost of a smile. But this one really seemed genuine. "You didn't have to."

Leaning in, she kissed his cheek. "Yes, I did. You deserve to get taken care of sometimes too, Mr. Zimmerman. Now, eat your sandwich. All of it."

He chuckled, though he still sounded exhausted. "Is that the way I sounded when I was making you eat these?"

"Maybe. But I'm glad you did it. Now, eat."

He didn't argue with her, and she sat with him as he ate in silence, just resting her head against his shoulder. Tristan sighed when he was finished. "Thank you," he said.

"Time for bed," she told him, standing and grabbing his hand. "You don't have to sleep on the couch."

He grimaced when he stood, but it was the sharp intake of breath that gave him away. He was in major pain.

Dread pooled at the base of her spine. "You're hurt. What happened? Are you okay?"

"Just what happens when your ass and an office chair make love for twelve hours." He said it lightly, but she knew that wasn't everything.

He was exhausted, so Alyse didn't push him for answers. Maybe he would tell her in the morning when he'd had a chance to rest properly. At least, she would ask. She didn't let go of his hand all the way up the stairs.

She helped him out of his jacket, and he stripped out of his pants to just a T-shirt and boxer briefs that made her mouth water. But tonight, she was just happy to have him there with her. Beside her.

"You need a break," she told him as they climbed underneath the blankets and she shut off the lights.

"I have a break," he said, pulling her close. "Remember? No shooting for three more days. Just me and you."

It didn't seem like enough until a sudden inspiration hit her. "I want to show you my world, Tristan. You took me somewhere I needed to go to show me that I could be normal. Will you trust me to take you somewhere I think you need to go?"

Tristan's lips found her forehead in the dark, and Alyse could tell he was already fading into sleep. "Of course."

Alyse knew exactly where to take him, where they could both take their minds off all this. It would be perfect.

Chapter 24

Sometimes being a celebrity had its advantages. In spite of everything she'd been through and all the anxiety that came along with it, Alyse was aware of the position she had and the privileges her life gave her.

For most people, chartering a plane and booking a private beach on very little notice was nearly impossible. Alyse was taking advantage of the fact that it wasn't impossible for her.

She wanted to show Tristan some of the perks of her life.

He'd fallen asleep almost immediately after they'd gotten into bed. She'd gotten back up and called Jared, explaining what she wanted, worried he might judge her for it. But she was happily surprised when he was willing to do it and even told her he thought it was a great idea.

That she deserved the break, and further, that Tristan and she deserved some time together.

She did. *They* did.

Jared's approval of them together was one more sign that gave Alyse hope. Jared was protective of her almost to a fault, and if he didn't like Tristan, he wouldn't be arranging this. Or at least strongly suggesting she do anything but this. He'd often done that when Alyse was dating Salvatore. Although, she'd ignored Jared's warnings because she thought she knew what was best.

Jared also had to run the plan through Zodiac, getting in touch with Mark Outlawson. Pulling a secret over on your own head of security wasn't an easy task. They needed help from the inside. Mark had, surprisingly, immediately agreed it was a great idea. The place they were going had its own security, but Mark would handle backup.

When she'd told Tristan about her grand scheme this morning—leaving out the details of where they'd be going— he'd been reluctant to go anywhere because of security issues. A conversation with Mark, admittedly terse and long, had changed his mind. Although Tristan hadn't much liked going in blind, he trusted his friend and colleague.

A little bit after taking off from a private airstrip outside the city, Tristan had been so stiff and distant, she'd finally put him out of his misery and told him where they were going. To her surprise, he'd not only heard of Santa Catalina, but he got more relaxed when he found out that was where they were going.

He relaxed back into the luxurious leather seat of the jet. "I was actually in Santa Catalina not too long ago."

"Guarding someone?" Alyse didn't want to sound like a snob, but the small island, part of the Channel Islands just off the coast of California, catered to the rich and famous. It had its own top-notch security system—nobody getting on the island without their approval—world-renowned chefs, spa programs galore, and lots of private beaches.

And a price tag to match all of the above.

"It was for work, but I wasn't actually guarding someone." He leaned back in his chair, wincing slightly. "I actually snuck on to the island."

"How'd you manage that? They don't allow any planes or boats without approval."

He grinned. "I swam from two miles out."

Alyse couldn't stop her bark of laughter. "Just out for a little exercise and ended up in the Channel Islands?"

"My friend Landon was undercover and needed some help. Callum was part of the mission too. Exciting stuff. I'm looking forward to seeing the main part of the island. The part I saw…wasn't for tourists."

He didn't say much more than that about it, but she was glad they were going there together. He still wasn't quite acting like normal, but hopefully the next couple of days would clear whatever was on his mind.

A few hours later, Alyse was turning her face up to meet the sun, sitting outside their private bungalow, no one around for miles.

A shadow suddenly blocked her light. "Join me in the water?"

Tristan didn't wait for the answer, scooping her off the chair and into his arms. She let out a giggle. "It seems I don't have a choice."

"I turned down your offer of a shower last night, and I regret it," he said playfully. "I need to get you wet and naked somehow."

Her eyes went wide. "I can't get naked out here!"

He glanced in both directions, down beaches that were entirely empty. "Why not?"

"Even here, there's always a chance that someone's watching."

Tristan's eyebrows rose. "You're worried about paparazzi here? Unless a reporter plans to swim in like I did, I don't think you need to worry about it. The resort's security is top-notch."

"Weirder things have happened."

"I suppose that's true." He lowered her into the warm water, thankfully not reaching for the tie of her bikini. He didn't even take off his own shirt. "I wish you didn't have to think about that all the time. Your job comes with a steep price."

Alyse smiled. "Sometimes. But it also comes with some pretty fancy rewards, like being able to afford this place."

"I won't argue with that." He leaned down and kissed her, walking them farther out.

They were shallow enough that Alyse could still stand, though the water was nearly to her shoulders. And that allowed Tristan to roam his hands freely over her body without any chance that the invisible paparazzi would see what he was doing.

Of course, stroking his hands down her sides and teasing her skin soon was making her think she didn't care about this phantom photographer.

He moved his lips to her neck, and every inch of her body woke up. After getting used to the pleasure of his body every day—often more than once—the fact that they hadn't had sex in almost two days had her thirsty for more. Alyse wanted him, and the way he was pressed against her told her he felt exactly the same way.

"What happens if you stay where you are?" Tristan asked huskily. "Nothing showing or visible? Plus, Mark will double-check that the resort hasn't missed anything security-wise."

He toyed with the ties of her bikini top. She raised an eyebrow. "You're very determined."

His lips brushed her ear. "I'm rested and have you all to myself, and I haven't been able to taste the fucking perfection of your body in two days. I'm not determined. Hell, I'm desperate."

Warmth pulsed low in her stomach, and she suddenly wasn't wet only from the ocean. This man made her feel things she had never felt. Just those words in her ear made her equally desperate for him.

She kissed him in answer, dragging his mouth to hers and making it very clear what she wanted. Those clever fingers undid the knot behind her neck with ease, dropping the skimpy material so it was only attached around her ribs. He pulled off his own shirt so they were skin-to-skin.

He started his path down her neck again, but this time, he did not stop. Down her neck and across her collarbone below the surface of the water. His lips never left her skin, and she gasped when he closed his lips around one nipple where it rested just under the water. And then the other one, not bothering to breathe in between.

It was erotic and freeing, and she let herself fall into the moment with him. Every part of her was now alive with desire and just as desperate as he was. She couldn't stop the low moan that escaped her.

His lips made their way back up her neck, before he pulled back and retied her suit. She let out a frustrated little sob.

"Let's get you inside."

"I thought you said there's nothing to worry about here."

He nipped at her jaw. "I'm not taking that chance. Especially not when I have the very strong urge to hear you screaming my name. I want you in the bed."

He grabbed her hand and pulled her toward the shore, and Alyse laughed, nearly going under. As they moved into shallow water, she noticed what she hadn't before since his shirt had been on, and she stopped abruptly.

Dark bruises ran along Tristan's spine and wrapped around his ribs. He was *hurt.* Badly. No wonder he was moving so stiffly last night.

Alyse grabbed his arm. "Tristan, what the hell happened to you? Why are you covered in bruises?"

His face went from turned on to shuttered.

"On the way back to your place last night, I was in a car accident. That's why I didn't end up coming back until later than I intended."

"Oh my God." Shock rolled over her body. "Are you okay? What happened?"

Most days, Tristan didn't drive Alyse to the set, but every time she'd seen him drive, his skills had been impeccable. She knew an accident could happen to anyone, but it was hard to think of Tristan losing control of a vehicle.

He pulled her against his body and wrapped his arms firmly around her. "I really am fine."

"Why didn't you tell me?"

"I didn't want you to worry. Especially since it was already over."

Anxiety fluttered in her gut. "I wish you would have told me. I shouldn't have dragged you all the way out here. We could have just…I don't know…stayed in bed. You need to rest."

He kissed her forehead. "That's why I didn't tell you. I'm fine, and I'm glad that we came here."

"But—"

He covered her mouth with his, cutting off her words. It was not a gentle kiss. It was fire and life and the absolute essence of who Tristan was. She resisted the pull for a minute, but then the kiss drove lust into her bones.

"Do I need to prove to you how healthy I am?" he whispered against her lips.

Alyse gasped for breath. "Yes, please."

He didn't hesitate, pulling her the rest of the way with him out of the water and up toward the bungalow. Once there, they didn't even make it to the bedroom.

They were too desperate, too needy, too wanting.

The bungalow was gorgeous and open—perfectly

designed for people coming in and out from the beach, with a luxurious outdoor shower. That small, enclosed space was where Tristan pulled Alyse, closing the door behind them, turning the water to scalding. It felt good, the heat amplifying the need driving through her veins.

Tristan's hands were on Alyse again as he kissed her, undoing the sloppy knots in her bathing suit and stripping her down to nothing. "No eyes here," she gasped.

"No," he whispered. "You're all mine right now."

Those words did funny things to her body. Dizzying emotion swirled in her stomach—terrifying and exhilarating at the same time.

Alyse was falling in love with this gorgeous, capable, caring man.

"I'm all yours," she whispered.

Pulling her under the spray of the shower, Tristan lifted her against the wall and pulled her legs around his hips. Alyse liked being on his level, chest to chest with the gorgeous details that she loved about him. His tattoo covered a scar, and she traced the lines of it as he ran his mouth across her skin.

"Alyse," he groaned her name and shifted them together so he was pressed against her. "The condoms are inside."

She kissed him, digging her hands into his hair and tangling her tongue with his. He made her feel reckless and free, and she wanted everything with him. But more than that, Alyse trusted Tristan not to hurt her. "Pull out," she told him. "I don't want anything between us."

The low swear from his lips was less a curse and more of a prayer as he pressed into her. Alyse moaned, the sound nearly lost in the water and Tristan's own groan of pleasure.

Tristan eased deeper until he was buried to the hilt and she was stretched to the fullest. Every bit of friction was delicious, and Alyse couldn't breathe. It was perfect. Tristan was perfect.

They were perfect.

For a moment, they were frozen together under the stream of water, eyes locked, and then they were moving together. The wood wall behind her rattled with Tristan's thrusts. This would be fast and bright and beautiful like they both needed it to be.

Tristan's mouth crashed down on hers, stealing the last of her breath as he drove home, driving her higher until she was dizzy. One hand slipped between them, fingers seeking her core, and Alyse groaned into his mouth, completely on the edge.

It had never been like this with anybody else. With others, she had been so worried about what they thought about her or how she looked to them that she couldn't focus on her own pleasure. With Tristan, Alyse just let go, trusting him to give her what she needed.

One more thrust and she was shaking under his hands, pinned against the wall by nothing but his body, and every movement wrung further pleasure from her.

He was close too. He pressed harder into her, movements erratic and desperate, and she held on to him, his pleasure making Alyse fall deeper into her own. Pressing his lips into her neck, Tristan groaned, pulling back and spilling heat across her skin to be quickly washed away by the spraying water.

They were both still, breathing together, unwilling to move and break this spell. Tristan finally reached out and turned off the water before twisting his fingers in her hair.

"I don't care what kind of accident I'm in. I'm not staying away from you that long again."

Again, that dizzy, buzzing feeling built in her chest. Alyse could hear a declaration in his words, but she didn't dare speak it out loud. She didn't want to risk this moment with him. Instead, she leaned close and kissed his jaw, hearing the hitch in his breath when she did.

"I guess we have some time to make up for, then."

He made a sound of agreement. "Yes, we do. And a perfectly good bed to do it in."

She laughed as he carried her inside the house, already looking forward to what was next.

Alyse leaned against the door that looked out over the beach, taking in the vibrant pink and purple of the sunset sky. It was beautiful, and she didn't want it to end. She didn't want to go back to reality. The past two days, she'd felt calmer and more alive than she could remember.

Not to mention well-loved. Her body was sore in ways and places she would never have thought could be so delicious.

Behind her in the kitchen, Tristan was cooking something that smelled amazing. Jared had made sure that the place was fully stocked before they arrived so they wouldn't need to go to the main part of the resort to eat unless they wanted to. Alyse really needed to send Jared on a vacation with Derek after all this was over. He continually went above and beyond, thinking of things she wouldn't.

But even here in paradise, Tristan was connected to his Zodiac team just in case. On the dining room table, his laptop sat open with his phone and hers—her original one she no longer used—and his gun. Alyse wasn't surprised he'd brought a weapon, even to a place considered safe.

Her old phone had been buzzing almost constantly. She had wanted to shut it off, but Tristan said he needed to know what the stalker was sending, so they left it on vibrate. Tristan checked it every once in a while.

And now it was buzzing again. "Another message," she called.

"I'll grab it in a second," she heard over the scrape of a spatula.

Alyse tried to ignore the phone, but the sound was ruining the beautiful view in front of her. She could feel that anxiety pressing in, and it pissed her off. She didn't want the stalker encroaching on their time there.

She was going to turn the phone off. Or at least give Tristan the phone so that he could do what he needed with it and be done.

As soon as she picked it up, Alyse wished that she hadn't. The message flashed on the screen, and the world crashed down on her.

Next time, your boyfriend won't be so lucky.

She read it in shock, trying to understand what the words meant. Another message came through while it was in her hand, causing Alyse to startle and almost drop it.

I can't believe you would go for such an obvious choice. Your mistake. But I'll fix it permanently.

What the hell?

I know who he is. He'll pay for touching what's mine.

Message after message came through, detailing how Tristan was going to die. How he was going to be killed for the crime of being with her.

She was going to be sick.

Tristan stepped into the room with two plates of food and froze. "Alyse?"

Alyse set the phone down and wrapped her arms around her stomach in an effort to hold herself together. "Why didn't you tell me this was happening? I know I said that I didn't want to know, but this is different."

Slowly, he put the plates down on the table. It smelled delicious, but she was no longer interested in eating.

He walked over and put his hands on her shoulders. "My job is to protect you. You didn't need to carry this too, you have enough you're already carrying."

Alyse jerked away. "But he's targeting you! Have you seen what he said? It's sick. Much worse than anything he's ever threatened to do to me!"

"Yes. We're analyzing all his threats. Everything he says gives us more information about him. That's why we haven't disconnected your number. Hopefully he'll eventually say something that helps us catch him."

Tristan was so calm, so rational. Meanwhile, she was shifting her weight from side to side and felt like she was about to crawl out of her own skin.

"How long has he been threatening you?"

"It just started recently. He sent an email while you were at the press junket. He'd gotten footage of you and me embracing. He didn't like it." Tristan sat down on one of the nearby couches. "Come here."

She did. He pulled her legs across his lap so she was leaning into him. They were tangled. Alyse knew that he was doing it to help stem her panic, and she hated that it was working. But she also couldn't pull away.

At least the stalker hadn't been targeting Tristan for weeks without her knowing. Just a couple of days. Between that and his accident, he'd had a rough time.

Wait.

She narrowed her eyes at him. "Your accident. Did that involve the stalker?" The timing would make sense.

"Someone ran me off the road," he said slowly. "I didn't get a look at his face, but yeah, it was deliberate, so I'm sure it was him."

Alyse felt ill, the room spinning. "He could have killed you. He *tried* to kill you. Oh my God."

His hand cupped her face and guided her gaze back to his. "He *tried*. He didn't succeed."

"But he could have," she gasped. "And it's my fault."

Here she was again, causing someone else pain, just like Deborah had always accused her of doing to her parents. Maybe she had been right. Alyse was poison to everything she touched. She ruined things.

The phone buzzed on the table across from them again. Tristan got up and grabbed it without looking at the message, and he threw it onto the other couch where its vibrations wouldn't be audible. And in a second, he was on top of Alyse, pinning her down with his body. She couldn't ignore him like this.

"It's not your fault. I can see that in your eyes, and you need to stop right now," he growled. "There is no one to blame but this psycho bastard. It's clear he views you as his and wants to make sure no one else can touch you."

His eyes were fierce, and he brushed the hair off her forehead before kissing her softly. "It's not your fault," he said again. "I don't know where you went in your head just now, but it's not true. This man has a poisonous fixation. When we cut off access to you, he got even more frustrated. Finding out you're close to me gave him a second target. This is his natural response. It's nothing you did, and I would never take back being with you."

Alyse tried to fight the tears that were swimming in her eyes, but she couldn't. "If he hurts you—" She cut myself off. "It makes me feel like I can't breathe."

"We're going to get him," Tristan said with such conviction that she had no choice but to believe him. "He's not going to hurt me or you."

"He already hurt you."

"He won't get a second chance. Being here allowed my team to tighten security for me as well as you while we're gone. Your plan worked perfectly."

They hung in that moment, and Alyse tried to push away the thoughts circling at the edges of her brain. But they were hovering there, waiting for her most vulnerable moment the way that they always did.

"Now, we're going to eat and enjoy that sunset," Tristan said softly, his lips gently pressing against hers. "And then I'm taking you to bed so I can spend our last night here doing my favorite thing."

"What's that?"

"Making you scream my name."

He was trying to distract her, and it was working. She decided that for one night, she would try to not let this get the best of her. She would resist falling into the trap that was her own mind. And even though the panic was still lodged in her gut, she nodded and kissed him back. "Okay."

But she knew tomorrow was back to reality.

Chapter 25

Tristan was ready to put his fist through one of Alyse's beautifully decorated walls.

"Tell me we have fucking *something*. It's been four days since we got home."

His main team was sitting around in Alyse's living room. Nathaniel's face was pale and haggard from lack of sleep. Mark and Callum didn't look much better.

"This guy knows what he's doing," Nathaniel said, staring at the screen in front of him.

"Do you concur, Jenna?"

Jenna Franklin had joined them via video conference. Her long blond hair was pulled back in a high ponytail, and the camera she was using to broadcast herself caught her at an angle. Even without most of her face showing, they could all see her eyes darting around. As usual, she was glancing at multiple screens almost simultaneously.

"Bastard is good," she said. "But no one is perfect. Nathaniel is doing everything I would be doing if this were my investigation."

"Thanks," Nathaniel muttered without looking up. They

all knew he meant it sincerely. It was high praise coming from Jenna.

"He'll eventually make a mistake, technology-wise. Everybody does." Jenna looked directly at the camera so he could see her face. "But as batshit crazy as he is with those messages, he's keeping himself locked down and focused in how they're delivered."

"He's going to get way more violent before we catch him through making an error," Callum finished for her.

"Exactly." Jenna nodded. "Dude seems about to lose his shit. Sending out an email or some fucked-up voice mail won't do it for him much longer."

In the four days since they'd gotten home from the island, things had been tense for Alyse.

Knowing the stalker was targeting Tristan was taking a toll on her. Some of her nervous habits had come back, and he had to make sure that she was eating. The only time she was fully relaxed was when they were alone and he took her to bed and held her.

Because if Tristan was with her there, then he was safe. It was so very Alyse to be more worried for him than for her own safety. And as misguided as that was, he couldn't deny how it made him feel to know she cared about him that much.

He'd still rather have the guy focused on him.

After their return, the escalation had been nonstop. Messages and emails coming at top speed. Blends of threats against Tristan and pleas toward Alyse.

Didn't she understand that he was doing it all for her? Didn't she see that he was the only one who truly understood what she'd been through? That her pain was his pain and he wanted to make it right? That he was the best one to help her do hard things today, not anybody else. That Alyse was being controlled and he wanted to set her free.

To be with him. To be only with him. To see, hear, and

know only him. He would help her forget about the past. Forget about all the rest.

The bombardment was overwhelming.

Alyse wanted to be kept in the loop, but Tristan tried to shield her from the worst of his messages. That night on the island had scared him. All the light had left her eyes. Even when he'd seen her panic, she'd never looked like that. Thinking that she was at fault triggered something deep, and Tristan didn't want her going back there.

But her physical safety had to take a front seat to everything else.

They'd upped all security. They'd already been taking different routes to the set every day, but now they had added decoy cars on multiple roads. They'd brought the studio in on the severity of the situation, so the film was now working with a skeleton crew and added security.

Late last night, the stalker had switched up his tactics, prompting their predawn meeting now. He'd sent pictures of dead couples—graphic cases of double murders or murder-suicides.

"Anything we can pull from those cases?" Tristan asked. "Was he somehow involved?"

Callum shook his head. "I don't think he was. I think he has a number of objectives with these photos. First is shock value."

Tristan scrubbed a hand down his face. "If Alyse had been the one to get them, it definitely would've spooked her. Hell, those images are jarring enough for us, and we're more used to this kind of shit."

"Agreed," Callum said. "I think the images are also a sort of catharsis for him. A way to help manage his rage. He may even see it as fair warning of what will happen if he doesn't get his way with Alyse."

Tristan didn't give a shit about this fucker's *warnings*.

Mark stretched his legs out in front of him. "And don't forget he could be using this to get us all chasing rabbits rather than concentrating on him."

He nodded. "I agree, and we're not going to let that happen. We stay focused on day-to-day physical security and finding this bastard."

"Roger that. We'll keep a couple people working on the images back at the office. If he has any connection to them, we'll find it."

"I don't think he does," Callum said. "I think he's just lashing out to prove that he's serious. And he is. This obsession is a lot bigger than I had originally thought, Tristan. He's not going to stop—" He cut off midsentence, and Tristan turned to see Alyse in the doorway.

He thought she had been asleep.

"He's not going to stop until what?" she asked.

"It's okay," Tristan said, standing and walking toward her. "It's not something that you need to think about."

She had her armor on, though she'd allowed herself to be a little more casual than normal in jeans and a less-dressy shirt. "I want to know."

He tucked a strand of hair behind her ear. "You don't need to see this. It won't change anything about your routine or what you need to do."

He could see the terror in her eyes, but also the determination. "I can handle it. This is about both of us now, right?"

He nodded.

"Then it's not fair for you to bear it alone."

Tristan couldn't argue with that, not after he'd said the exact same thing to her before.

"Please finish," Alyse said to Callum as they came back to the group. He kept her hand in his.

Callum cleared his throat. "He sent a few pictures of

murder cases. I think part of why he did that is to show he's not going to stop until one or both of you are dead."

"Can I see the images?" she asked.

Tristan didn't want to agree. Everything in him wanted to protect her from this, but he wouldn't. If any other client asked to be more informed about the threat against them, Tristan would never withhold that info. He couldn't do it now.

"Jenna, can you send them to my tablet?" he handed it over to Alyse. "They're all real cases ranging from fifteen years to six months ago. None of them seem to have any tie to you."

"We've also looked through anyone you've been connected to for the past five years," Mark said. "So far, that hasn't resulted in anything. But this guy is connected to you in some way. We can all feel it."

They all watched as Alyse looked through the pictures. Her face was tight and pale, but she kept it together.

"None of these are familiar to me. I don't recognize any of them or remember hearing about them." She shrugged one shoulder. "But I don't watch the news very much if I can help it."

"They may be a decoy, attempting to get us to focus on something rather than him," Tristan said. "Or like Callum was saying, these may be some sort of outlet for his rage."

She nodded. "Do you have a transcript of the messages he's sent? I don't want to hear his voice, but I'd like to look through them."

Immediately, they came up on the tablet, thanks to Jenna or Nathaniel. Once again, he wanted to protect Alyse from what she would see, but ultimately, that wouldn't help. Besides, the phrases weren't nearly as jarring as the images she'd just looked through.

While she was reading, Mark leaned forward toward him. "You're not going to want to hear this, but it needs to be said.

You're not just her bodyguard anymore. You're also a client. You're in just as much danger as she is."

Tristan bristled, just like his friend knew he would, but Callum nodded in agreement. "Outlaw is right. Until we catch this guy, you need to be under protection."

Mark held up a hand before Tristan could speak. "We know you can take care of yourself. But this is way beyond what you can do personally."

Alyse looked over at him too.

Tristan took a breath and forced down his objections. His friends were right, even if he didn't want them to be. "Fine. Set it up. I'll be primary for Alyse, but we'll also have multiple agents with us at all times."

Tristan wasn't going to let this guy touch him or Alyse, but having backup wasn't something he should turn down. The accident had already been too close.

Alyse went back to reading the stalker's texts.

"The most important thing is getting a lead on who this guy is," Callum said. "We can't combat a ghost. Especially when he's running digital circles around us and only shows signs of further escalation."

"Agreed. But how?"

Alyse let out a grumpy breath at the screen. He turned to her. "What? Had enough?"

She rolled her eyes. "I'd had enough after the first one. But once he started talking like my psychologist, it really pissed me off."

Both Mark and Callum sat up straighter in their chairs. "What line reminded you of that?"

She handed the tablet back to Tristan. "The one about him helping me do hard things today. That's how my psychologist and I end our sessions usually. With her asking me what hard thing I can do that day."

He met eyes with Mark. "You looked at Dr. Elliot?"

"No," Alyse gasped. "It can't be her. She's a woman, and I've known her since I was a preteen."

"Not her," Tristan said. "But the messages are personal. They're about understanding you and sharing your pain. Who do you tell your pain to?"

Understanding dawned in her eyes.

"Dr. Elliot is definitely clean," Mark said. "We also ran the employees in her office, but there were no red flags."

Tristan looked at Nathaniel and Jenna. "Can we check her systems? Rerun everything on people in her office? Maybe this guy is one of her patients and found out Alyse was too."

Callum crossed his arms over his chest. "She's not going to just offer you a list of her clients."

Alyse nodded in agreement. "That's why so many celebrities go to Dr. Elliot. She goes out of her way to ensure discretion."

"Let's do what we can," Tristan said.

Callum was studying his tablet again. "It's certainly worth a look. You're right, these things he's saying are personal and definitely lean toward him understanding Alyse. He wants to be the one she turns to."

Jenna spoke up from her screen. "Nathaniel and I will start probing her system, looking for holes. We'll try to keep it on the legal side."

Tristan nodded. They would cross into the illegal side if needed, but none of them wanted to say that out loud, putting Callum—a federal agent—in a sticky situation.

It felt like a step in the right direction, at the very least. Tristan was done waiting. Waiting made you a sitting duck. It made you vulnerable.

It was time to go on the offensive.

Chapter 26

Two days after that predawn meeting, they were nowhere closer than they had been. Nathaniel and Jenna hadn't found anything in Dr. Elliot's system that suggested a leak of data. A full work-up of everyone at her office had been a dead end too.

He'd personally gone to the psychiatrist, explained the situation, and asked if she'd be willing to share her client list.

Tristan hadn't been surprised when she'd said no.

She did reassure him that she had no clients who had ever mentioned Alyse. She promised if she discovered anyone who meant Alyse harm, she would notify the authorities immediately. Safety from harm superseded doctor-patient privilege. He gave her Callum's number.

Driving back with two guards of his own, Tristan could feel frustration eating at him. He'd felt like he was watching Alyse waste away more each minute. She was jumpy, nervous, almost nauseous. Every second they sat passively waiting for the next scene from the stalker's horror show was another they let themselves be victims.

It was still time to go on the offensive. And Tristan had the perfect bait to draw the stalker out.

Him.

There Tristan was for the third night in a row, nursing a beer in one of LA's more popular bars. Places with cameras and plenty of people the stalker could blend in with if he was casing him. Which Tristan very much wanted him to do.

But he wasn't there. Tristan felt it in his gut that tonight was going to be just as fruitless as the other two nights they'd tried this. Yet another night he could have been at home with Alyse, comforting her and loving her, instead of being at a bar trying to lure the bastard out.

Maybe they'd been too obvious. He'd broken radio silence with the office to make sure his plans for going out could be heard by anyone who happened to be listening. But for whatever reason, this guy wasn't picking up what they were putting down.

Mark and Callum were with him tonight, just as they'd been the last two nights, although they weren't sitting anywhere close. Callum was at the other end of the bar, and Mark was at a table in the back corner where he could see anyone coming in and out.

"We need to catch this fucker." Tristan said into his hidden comm unit behind the beer he was sipping. This channel was private to the three of them. They had another six Zodiac agents outside surrounding the building and scouting the nearby area, ready to move on their command.

Mark's chuckle held no humor whatsoever. "No one is going to deny that fact."

Tristan glanced around the room again, hoping to find somebody—*anybody*—who was taking an interest in him. He felt like he was fucking trolling.

"This is killing her," he said, not having to specify that he was talking about Alyse. "I'm watching her wither in front of my eyes, and there's nothing I can do about it."

"Does she know what you're doing right now?" Mark asked.

"Not the specifics. She knows we're working on a plan to catch the stalker, but not that we're attempting to bait him. That would throw her over the edge. She's already not eating again and jumping at every sound. It's killing me too."

Tristan didn't mention she wasn't sleeping well. Neither was he. But Alyse woke regularly, snapping awake with terror even when she was in his arms—as she was every night. The knowledge that the stalker had turned his gaze on Tristan worried her much more than when he had only been targeting her.

"Of course it's going to bother you," Callum said. "You're half in love with the woman already. I don't blame you for not wanting to see her in pain or frightened."

Half in love with her. That wasn't the truth at all.

Tristan was *all* the way in love with her.

Truly, fully, deeply in love with Alyse Peterson. America's fucking Glamour Princess. Although he couldn't give a shit about that. What Tristan loved about her was underneath the outer package.

Her delicate strength and sweetness. Her honesty and kindness. The way she met her problems head on and tried to keep herself down-to-earth in spite of her fame. Everything.

This was far beyond a simple job now. He needed Alyse to be safe. Because he wouldn't survive if she wasn't.

Tristan took another sip of his beer. "You're only half right, Callum."

"On not wanting to see her scared or hurting?"

"I'm not half in love with her. I'm completely in love with her."

There was silence on the other end of his earpiece. That hadn't been what they were expecting. Tristan wasn't surprised. He was a crabby bastard, and the last thing he would have said a couple of months ago was that he would fall in love with anyone.

Particularly someone like Alyse.

"Holy shit, man," Mark said. "Really?"

Tristan knew he was grinning like an idiot into his beer. "Yeah."

"I'm happy for you," Callum said. "I really am."

"Me too." He could hear the laughter in Mark's voice. "Although as soon as this is over, I'm going to give you so much shit."

"I need her to be safe. I can't function otherwise. I can't lose anybody else."

Another beat of silence from his friends.

"You're already too much on edge," Mark said. "You're running yourself ragged. Hyperfocused guarding Alyse every second during the day and then not getting much sleep being out here with us the last couple nights."

"Something has to give," Callum chimed in.

"I know. And the bastard isn't going to show up again tonight. But I had to try. Every time I think about something happening to Alyse, I see Cliff."

They both knew who Tristan was talking about. They'd been with him. Cliff Johnson had been a dorky, sweet kid barely out of training who'd latched on to him like a puppy in Afghanistan. Tristan didn't mind, and part of him liked the way he idolized him. It made Tristan feel like a hero. He shouldn't have accepted it the way he did. If he hadn't, maybe Cliff would still be alive.

The kid had followed him to an expat bar when he was off duty. Tristan had wanted a little space from the unit and a drink that was better than the bullshit they had on base. Every regulation said that he should have sent Cliff back to camp. He wasn't supposed to be off base, but Tristan thought he deserved a break too. So, he bought him a drink.

And then just shit luck. Two strangers got into a fight at the bar, and hot tempers led to a firefight Tristan hadn't seen coming.

His instincts failed him.

Tristan tried to get them out but couldn't. He'd dropped to the floor, but Cliff had been a half second too slow. The stray bullet in his direction happened so damned fast. He was dead before the fight was even over. Died right on the floor next to Tristan—his eyes wide with terror and confusion.

Blue eyes. Not nearly as compelling as Alyse's, but the thought of her eyes lifeless like Cliff's caused him to break out into a cold sweat.

"Tristan." Mark cut into his thoughts. "Cliff was a good kid. But he was also a dumbass who had no business breaking regs and following you that day. You couldn't have known what would happen."

"Yeah." But the fact of the matter was that Cliff was still dead, and Tristan didn't stop it.

That couldn't happen to Alyse. Nothing could happen to her. He wouldn't survive it.

He'd wanted this fucker to come after him like he'd promised so Tristan could put him in the ground. But evidently, that wasn't going to happen.

He tapped his earpiece to activate it to change the channel so everyone could hear, not just Callum and Mark. "No sign of this guy. Let's wrap it up for the night, everyone. Thank you."

He heard a chorus of affirmative responses from the men and women stationed outside. Mark stood up from his table, giving Tristan a barely noticeable nod as he walked toward the door. He would supervise everything outside. A couple minutes later, Callum did the same.

Tristan hated that he had to stay here until he was given

the all clear and a car was ready for him, but he wouldn't deviate from the plan.

Since this hadn't worked, they needed to figure out something else. He was done letting the stalker dictate the terms of this battle.

They had to turn things around, and evidently, Tristan wasn't enough to draw him out.

An idea was forming in his mind, and he hated it. But still, anything was better than waiting in limbo and watching Alyse waste away to nothing.

They needed to take the fight to him so they had the tactical advantage.

And Tristan knew just how.

~

Alyse

Alyse was falling apart.

And it seemed like the more she tried to keep herself together, the worse she got.

This whole week had been a nightmare. Once she knew Tristan was also in danger, it was like she couldn't turn off her mind. She hated that he had to deal with this monster also.

Her nerves were on a hair trigger. Alyse jumped at everything, even when she was at home. While on set, even with the skeleton crew, it was a continual onslaught of too much stimulation, and work that would normally only make her pleasantly tired had her utterly exhausted by the end of the day.

Tristan was tired too, running himself ragged trying to protect her and find this man before they both wound up dead.

The only solace Alyse found was when they collapsed into bed together, too exhausted to do anything but hold each other. But even the safety she felt in Tristan's arms didn't keep the nightmares at bay. She had woken up sweating and panting in nameless fear more times than she could count.

Tristan loved her back to sleep. Sometimes with drugging kisses that warmed her body and made her ache, and sometimes with more until they were even more exhausted, but spent and panting together.

The messages from the stalker had gotten more frequent and desperate. Alyse didn't want to know what they said, but she couldn't stop herself from asking now. She needed to hear them so she could protect herself and Tristan if she could.

The stalker seemed to know things that he shouldn't know. He dropped snippets about Alyse not feeling good enough. Like she would never measure up.

It could be a brilliant guess, but it also could prove that he had access to something private. Tristan assured her they were still investigating Dr. Elliot and her office. Alyse knew the stalker wasn't her, but she also knew she had opened up to her about all those things. And Dr. Elliot took notes. Most therapists did. Maybe the stalker had somehow gotten those.

The fact that Tristan had been gone the last few nights was slowly eating at her. Knowing he was being targeted made her sick. Tristan didn't give Alyse specifics about what he was doing each night, but just his being away from her was enough to send her anxiety spiking.

At least if he was there with Alyse, she knew he was safe. Away from her presence…

Alyse could still remember the bruises from when the stalker had run him off the road. What might happen next?

Last night, Tristan had stayed home, and while her relief had been palpable, something had been off. He'd been with her, but also…hadn't been. He was colder and more calculated. More like the intimidating man she'd first met, rather than the man who'd been holding her through her nightmares for the past week.

She knew she shouldn't read too much into his coldness. He was preoccupied with everything that was happening. But there was a smaller, darker part of her mind that whispered it had all become too much. That she was no longer worth the pain or stress that being with her caused, and he was starting the separation early.

Alyse didn't want to believe it. But it was hard not to.

When she woke that morning with Tristan's arm slung across her waist, Alyse nearly wept in relief. At least in sleep he wanted to be near her. Rolling over, she tucked herself into his body, and he pulled her closer.

"Good morning," he said, lips pressed into her hair.

"I missed you." He'd been hard at work in his room when she'd gone to sleep. "I wasn't sure if you were coming to bed last night."

He groaned softly. "I always miss you, Alyse. Every second I'm not with you."

"Really?" She hated how vulnerable her voice sounded. She hated the voices in her head that made her doubt him after he'd proven how much he cared. But the anxiety and panic had Alyse in their grip, and they wouldn't let go until she'd heard his answer.

Tristan opened his eyes more fully and looked down at her. Up close, Alyse could see the exhaustion. It only piled on the guilt, because the exhaustion was because of her. For her.

"Yes, really." The look in his eyes gave her no reason to doubt him.

Alyse got lost in the kiss he pressed to her lips, and her panic faded a little.

"I want to take you out to dinner again," Tristan said softly after a moment.

That wasn't what she'd expected. "Are you sure that's a good idea? With…everything that's happening? The way he's escalating?"

A kiss was gently placed on her temple. "I think we could both use a little normal."

His voice sounded fine, but he didn't meet her eyes when he said it, and that subtle dread was back, resting against her spine. He was offering to take her out, but Alyse didn't feel like he really wanted to.

"We're both tired," she said. "Exhausted. We could have some normal by staying here and watching some TV. Or staying in bed. You don't have to do anything you don't want to. And I can understand if you don't want to take me out right now."

That brought his eyes to hers, and Alyse saw her Tristan again. He was there with her. "I want to take you out every single day, and I will once we catch this bastard."

"Until then, we can wait. I'm okay. I just like being with you."

He kissed her on her forehead, and she thought that might be the end of the discussion. But then his face hardened again. "No. Tonight, we'll go out. I want to take you out."

Before Alyse could say anything further, he shifted his body over hers. She sighed as a wave of relief crashed over her. Every touch and kiss eased her mind and shut off the voices in her head whispering that she wasn't good enough for him.

Though Alyse wasn't ready to say it out loud, she loved this man. Wholly and completely. She wasn't sure when it happened; all she knew was that it had.

And she was never going to be the same.

Tristan moved again, teasing her body in the way that only he could, and there was no more thinking.

Chapter 27

Tristan hadn't told her what to wear for their date this time, but Alyse knew he preferred her in plain and simple clothes. So she went with what had been so successful with their first date. Jeans and a T-shirt, this time with an added sweatshirt. Hair pulled up in a messy bun. No makeup.

America's Glamour Princess was anything but.

The thought of setting foot outside the house like this still made anxiety claw at her throat, but it was the thought of Tristan that steadied her.

Alyse walked down to the foyer, where he was already waiting. She stopped hard when she noticed the surprised look on his face when he saw her before he quickly covered it up.

Oh no. Had she messed up? Maybe she was underdressed for what he had planned. He was more dressed up than her—slacks and a jacket. It was what he had to wear to easily conceal his gun, and Alyse knew there was no way he'd leave it behind.

"What's wrong?" She asked.

He shook his head. "Nothing."

"I thought tonight would be like our last date. Am I underdressed? Should I go change?"

He gave her a tight smile and reached for her hand. "There's no time to change."

The floor fell out from underneath her. She thought that he would joke it off or tell her she was being silly.

Honestly, she'd thought he would yank her into his arms, kiss her, and tell her—once again—that he preferred her like this.

Tristan's words threw Alyse for a loop, and suddenly, she was back with Salvatore, watching him sneer when she appeared without makeup for the first time.

Tristan saw her face and reached for her. "Hey, that's not what I meant. Absolutely not. We have a reservation, and I don't want us to be late." His voice was gentle, and he pulled her closer. Alyse let him, even though she couldn't relax. "Don't ever doubt that I love you like this, Alyse. I swear it."

Love. Alyse wasn't sure how exactly he meant the word, and she sure as hell didn't want to ask him right now.

"Okay," she whispered, trying to breathe through the screaming in her brain.

"Do you believe me?"

She nodded, but it was just a motion. She did believe him. She was overreacting and she knew that, but she couldn't seem to stop.

Either way, there wasn't time to dwell on it. They were ushered to the car, this time being driven in case they needed backup.

From next to her in the back seat, Tristan intertwined his fingers with hers then brought their joint hands to his lips. Her anxiety settled into a dull roar.

Alyse wanted what he was offering—a night of normalcy with him while getting out of the house.

"Are we going back to Maddox's?" That would suit her

just fine. It had been one of the best nights of her life—and certainly the best date of her life.

Tristan's eyes moved away from his focus outside the car, constantly looking for danger, and met hers. "Not tonight. But I'd like to take you there again soon."

Alyse nodded then he turned back to the window. At least he was holding her hand, thumb running absent circles across her palm.

She tried not to tense as they got closer to downtown LA. The restaurant they stopped in front of was definitely more populated than Maddox's. Not a well-known celebrity spot, but not a hole-in-the-wall either.

Had he thought this through? "Do you know the owner of this restaurant too?"

Tristan didn't take his eyes off the outside world. "No, but I've been coming here for years. They have some of the best Italian food I've ever eaten."

Her stomach growled softly. It had been hard to eat lately. Her appetite seemed to disappear whenever Alyse thought about the stalker. Italian sounded good. Not that the type of food mattered. Tonight was about her and Tristan.

Alyse squeezed his hand. She trusted him and wanted this time with him.

She felt better when they were ushered in through the back and out to a patio shaded with trees. Candles lined the tables, giving the space a comfortable glow as the last of the sun faded from the sky, and to her relief, the patio was entirely empty.

The hostess seated them, and soon, a glass of wine was placed in front of her. Alyse immediately took a sip. She was safe with Tristan, and the wine would wash away some of her nerves. At least, she hoped it would.

Tristan didn't touch his wine, but she wasn't surprised

since he was on duty. Even after they placed their order, he didn't relax in the slightest.

His eyes were flying all over the place, and he hardly touched their appetizer—fried calamari—when it arrived.

Alyse took another sip of the wine.

"Maybe we shouldn't be here," she said quietly.

"What?" Tristan looked at her for the first time since they sat down.

She swallowed. "We can just go. We don't have to wait for our meal. If we were at home, maybe you'd be less on edge. This isn't what I want for you." It wasn't what she wanted for *them*.

For just a second, Alyse swore she saw guilt flitter across his handsome face. But it was gone so quickly, she figured she must have imagined it.

"I'm sorry," he said, reaching for her hand across the table.

"It's okay," she said. "I understand. Let's just go home."

And Alyse did understand. He wanted to keep her safe, and doing that in public, even isolated like this, was more difficult and stressful.

"No, we need to stay."

They needed to stay? Before Alyse could ask what he meant, she blinked against the flash that suddenly blinded her.

Shit.

She knew immediately what it was. The press. Paparazzi. They'd somehow found them. Her hands rose instinctively to cover her face.

"Tristan, can you get them to leave?"

He was on his feet in a second, but the photographer was already gone.

"Don't worry," Tristan said. "I'll have the rest of the security team stop the guy and delete the images."

Alyse tried to steady her breathing when all she wanted to do was leave. Tristan said something into the earpiece he was wearing.

"It's okay. They got him. You're okay. Let's just keep eating."

Despite his reassuring words, her appetite was gone. But she forced herself to eat a few more bites. When the waiter brought out their main course a few minutes later, Alyse wasn't sure how she would make it through.

But she forced herself to try. This night was supposed to be for her and Tristan. One camera flash from a paparazzi, that had been handled, shouldn't ruin it.

Tristan wasn't eating much either. The longer they stayed, the more tense he became.

They were only a couple bites in when there was another flash. This time, Alyse put down her fork.

They had found her. There was no going back. If there were two paparazzi here, the rest would soon follow.

Oh my God, she looked awful. And the camera had caught her mid-bite. Alyse could already imagine what would be splashed all over social media in an hour.

America's Glamour Princess…not so glamorous anymore! Look at the mess she's been hiding!

"Let's go," she said. "They won't stop now that they found me."

She tried to make it look like no big deal. A small smile and a shrug of her shoulders, but she was swallowing down bile. Tristan might love her looking like this, but the rest of the world wouldn't.

"Okay," he said, reaching for her.

There was that trace of guilt again before he was guiding her back through the restaurant toward the back entrance, hand at the small of her back. They stopped briefly out of sight, and Tristan had a few words with the owner. He understood, and then they were moving again.

It was going to be okay. They hadn't gotten many pictures, and hopefully none of them would be too worthwhile. The rest of the security team would keep them away from them as they headed out the back door.

But as soon as the door opened, they were bombarded. Screaming fans called her name, and flashing camera lights made it difficult to see.

Terror, deep and true, ripped down her spine. How did they all get there so quickly? They'd not even been at the restaurant a half hour. She'd thought the first photographer got lucky—maybe saw them sneaking in the back.

But there were upwards of fifty people all crammed into the tight space that blocked their way out now. The car they'd arrived in was nowhere to be seen. They were trapped.

Turning her back to the crowd, Alyse tried to breathe through the stabbing panic that made her want to drop to the ground. There would be pictures of her like this. Her image would be ruined.

Alyse waited for Tristan to pull her inside to get them out a different way. She waited for him to execute the perfect backup plan she knew he always had. She waited for that solid arm around her waist and whispered words of comfort in her ear.

None of it came.

Tristan made no move to escort Alyse somewhere else. He wasn't even looking at her. His sharp eyes scanned the crowd. He was looking for something, or someone.

He wasn't caught off guard, trying to move to Plan B. There was no surprise or anger whatsoever. There'd been no reaction from him when the photographer had found them on the patio either.

Because Tristan had known.

Black dread swam behind her eyes, and Alyse thought she was going to be sick as it all clicked into place.

Tristan had set this up.

He'd leaked their location to the press to draw the stalker out, hoping that the idea of seeing her in person would be too much to resist.

And now Alyse was there with no hairstyling or makeup and clothed like some sort of hobo—everything she'd branded herself as *not* being.

This was her nightmare. Worse, it was the nightmare Tristan knew about.

The looks of guilt and his shock at her attire now made total sense. They couldn't be late because they couldn't miss the press sneaking up on them.

He could have told her. Alyse would have done it. She would have done anything to catch the stalker. But this…

She felt like she couldn't breathe. All the oxygen around her was suddenly water, and she was drowning.

The crowd hurled questions at her, but Alyse didn't hear them. It was just a wash of noise. She focused on Tristan as all the ground around her seemed to slip.

"This was you."

Her words were so soft she was surprised he heard her.

He hesitated, then nodded, his jaw hard, cheek twitching from his gritted teeth. "Yes. Every person Zodiac Tactical could spare is here as well."

He used her as bait. A means to an end. And there was nothing Alyse could do about it, because he had made the choice for both of them without giving her a say or any chance at all to prepare herself.

Straightening, she pulled the shell of Alyse Peterson around her. Yes, she looked awful. Alyse was sure every single one of her flaws would be on display in these pictures and footage. And yes, these images would be splashed all across the world tomorrow.

But there was nothing she could do about that now. All Alyse could do was try to salvage the situation. She shut down everything inside and turned back to the crowd, giving them her best smile.

America's Glamour Princess might not be very glamorous right now, but somehow Alyse would survive.

Chapter 28

The chatter in Tristan's ear was near constant as his men—way more of them than Alyse had known about—searched for the stalker in the crowd they'd allowed to be created.

The plan had worked near seamlessly. Since feeding the stalker info via their own channels hadn't drawn him out, they'd used the press. Undoubtedly, he spent time scouring the internet for any live sign of Alyse out and about.

As soon as they'd arrived at the restaurant, Nathaniel had very subtly let the electronic cat out of the bag. A ghost mentioning that Alyse had been spotted out on the town for the first time in weeks. Paparazzi had taken the bait.

They could've easily kept those cameras out of the restaurant. Tristan could've gotten Alyse out through another exit. They could've stopped the whole thing at any moment, but they'd let it build.

They wanted to give the stalker somewhere to go, confident he'd be able to catch a live glimpse of Alyse while blending in with a crowd. They had to seem like they were a little caught off guard, that a photographer had found them and snapped the shots before they could get things under control.

In essence, look like they were incompetent. A little unprepared.

Nothing was further from the truth.

They'd chosen this restaurant specifically because it assisted in their mission: spotting the stalker. The restaurant had four entrances and exits, so if needed, they could get Alyse away from the crowd and out in mere seconds. Despite what they were attempting to do, her safety was the most important thing.

The restaurant was on a relatively quiet street in east LA. It had two banks surrounding it, both with ATM cameras that would capture footage. There were also three traffic cams they were plugged into.

Before coming there tonight, his team had wired multiple cameras around the entrances to the restaurant and the surrounding areas.

If that bastard was there, they were going to catch him. Or at least catch an image of him. There was no clear sign of anyone who might be him, but they were getting photos of every man's face in this crowd.

He was there. Callum had agreed, after so long without access to Alyse, he wouldn't miss this opportunity. Especially one that seemed like an accident.

Tristan wanted him to try something right now while they were prepared so they could take him down, but he knew the guy was too smart for that.

But they were going to catch him because of what happened tonight.

Alyse gracefully took questions from the crowd and her fans, that brilliant, perfect smile on her face.

But not her real smile. Nowhere near her real smile.

Right now, Tristan was actively ignoring his response to

the look she'd given him a few minutes ago when she'd realized what he'd done. That he'd set this up. Set *her* up with no warning whatsoever.

It echoed the look she'd given him when he'd made her show him the home gym for the first time. Terror. Pain.

But this time, it had been mixed with betrayal.

Tristan swallowed back his gutted response once again. Catching this bastard would make that look worth it. He couldn't lose Alyse, and she couldn't keep going with the threat constantly hanging over her. This needed to end.

It would be worth it.

Jesus. It *had* to be worth it.

When she'd come down the stairs for their *date* looking perfect and delicious in her casual clothes—messy hair, no makeup—he should've made her go change. But there hadn't been time. They'd already leaked where they were going to be, and their timeline had to be perfect in order to pull this off.

Tristan couldn't tell her what they were planning. It was crucial that she be caught off guard by what happened. It was the key for them to figure out who in the crowd was the stalker.

But when she'd come down, he'd realized he'd made a tactical error. She'd thought—and why would she not?—that this would be another date like their previous one.

She'd trusted that it would be just her and him. That he would protect her from the prying eyes of everyone else. She'd looked downright delectable to him, but she definitely wasn't in her armor.

And Tristan had sent her straight into the battle arena without it.

Fuck.

It had to be worth it.

A loud question from the crowd flew toward them. "Is this how you normally look?"

She made a soft joke about waking up like this, causing people to chuckle.

She was fucking amazing. After the first brief moment of panic, she'd turned and handled it like an absolute champ, even not dressed like she was generally expected to be. She'd calmly answered questions and charmed the reporters and fans alike.

"Okay, Tristan, we've got everything that we can right now," Mark's voice said in his ear.

"You're sure?" Tristan asked. Almost every employee on his payroll was there right now, surveilling every inch of the surrounding six blocks.

"Yeah," he said. "If he's here, we have a picture of him. If he was going to make a move, he would have by now."

"Roger that." Tristan hadn't expected the asshole to make a move tonight, but how he wished he'd tried. They could've wrapped this up with a pretty little bow.

But they'd known it wouldn't be that simple. And now it was time for him to get Alyse out of there and talk through what had happened.

"Thank you, everyone," he said, addressing the crowd loudly. "Miss Peterson has to leave now."

Tristan didn't waste any time getting her to the car at the other actual secret entrance of the restaurant in a hidden underground garage, and thankfully she didn't resist in any way.

But neither did she touch him. He couldn't blame her for being a little pissed, but she'd handled it so well he was sure she'd understand why he'd made the call.

Tristan opened the door for her and let her slip inside before going around to the other door.

"We're ready," he told their driver and the other Zodiac agent sitting next to him, studying for any vehicular attacks.

"Wait," Alyse said, opening her door and leaning out. The sound of her vomiting reached him, and he froze in the process of entering the car.

Oh shit.

Reaching out, Tristan put his hand on her back, and she flinched.

"Don't touch me," she said as she pulled herself back into the car and shut the door. "Now I'm ready."

As the car started to move, she curled herself into the corner of the seat—as far from him as she could physically be in the same space.

Now out of the bright glare of the flashbulbs and lights of the restaurant, Tristan could see how pale she was. The fine tremors in her hands. Her skin was flat white and pasty. Like she was ill.

He'd been so wrong. She hadn't been taking it well at all.

Tristan reached toward her but dropped his hand when she flinched. "I'm sorry, Alyse. Nothing else was working. We were playing on his terms, and I needed to change the game. We needed somewhere we could get eyes on him. But I swear to God, your safety was never at risk. I literally had dozens of agents around who could've stepped in if needed."

She didn't say anything, just wrapped her arms around herself like she was trying to stop herself from shattering.

"Alyse." He tried again. "Your safety is the most important thing to me. I couldn't—" He stopped, taking a breath. "I couldn't live with myself if anything happened to you. I don't want you to think I deliberately put you in jeopardy."

Tristan didn't say that he loved her. Not in this moment. Those words deserved more than to be an explanation. They deserved warmth and touching and privacy. Not the back of a car when he wasn't sure she wouldn't jump out at the first opportunity.

"This is not about my safety," she whispered.

"Everything is about your safety. Catching this bastard is about your safety."

She shook her head. "You should have told me." Her voice was raw and broken in a way he'd never heard before. "Did you think that I would say no? Did you think that I wouldn't be willing to help you catch this monster?"

"No, I—"

"I don't even mind that you used me as bait. Hell, I would've offered if I'd even known the option was on the table."

"You needed to be surprised. Callum is convinced your sincere reaction is what will help us pinpoint the stalker in the crowd."

Those sapphire eyes pinned him. "You took my worst fear and made it reality for me. You shouldn't have sent me out there naked. You could have planned this in a way that didn't prey on my biggest insecurity."

Tristan felt sick. "Everything had to feel authentic. If you'd known, people might have known it was a setup."

"It's always a setup," she snapped, voice suddenly loud. "You know that. My entire fucking life is a setup. Every date. Every shopping trip. I'm an actress. You think I couldn't have acted surprised? Let me tell you, of all the things to act, surprise isn't hard."

He hesitated. She was right. "You handled everything perfectly. I had no idea you were struggling."

"And there's the lie," she said, laughing without humor. "You fell for it, and so did everyone else. But it all comes with a price. One I'll keep paying."

She turned back out the window. "I thought you understood."

The pain in those words undid him, but he knew better than to reach for her right now. He wanted nothing more than to pull her into his arms and make her feel safe.

The thought that he'd lost that right destroyed something in him.

"I didn't mean to hurt you. But your safety is the most important thing in the world to me. More important than anything else, even your image."

They pulled into the driveway of her house, and Alyse barely waited until the car was still before exiting and making a beeline for the door.

Tristan followed, but she turned before he could take three steps. "You're so concerned about my safety? Fine. You can stay in the security office and do your job as my security guard."

The door closed behind her with a finality that shook his core. He did this. He'd thought he was doing the right thing, and now he wasn't anywhere close to being sure.

The only thing that he could hope was that this led to a breakthrough. If not…

Tristan pushed the thought away. They were going to find the stalker.

They had to.

Chapter 29

Tristan hadn't set foot in the garage apartment turned security suite in weeks. There'd been no need to since he'd been inside the house with Alyse. Now that he was here, he hated the combined space and the seven steps that he could take from one end of the room to the other.

Mark and Callum had joined him there after wrapping up at the restaurant. Between them and the two guards already stationed there at the house, this apartment was pretty damned cramped.

The footage and photographs from the paparazzi setup were running across the monitors. They, and a dozen more people back at the office, were poring over them. Every second of footage needed to be analyzed for anything out of the ordinary. they'd all be working around the clock.

Tristan could barely focus. This was not where he wanted to be. He knew he'd be sorting through footage, but he'd planned to do it inside the main house. Not be stuck outside while Alyse was hurting.

His hands were twitching with the urge to hold her. Comfort her.

"You need to stop pacing," Mark said softly.

"If I stop, I'm afraid I'll put a fist through a wall."

He didn't look up from the screen he was studying. "I assume Alyse wasn't too happy about being used as bait."

"More that I didn't forewarn her." Tristan scrubbed a hand down his face. "I wanted to protect her. But I fucked up."

"How so? She's okay, right? Looking at this footage, she handled everything like a champ."

Tristan thought of the sound of her vomiting when they got to the car. "I sent her out to the wolves with no protection. Makeup, hairstyle, glamour…that's her armor, and it didn't occur to me how important it would be to her in a situation like this."

Mark paused the footage and spun around to face him. "Sometimes we get so caught up in physical safety, we forget about mental and emotional safety."

"Yeah." God, now *he* felt sick.

He'd taken steps, all the steps needed to protect her body, but none to protect her soul. The thing that was most precious to him.

"I fucked up."

Mark's code name might be Outlaw, but there was nothing outlaw about him now, just his friend.

"Yeah, you did."

A friend who didn't lie to him.

"But you move forward, make it worth the price you both paid, and then you grovel like hell once we catch this asshole."

"Roger that." Tristan sat down to get to work. Mark was right; pacing wasn't helping anything.

Every person they had available had been in place, including in the gathered crowd so that they could step in if physically necessary. They were looking for someone who wasn't on their list of vetted contacts, who was male, and who showed up after the information had been leaked to the public.

Or if he had somehow gotten access to the information before it was released—a possibility given the advanced technological skills he'd shown—they were looking for anyone who was out of place. Anyone who was calculating, looked like they weren't there just to get a photo or an autograph.

But what would he do? What would he be willing to do in public? Tristan looked over at Callum. "What kind of action would you expect him to take?"

Callum's eyes remained glued to the screen. "At this point, it could be anything. He's not rational. The anger he feels at both you and her is overriding his reason. He was there tonight, I'm sure of it. He can't wait much longer to get near her."

"Agreed. But that's tricky to pin down with just a facial expression."

He nodded. "I'd look for someone who's calmer than the rest of the crowd. He's too smart to be standing alone, probably, but he won't be caught up in all the excitement."

They worked all night. Three times, they found potential suspects—male, somewhat aloof, potentially alone. The first two we were easily able to identify through facial recognition software. Almost as quickly, they were able to eliminate them as suspects—one had been in South America during the time they knew the stalker was in Paris. The other's wife had a baby a few weeks ago. They'd been able to trace his locations enough to eliminate him as a possibility.

The third man gave them much more of a runaround. He didn't have much social media presence—normally, they could gather as much detail about someone as they needed from that—and was single and worked in finance.

He roughly fit the description they had, based on the footage in Paris. Dark hair, not quite six feet tall, hefty build.

Tristan studied the picture they got of him at the restaurant. He wasn't looking directly at Alyse in it. As a matter of fact, in most of the footage they had of him, he wasn't really looking at her.

What did that mean?

"Is this the guy, Callum?"

Callum was studying the same image. "Guy's name is Todd Perry. And yeah, I think he could definitely be our perp."

"Want to ask if she recognizes him?" Callum said.

Tristan shook his head. "Let's see what we turn up on him first." He hated that the distance between Alyse and him was so great that getting her input wasn't an option.

That was on him.

In the end, it was better that Tristan didn't ask her anyway. As Nathaniel and Jenna dug further into Todd Perry, they found some pretty sketchy stuff.

But not the sketchy they were looking for.

His white supremacist affiliations were definitely cause for concern, but not *their* cause for concern. And meetings with his buddies provided an alibi for two separate stalker events concerning Alyse.

By dawn, they were back to square one.

An unfamiliar sensation of panic ripped through his chest. He was on his feet again and back to pacing. "Everything we did was just to get a lead on this fucking bastard. There can't be nothing."

"We're going to figure this out, Pisces," Mark said. "I promise."

"You didn't see her face." His voice ripped through the room, taking all the air and sound with it. "I fucked up. She paid a high price for this. Higher than I thought possible. And I might have screwed up what we have. For nothing?"

Tristan was a second away from putting his fist through

the wall. The only thing that held him back was that this was still Alyse's home, and he wouldn't disrespect her by damaging it. But he was not in control. He should have known better. Done something different.

Just like with Cliff. Tristan should have seen that his choice was wrong long before Cliff's lifeless eyes were staring up at him from the floor. He'd misjudged that and then misjudged this.

What had he done?

Mark stepped closer to him, and Tristan could see wariness in his eyes. He and Callum knew him better than almost everyone. They knew his past and what was going through his head. "It's going to be all right."

"I can't lose her."

"You won't," he said. "She will be okay. Alyse is amazing, kind, and smart. When this passes and we catch the bastard, she'll understand why you did this."

"In the meantime, we'll check the footage again in case we missed something," Callum said softly.

Tristan forced himself to sit down on the cot at the side of the room and not move. This was the last place he wanted to be. Not knowing how she was killed him. Every instinct he had concerning her told him she wasn't okay.

Was she still sick? Throwing up? Checking and rechecking social media to see what photos had been posted? Was she crying? Tristan almost leaped to his feet again. Should he go to her? The thought of her sick and alone made him ache.

Fucking hell.

He'd hurt her. As if she hadn't been hurt by enough people.

She was the last person who deserved any more pain.

Tristan had been so sure—*so sure*—this would work.

Pulling out his phone, he sent her a text, though he didn't have hope that she would actually respond.

I'm so sorry. I know there's nothing I can do to make it better. I was wrong to do that. I hope you can forgive me.

Tristan wanted to say more. He wanted to tell her how he truly felt. But mentioning love for the first time over text in an apology would make the words feel shallow and manipulative.

He could only hope she'd let him say them to her in person at some point.

His phone rang as soon as he pressed send on the text. Nathaniel. He put it on speaker. "Nate, you've got me, Mark, and Callum."

"I found something," Nathaniel said.

"From the footage tonight?"

His voice was dark. "No. From Dr. Elliot's office."

Tristan hadn't been expecting that.

"Actually, Jenna found it," Nathaniel continued. "Someone has been very subtly hacking Dr. Elliot's system, and it looks like the same footprints as the guy messing with ours."

It was thin, but it was a lead. And it was more than they'd had on him. Ever. "Go."

"Name is Garland McDowell. Ring any bells?"

Tristan looked at Mark and Callum to see their reactions, but they showed no recognition. He'd never heard of him.

"None here." But there was something in the back of his brain. The name sounded familiar. The last name. "McDowell." When he said it aloud, it clicked, and he felt sick again. "Any relation to a Deborah McDowell?"

Surprise entered the faces of his friends. Alyse's acting coach was not someone he had brought up to them, because that wasn't his story to share, and she had been so thoroughly excised from Alyse's life that there was no reason to do more than a cursory check. They'd looked into her briefly when they'd done the rundown and gone no further.

Nathaniel sounded surprised too. "Yeah. That's his mother."

Fuck.

"And that's the guy who hacked Dr. Elliot's system?"

"Yep," Nathaniel said. "Honestly, I wasn't even sure this was the guy we were looking for."

"It is." Tristan locked eyes with Callum. "We need a warrant. Now. To get into his house and computer."

"We don't, actually," Nathaniel says. "I got a trace, and the address is an office building that's been abandoned. Since there are no registered businesses on the property, no warrant necessary."

"I owe you one, Nathaniel," Tristan said as he hung up. "Let's go."

Chapter 30

If it weren't for the lack of lights in the building, Tristan wouldn't have known this place was empty. It looked like a relatively new building—bland, office-park architecture with abstract bricks and dark windows.

A great place to lie low if you didn't want to be found. Clever.

Callum called for backup on the way, but Tristan wasn't going to wait. If Garland McDowell was inside this building, he and Tristan were going to have a chat before a whole host of law enforcement showed up and spooked him.

They came around from the back of the building. "He's too smart to just sit here and wait for law enforcement to show up and take him," Tristan told his friends. "He's been one step ahead of us the entire time. We need to go in quietly."

Callum shook his head. "Tristan, the guy wants to kill you and won't hesitate to do so. Waiting for backup is the safest play."

Tristan didn't say anything, but he wasn't waiting. They had this chance, now, and if they caught him by surprise, they could finish this right now. Everything he had put Alyse through would be worth it if they could get their hands on him.

Tristan looked over at them in the car. "You know I'm going in now."

"Yeah," Mark said, pulling out his gun. "And that's why I'm going with you."

Tristan managed a grim smile. Mark was called Outlaw for a reason. "Thank you."

They'd parked the car far enough away that the shadows obscured the vehicle, though the sky was lightening with the first stages of dawn. It was now or never if they wanted the element of surprise.

"Fine," Callum said. "I'm not letting you two go in alone. But Mark and I take point. You can't make yourself an easy target for someone who has already proven he wants to try to kill you."

Tristan's jaw creaked from how hard he was gritting his teeth, but Callum had a valid point. He couldn't do anything to help Alyse if he was dead. And he wasn't about to let this fucker get what he was after. "Fine."

Weapons loaded, they got out of the car. They only stopped to put on vests from the trunk and add comm units to their ears before heading in. Instinct and training took over the three of them, and Tristan faded back as Callum took point. They kept to the shadows as they approached the building.

It was likely that McDowell had cameras covering every inch of this building the same way they had them covering Alyse's home. But maybe they would get lucky. Tristan hated luck, but it was all he had right now.

They split their approach, two of them going to the front of the building while Mark covered the back entrance in case Garland decided to run.

"Back door is locked," Mark said.

"Roger," Tristan said. "Any signs of rigging?"

"No," Mark said.

"Then it's probably here," Callum said, looking by the door.

Tristan raised his eyebrows. "You think he's booby-trapped the place?"

"A guy this paranoid and deadly?" Callum asked. "Yeah, it's likely. One of the reasons I wanted to wait for backup."

Tristan shook his head. "You know that we don't have that kind of time. He's too slippery."

"I know. But we have to be careful."

They moved forward. The double glass doors looked exactly like every other office building he'd ever seen. He didn't see any cameras, but that didn't mean there weren't any. Callum cautiously approached the door and looked through, examined the edges and hinges while he hung back. Tristan had to force himself to keep still and not burst through before they did this check. It was only the years of training that held him in place.

He was able to get out of his own head enough to realize this exact situation was why Tristan didn't get involved with clients. Why nobody should. His emotions were spinning too rapidly, his desperation too high.

He was a liability, and his friends were having to compensate for it.

Callum looked closer through the glass and slowly, gently, tried the handle. "Unlocked."

"Is it wired?"

He nodded. "I can see the hole that was drilled, no light visible though."

Clever. An invisible trip wire that most people wouldn't think to look for. Thank fuck they weren't most people. They didn't waste time checking what kind of trap he'd laid, just continued moving forward, looking for the next one. They stepped over the invisible line and gave it a wide berth.

"Outlaw," Tristan said into his comms unit. "Trip wire on the front door."

"I'll tell the backup."

"We're on our way up to the third floor." That was where Jenna and Nathaniel had pinpointed McDowell's location.

"Watch your six," Mark responded.

"Roger that."

The stairs were clear, and they took them two at a time up to the third floor. Another trip wire, this one a laser lining the inside of the doorway. This trap was easily visible. Holes drilled into the doorframe and barely hiding the muzzle of a gun. If law enforcement had torn in here, weapons blazing, they would've gotten a very ugly surprise.

That thin red line on the floor and the near-invisible trip wire at the front door told Tristan everything he needed to know about Garland McDowell. He knew exactly what he was doing, and that people were going to come after him.

He didn't care who he hurt. There were dozens of ways he could've set up his trip wires to notify him if someone entered, without hurting anyone. But he'd gone for methods that would cause as much damage and as many casualties as possible.

This was him trying to take down as many people as possible if anyone found him.

Tristan wasn't remotely surprised. But he was more determined than ever to end this as soon as possible.

Callum and Tristan fell into step together, clearing one room at a time in total silence. The quiet on this floor was so complete it was almost eerie, and the closer they got to the room that was Garland's, the more his internal alarms were screeching at him.

He was either lying in wait for them, or he wasn't there at

all. Tristan was betting on the latter. His gut told him that McDowell was gone. Callum seemed to feel the same, his stance and tension easing slightly as they approached the final door, which was closed and locked.

Tristan took up a position with his gun pointed at the door and nodded to Callum. On a silent count, he kicked the door and pushed through the opening.

It only took them seconds to clear the room. He wasn't in there. But looking around, he knew right away they weren't leaving empty-handed.

"Fuck. He's not here, Outlaw, but we need you. Trip laser on the third-floor stairs, so be careful. Have everyone else clear the other floors."

If they'd had any doubt that they'd found the right guy, this room erased that. Everything that was in this room was Alyse. The walls were covered with pictures of Alyse. The images of her in the bath that had been plastered on the gate. Photos of her at home. Of her at the studio. Screen captures of every camera feed that she had been featured on in the last month, including the blurry picture of their kiss.

There were pictures of Tristan too. Photos that looked like surveillance, any time that he'd been apart from Alyse. Going to the office. Returning to her at home.

The only segment he didn't have pictures of was his and Alyse's trip to Santa Catalina a couple weeks ago.

Good. Those days were just for them, and Tristan didn't want to share them with anyone. Especially this bastard.

Mark stepped through the door, and the look on his face was what Tristan was sure his own reflected. "Holy fuck."

Tristan's jaw was locked tight. None of them touched anything since it would all need to be processed by forensics.

But they knew who the perp was. That was more than they had yesterday.

"Tristan," Callum called him over to a corner of the

room. There was a map on the wall. A piece of land that looked like desert, but there was nothing to identify where it was.

"What is this?"

He tapped a picture nearby. "Cabin, it seems like."

Mark rolled his eyes. "Dude planning to take a vacation?"

Callum studied it closer. "More like he's got somewhere planned to take Alyse if he can get to her. He wants an environment that won't be easily found, and one that he has complete control over. This fits the bill. Especially since it looks like it's pretty isolated."

Panic spiked through Tristan's chest, and he pushed it back. There was no fucking way he was letting him near Alyse.

Tristan pulled out his phone and dialed Nathaniel. He answered on the first ring. "Yeah."

"McDowell's assets. Does he have any property?"

"No," he said. "Nothing besides where you're standing."

"Anything strange for the mom? Random bits of land that wouldn't make sense?"

"No."

Tristan snapped a picture of the map and sent it to him. "See if you can dig up any property records for this place. Or a location. We need to know what we're dealing with there."

"You got it, boss."

Mark looked at him. "What are you thinking?"

"I don't know," he said. "But I don't like any of this."

Tristan walked around the room again. "We need everything on Garland McDowell. He wasn't planning on being found here. That's clear. I doubt he would have left everything out in the open if he'd had any clue. So, where is he now?"

"Is there a computer on-site?" Nathaniel asked, and Tristan switched the phone to speaker as he sat down in front of the dark desktop. "I can see when he last accessed it."

"Yeah."

Callum cut in. "We need to check it for traps first. I wouldn't put it past this guy to have a surprise waiting for the first person to power it up. And inspecting it is above our pay grade."

Tristan swallowed his snarl. Callum was right. "I'll contact you as soon as the bomb squad gets here and clears the computer, Nathaniel. In the meantime, focus on anything about that cabin."

Realistically, Tristan knew the bomb squad was quick to arrive, but every minute they waited grated against his skin. Once it was clear, he immediately had Nathaniel back on the phone.

"Here's what I need."

Callum and Mark continued collecting any information they could from all the stuff pinned around the room, while Nathaniel led Tristan through the steps to help him splice into the computer so he could access it remotely.

Finally, he connected. "Okay, got him. Checking the last log-in before ours."

Callum and Mark joined him as Nathaniel got the info he needed.

"Garland last accessed this particular computer early yesterday evening," Nathaniel said.

My stomach dropped. "When?"

"Activity stopped right after you released Alyse's location."

Mark shook his head. "So, our trap did work."

"Then why the fuck didn't we catch him? He wasn't on-site."

Nathaniel's keys sounded through the phone. "I ran all the footage again while we were waiting for the bomb squad. Definitely no sign of Garland, unless he was wearing facial prosthetics that would cause our software not to recognize him."

Tristan looked over at Callum. He shrugged. "It's possible, although I wouldn't profile him as someone quick to change his appearance. But we may need to manually sift through the footage again, in case he was being cautious."

He took one last look around the room, at the pictures of Alyse and the telltale signs of madness. "I need to get back to Alyse's house. I need to talk to her."

Knowing exactly who they were looking for changed everything. Maybe Alyse could give them some insight as to who Garland was or where he might go. Tristan wanted to check the footage himself now that he knew his face. He trusted his team, but his mind wasn't going to rest until he looked at every frame.

Most of all, Tristan needed to tell her that they'd found him. That at least part of this was worth it.

The sun was full in the Los Angeles sky as Tristan stepped out of the office building. But he didn't feel any relief, because the same question kept circling on repeat in his mind.

Where the hell was Garland McDowell?

Chapter 31

Alyse rested her head on the cold tile of the bathroom floor, exhausted. At some point in the middle of the night, she had given up on trying to stay anywhere other than near the toilet, the memories swimming and sickness making her retch far too often.

She had cried when she shut the door in Tristan's face, because of all the things Alyse wanted in that moment, she wanted most for him to hold her.

And she couldn't have that. Not after what he had done.

Half of her expected he would come after her, but after an hour, Alyse realized that he wouldn't. He would honor the boundary she set so clearly.

But Alyse still wanted him to fight for her, even though at the same time she wanted to scream at him.

Lying on the floor, she kept wondering how she had gotten there. Alyse had made so much progress—much of it to do with Tristan's encouragement and support…and *love*. That was why everything hurt so much—why it felt like her heart was imploding. But even then, as much as she hated what he'd done, she understood.

Tristan was a man with a mission: protecting her. Like the Navy SEAL he'd once been, he wouldn't let anything cause him to falter in his mission now. He thought he was doing the right thing so Alyse could finally be safe and they could be together without this shadow over their heads.

But he still should have told her. They could have planned it together. Alyse wasn't so fragile that she wouldn't have been willing to use herself as bait. She wanted to catch the stalker as much as Tristan did. And she definitely could've acted however surprised he needed her to.

Her throwaway phone dinged, and tears pooled in her eyes once again as she saw his message.

I'm so sorry. I know there's nothing I can do to make it better. I was wrong to do that. I hope you can forgive me.

Could Alyse forgive him? She wasn't sure. She desperately wanted to, but everything was so raw and brutal and painful that Alyse couldn't see beyond the next time her stomach rebelled against her.

At some point, she must have fallen asleep, exhausted beyond anything. When she woke up, she was still in the bathroom. Alyse forced herself off the floor. She needed some water. Food was definitely not an option.

The sun was up, but it was still early. She almost never woke up this early if she didn't have to work, unless it was Tristan deciding to wake her up for some delicious morning sex. Pushing the thought away, she made her way through the house to the kitchen for the water.

Alyse thought she heard a noise coming from the gym, and she couldn't help herself, she rushed in that direction. Maybe Tristan was there working out. Seeing him wouldn't change anything that had happened, but she needed to see him anyway.

Just needed to know...*something*. Alyse wasn't sure exactly what.

Had she and Tristan broken up? The thought took her breath, and Alyse placed her hand on her stomach against the sharp pain that was nearly physical. It let her know one thing very clearly—Alyse didn't want their relationship to be over.

She wasn't okay with what he'd done, and they were going to have to have a long talk about respect and boundaries... even if he thought he was protecting her.

He might not like or agree with how Alyse handled her professional image publicly. And she truly believed he thought she was beautiful with no makeup or styling. But he couldn't make decisions about her public image without consulting her first.

The amount of damage control her team would need to do almost had Alyse sick again. She'd been in touch with Jared already, and he'd assured her the social media response wasn't as bad as it could've been. People were pleasantly surprised to see Alyse more casual than they expected.

Of course there were also some trolls, but there always were.

Jared insisted she just worry about staying safe and help catch the stalker. He and the team would handle the media fallout.

Alyse didn't know exactly what she would say to Tristan when she saw him, but she knew she wasn't just going to avoid him. They needed to talk. Maybe yell. But clear the air and see where they stood.

So she was disappointed to find he wasn't in the gym. Maybe she would try to sleep more—this time in her bed— and hope he would come back while she slept.

The house felt too quiet without him. The living room seemed too big and too empty without his presence, and Alyse wondered as she walked through the room how she had ever lived there completely alone.

"Hello, Alyse."

Alyse spun, nearly tripping over her feet, dropping the glass and cracking it as water splashed across the carpet. Her stomach plummeted, and adrenaline slammed through her system.

It was him. Alyse knew that voice from the voice mails. The way he said her name made her skin crawl.

God, how had he gotten in here?

What could she do?

Why didn't Alyse let them put cameras in the house?

Why had she sent Tristan away?

All the thoughts swirled through her mind in a second as Alyse took in the man in front of her. Tall—nearly as tall as Tristan—but wiry. Thin, but strong. Dressed all in black. His eyes made her shiver. They were dark, and the way he looked at her made her want to run back to the toilet and vomit all over again.

Alyse was very aware that she was only wearing a thin nightgown. Something that she might have been happy to have Tristan see and slowly strip her out of.

The way this man looked at her felt like a violation, even more than he'd already done. Terror ripped through her like ice, her entire body cold and shaking. Alyse tried to take a breath. Panic wouldn't help. She knew it wouldn't. It didn't help, even if there was nothing wrong. Now it could get her killed.

In her mind, Alyse imagined Tristan's voice, warm and soothing and confident, telling her to focus. It cleared the fog just enough for her to swallow her panic.

She could do this. There was no use screaming. Tristan wouldn't hear her even if he were still there. None of the guards would hear her either. Alyse needed to get to one of the panic buttons.

She swallowed. "Who are you?" She wanted to know his name. Needed to know.

"You know who I am."

Taking a deep breath, Alyse managed to keep her voice even. "I know you're the asshole who's been terrorizing me for months. That's all I know."

He took a step toward her so fast, she flinched. "Terrorized? Is that what you think I did?"

The panic button for the living room was behind her, just out of reach. Alyse made a point of not looking in that direction so he wouldn't see her thought. She needed to make it over there.

"I'm the one who knows you. I'm the only one who understands who you really are."

Alyse swallowed. "That's not true."

"It is." His voice was still eerily calm. "I'm the only one who understands what she did to both of us. She made us."

She.

"Who?"

The man shook his head. "If you thought she was bad to you, you should've tried being her child."

It clicked in her brain like a key in a lock. "Deborah McDowell. You're her son."

She had mentioned having a son a few times, but Alyse had never met him. She never even knew his name. The man in front of her smiled. It would have been a handsome smile without the crazed light in his eyes.

He bowed slightly. "Garland McDowell. It's good to finally talk to you face-to-face, Alyse. Although I feel like we've known each other forever. We're soul mates, you and I. Cut from the same cloth."

"Garland…" she said, trying to stall, to use anything she

could remember that Deborah had said to her to delay him, but she had nothing.

"That's right," he said. *"Garland.* Because my bitch of a mother was so obsessed with old Hollywood that she had to name her son after one of her idols. Judy."

There had been a poster of Judy Garland in Deborah's office the few times that Alyse had gone there. It didn't seem strange to her at the time, but now it made even more sense.

"How did you get in here?"

His smile was nothing short of disconcerting. "I took advantage of your boyfriend while he was trying to take advantage of me."

"I don't understand." Alyse really didn't, but mostly she wanted to keep him talking.

"His attempt to use himself as bait was laughable. I knew he was laying a trap. Then your sudden public appearance definitely didn't sit right. Although I have to admit, it was almost more than I could take, knowing you'd be available for me to see in person."

He closed his eyes in some sick pleasure. If there had been anything left in her system to vomit, she probably would've.

Alyse had to get away from him. She inched back toward the panic button.

Garland's eyes popped back open. "I knew I had to be patient. Mother always wanted immediate results, but I've learned patience since I got away from her. I used that."

She slid back a little farther. "Yes, patience."

He stroked a finger down her arm, and she barely avoided shuddering. "You have a basement crawl space."

Alyse didn't understand the change in subject. *"What?"*

"Your security team checked it, of course, when they originally secured this place. But they were so busy trying to figure out who I was in the crowd last night that they weren't focusing their efforts here at the house. A relatively simple security camera hack and I was able to get into your basement crawl space. Then, all I had to do was be patient. Wait for the perfect time to get to you. It might involve killing Zimmerman in the process, but I was willing to do that if necessary."

"You've been in my basement all night?"

That smile again. "I was prepared to stay days if necessary. Only having to wait a few hours was nothing. I don't know what had Zimmerman and his team speeding out of here. I guess something they saw in their little trap. Whatever it was, wasn't me."

He took another step right into her personal space. When Alyse tried to step away, he grabbed hold of her arm. "I've been ahead of them from the beginning. I have Mother to thank for that. I may hate her, but she made me stronger and smarter than I would've been otherwise. You too. We both have her to thank for that."

Slowly, Alyse took a breath. "I'm sorry for whatever your mother did to you. You obviously know about what she did to me."

Her words seemed to calm him, and he smiled again. "I do. When I found out that she'd abused you in the same way she did me, I knew we were meant to be together. No one understands but us, Alyse. We can heal each other."

Oh God, what was she supposed to do?

"Garland, I'm so sorry for your pain. For both of our pain at the hands of your mother." Alyse wanted to get him to focus on the fact that she knew him. Was acknowledging him. "But that doesn't mean we're supposed to be together."

She saw his eyes harden and knew she'd said the wrong thing.

Alyse made her move. Shaking off his arm, she turned and sprinted for the panic button, but a solid weight slammed into her before she could reach it. Alyse opened her mouth to scream, but all the air was knocked from her lungs as Garland landed on top of her.

Get away. Get away. Get away.

"It's time for us to go, Alyse. You don't understand, but I will make you see that you're meant to spend forever with me."

She clawed at the carpet, trying to get closer to that button, to the door, anything. She wasn't going to let him take her. There was a moment when Alyse managed to wrap her fingers around the little table in front of her—the one near the panic button. But she barely moved it an inch. His weight was too heavy, and she was weak from nothing to eat and throwing up her guts all night.

Still, Alyse fought until she felt the sharp point at her throat.

"I didn't want to have to do this," he said with a growl, flipping her over on the floor. It wasn't a knife; it was a needle. Oh God.

This close, Garland's eyes were manic, and the sinking in her gut told her there was no way out of this. Not unless a miracle occurred. "I was hoping I'd eventually be able to talk you into coming with me willingly, Alyse. Getting you to understand that we're meant to be."

Alyse whimpered as the needle pressed into her skin.

"But then you met that bastard Tristan Zimmerman. He confused you. Clouded your judgment. Kept you from me. Touched what wasn't his to touch. For that, he'll have to die."

"No, please."

Where was Tristan? How would he know something was wrong? The only encouragement she had was that Garland wasn't telling her Tristan was already dead. So maybe there was still hope.

No matter what, Tristan wouldn't want Alyse to allow Garland to take her.

So, she fought.

Garland shook his head, disappointment clear in his dark eyes. He'd wanted her to go with him of her own accord.

Wasn't going to happen.

He blocked her hits easily, keeping her pinned with his weight.

The sharp pinch of the needle was the last thing Alyse felt as the world faded to black.

Chapter 32

"Alyse?" he called out as he pushed open the front door. They were all exhausted, but Tristan needed to tell her about Garland.

They'd found him, even if they hadn't caught him yet. That didn't make up for what he'd done, but God, Tristan hoped it would help his fuckup seem a little more bearable.

He needed to see her face. To apologize. However many times it took. Tristan was under no illusions that all would be forgiven, but he wanted to let her know that he was going to fight for them. To do whatever it took to get her to forgive him.

If Tristan could get her to answer him at all.

"Alyse?" Jogging up the stairs, he went to their bedroom. The fact that Tristan already thought of it as *theirs* was proof enough to him how fucking in love with her he was.

The upstairs was quiet too. Where was she? The bed wasn't made, and her phone was on the nightstand.

Tristan stopped. That was strange. Not the phone, but the bed. Alyse always made the bed. He'd teased her about it on some mornings, the fact that a star like her made her own bed. She'd told him that it was a long-held habit ingrained from what her parents taught her.

So the messy comforter and sheets set Tristan on edge. Had she just gotten out of bed and gone to the kitchen for food? There was no sound coming from the bathroom.

His instincts were screaming, but Tristan couldn't put his finger on why. They hadn't gotten any calls about the house. Everything was fine. Except Alyse wasn't in the kitchen. Or the gym. She wasn't anywhere in the house.

Had she left with Jared? Tristan hadn't checked in with the house guards. Maybe she'd called Jared and had him come get her.

They were her security, but they didn't dictate where she could or couldn't go. If she'd decided to leave, they couldn't stop her. But surely she wouldn't have left without a detail with her.

Something wasn't sitting right in his gut.

Tristan grabbed his phone, about to call the garage security suite, and saw there were a number of messages from Jared he'd missed in the course of hunting down Garland McDowell. Tristan called him, praying he knew where Alyse was.

"I should fucking fire you right now," Jared answered without any greeting. "How could you do this to Alyse? Do you know she's been up all night vomiting?"

Tristan scrubbed a hand down his face. "I made a judgment call and it was the wrong one, and I'm fucking sorrier than you can possibly know. Can I talk to her?"

He'd rather tell her about McDowell in person, but getting her the information was more important than his personal feelings.

"Why? Is she not taking your calls? I don't blame her."

Tristan stiffened. "Jared, this is important. Is Alyse with you?"

There was a silence on the other end of the phone. "No. Believe me, I wanted to come get her, but she wouldn't let me. The social media team and I have been up all night doing damage control from your little stunt. She's at her house."

No, she wasn't.

"I have to go. You can kick my ass for the restaurant thing later."

"Tristan—"

Tristan hung up before Jared could ask more questions. His instincts were screaming he didn't have time. He walked back into the kitchen, and there was a glass in the sink. Just like with her bed in the morning, Alyse didn't leave dishes around. When she was finished with them, she put them into the dishwasher.

Tristan called the guard house. No answer.

Fuck.

He ran for the side door as his phone started buzzing with a call from Mark.

"Something's wrong!" Tristan yelled as he ran.

"No shit. I'm at the guard room. Eric's unconscious. Needle literally sticking out of his neck."

Tristan's entire body went cold. "Alyse isn't here, Mark. Her phone is in the bedroom, and there's a cracked glass in the sink. He took her, Outlaw. We missed something, and he got to her."

Dread sucked the oxygen from the room.

He didn't hear anything from Mark. A few seconds later, he was running to the house, already barking orders on his earbud. Through the roaring in Tristan's ears, he could hear him calling in reinforcements, getting medical attention for Eric, demanding reports and footage from everything they had set up around the house.

Demanding confirmation that Alyse had, in fact, been taken.

Tristan didn't need confirmation. Eric being unconscious was more than enough proof.

This was his fault. Someone else had paid the price for Tristan's actions just like Cliff had.

Outlaw got right up in his face. "Whatever is going on in your head, you need to shut it down. Work the problem. If we have to grieve, we do it after the mission."

Tristan nodded. He was right. Falling apart solved nothing. "He wants her alive."

Mark nodded. "Hell yes, he does. We use that to our advantage and get her back."

They both looked around the living room. "There's a damp mark here. Must be the water glass."

Tristan's eyes went to the table with the lamp nearby and noticed that it was out of place. To anyone else, it would look fine. But he had been living there the last month, and he knew it wasn't right. She had struggled. She had fought him.

Good girl.

She had fought, and Tristan would fight for her now.

His phone buzzed in his hand. "Give me some good news, Nathaniel."

"I wish, boss, believe me. I have the opposite of good news. I was able to access McDowell's computer. As you know, his last access was right as you released the info about your location at the restaurant last night."

Tristan was listening as he looked around the room for any further clues. "So, he was there? No one has spotted him in the footage."

"That's the bad news. The last thing he looked at before shutting down his computer was the building plans of Alyse's house. Specifically the crawl access area of the basement."

"Fuck."

"It's a potential weakness, I've already checked. Not necessarily when we were fully manning the house, but last night…"

Last night they'd been all hands on deck at the restaurant. Minimal coverage there at the house. "He was here. He took advantage of my plan and planted himself here."

"How do you kn—" He cut off as someone else said something to him in the background. "Oh shit, Tristan. I just heard Alyse is missing."

"He took her." Tristan studied that misplaced lamp again, his teeth grinding together. *Work the problem.* "I need anything you can find on that desert property. Taking her there has been his plan all along. It's our only lead now."

"Jenna is on it and has Blaze and Neo helping her."

Good. Kendrick Foster—aka Blaze—and his wife, Neoma LeBarre, were part of the Linear Tactical team, and both were tech gurus like Jenna. There were very few people in the world who were more proficient in all things computer—legal and illegal.

"No holds barred, Nate. I don't care what laws they have to break to get the intel. I will personally take responsibility so it doesn't blow back on them."

"Between Neo, Blaze, and Jenna, I don't think anyone would be able to trace it back to them anyway. We'll have something for you soon, I promise. Be ready."

Callum came running in. "I just heard. I've got any backup we need on standby."

He was right; so was Nathaniel. They needed to be ready for once they got word. Tristan had to trust his team now.

Tristan turned to Mark. "Have our people clear every inch of this house from top to bottom and report anything they find."

He nodded. "There were signs that he planned to be in

that crawl space for an extended period. Water, provisions. He was ready to stay as long as he needed."

Tristan scrubbed his hand down his face. "I should've been here. I never should've left her alone last night."

Both Mark and Callum shook their heads. "There's no guarantee he wouldn't have killed you outright," Callum said. "He was prepared to move when he had the opportunity."

Even knowing that was true didn't help much. Tristan still should've been there with her.

She had to be terrified. Had he hurt her? Touched her?

Mark got in his face again. "Work the problem."

Tristan nodded. "Let's go. We'll gear up at the office and get ready to move."

All three of them had been SEALs. They knew what it was to prep for a mission then stay in a ready frame of mind until it was time to go. They would do it again now.

They headed back to the office, dressing out in full tactical gear and weapons. Nathaniel had provided all the details he had about Garland McDowell, and they were all studying the digital files.

"The fact that he didn't kill Eric is a good sign," Callum said. "He's not a complete sociopath."

That helped everyone but the person who needed it the most: Alyse.

But Tristan nodded. "Do we have someone with Eric so we can get a statement as soon as he's conscious? He might have intel."

Mark looked up from double-checking his weapon. "We've got a man at the hospital with him. As soon as he's awake, we'll get his statement."

When they were as ready as they possibly could be, Tristan went upstairs to the security suite. Nathaniel didn't even look up when he walked in, fingers flying across the keyboard and things flicking across the screen faster than Tristan could follow. He looked exhausted but determined.

"Anything?"

"Not yet," Jenna's voice came through a speaker. "But we're close."

Tristan tamped his instinct to tell them that every minute they didn't know Alyse's location was one when she could be in pain and danger. They knew that. Everyone knew that. The knowledge was steeped in the very air.

Rubbing his hands over his face, Tristan stepped out of the room. He couldn't stay still, and his manic energy wouldn't help them do their jobs. The pacing gave him a physical outlet but not a mental one.

Had he hurt her? Touched her? Was she already dead?

The thought stopped Tristan as pain cracked through his chest. No. She couldn't be dead. He had been an idiot for not telling her that he loved her, and once he found her, Tristan would make sure to say it every day. More than once.

If she was alive, she was going to hear those words from his lips as soon as possible.

Stay alive, beautiful. I'm coming for you.

He put every ounce of resolve into the thought.

"Tristan," Nathaniel called.

He was through the door in a second. "You found it?"

"North about two hours," he said. "We found a probable match. It's some land not registered to anyone that I can find, not even on government property or parkland. Literally no-man's-land."

"Are you sure that's it?"

Jenna came on the speaker. "It's an excellent match to geographic data. We're still pinpointing the exact location of the structure, but based on the images in McDowell's hideout, I would call this actionable intel."

If Jenna called it actionable, that was good enough for

Tristan. Zodiac Tactical had planned full missions, even without one hundred percent assurance, based on her judgment and data.

"Then we'll roll. Send the exact location when you get it." At least then they'd be closer.

Tristan prayed it would be enough.

Chapter 33

Alyse woke slowly, but it didn't take long for the panic to catch up with her. The last thing she remembered was Garland on top of her and the threats, but that had been at her house.

She blinked, looking around. They definitely weren't in her house now.

And she couldn't move.

Alyse couldn't feel anything holding her down or tying her, but she remembered the needle. The bastard had drugged her. That was why she couldn't move. She was able to wiggle her fingers and toes. That was good. At least whatever Garland had given her wasn't permanent.

The fact that Deborah's son was Alyse's stalker made a sick sort of sense. And also terrified her. She could feel bile working its way up her throat.

What would Tristan tell her to do right now?

First would be to keep as clear a head as possible, not to let fear overwhelm her. To stay aware, look for any opportunities.

Not to panic.

Did he even know Alyse was gone yet? How long before

anyone entered the house and discovered her missing? And even if they did, how in the world would they know where Garland had taken her?

Her eyes felt heavy, but Alyse managed to keep them open, staring at a bare wooden ceiling above her. Definitely not her house.

Alyse blinked, focusing on wiggling her fingers and toes. It wasn't much, but as she was able to move more and more of her body, her panic receded slightly. She didn't know where Garland was, and she wasn't waiting around to find out. As soon as Alyse could manage it, she would run.

Eventually, she was able to force her body to sit up. Everything felt stiff. She'd been lying on this tiny bed for a while.

The room around her was actually nice. Tastefully decorated in a classic country style. The wooden walls made her think this might be a cabin of some kind, and the room seemed quite feminine. Flowers on an antique dresser, lacy bedspread, pieces of art depicting floral landscapes.

It might have been a nice getaway, if Alyse weren't there because of a stalker.

When she looked down at herself, her stomach rolled. Alyse wasn't wearing her nightgown anymore. Which meant he had changed her—*touched her*—while she wasn't awake.

What did he do to her?

Her stomach revolted again, and Alyse had to force herself to breathe and get herself under control. She was alive, and she was somewhat mobile. She needed to focus on that.

Alyse sat up farther, trying not to make any sound. She froze when she got a clearer glimpse of what she was wearing.

It was a costume Alyse had worn for years as a teenager when she was on a television show. She was once again dressed as Corey Gable, the character who wore a school uniform and was sassy and cute. The main character's best friend.

That role was the one she had played while Deborah had been abusing her. Alyse forced her way off the bed and stumbled on shaky legs over to the mirror on the dresser.

Garland had done her hair and makeup. She looked like a perfect doll version of Corey Gable. Something she had hoped never to see again.

Alyse wasn't sure if she was shaking from the drugs, sickness, or adrenaline. It didn't matter. She had to move. She needed to get out of there and figure out how to get help. Hopefully Garland didn't know she was awake yet. This would be her best chance.

Alyse took more shaky steps to the door. She let out a shuddery sob of relief when she realized it wasn't locked, and she opened it slowly. The hallway was empty, and Alyse heard nothing.

She crept out of the room, doing her best to make no sound at all. Her heart pounded in her ears, and Alyse was sweating from the effort of moving with the drugs still inside her system.

Alyse had been through worse, ironically, at the hands of Garland's mother. She could do this. She wasn't going to let this break her.

She kept her focus on Tristan. He would want Alyse to keep moving forward, to take advantage of an opportunity to escape. He was looking for her—or would be as soon as he knew she was gone.

She needed to tell him she loved him. She didn't want their fight to be their last words.

Alyse opened another door and let out a gasp, leaning against the doorframe for support. No one was in the room, but it wasn't empty. A gorgeous four-poster bed was made up like a set for a romantic movie. Shining silk sheets and rose petals scattered across the bedspread. Studio lights and a camera. It all looked very familiar and perfect, except for the chains attached to each post.

She was about to be sick.

"Do you like your surprise?"

Alyse jumped, nearly falling, spinning to face Garland. If he touched her now, she would definitely vomit all over him.

She sucked in breath after breath. She needed to keep him talking. That was the goal. If he was talking, he wasn't doing whatever he was planning. "It was a surprise?"

"Of course." His smile was huge. "This is the start of our new life together, Alyse. I wanted to make it special."

Alyse braced herself against the doorframe. "Then why these clothes? If you want me to like you, why would you change me while I was asleep? If you know so much about me, you know that I hate this character now."

He moved so fast Alyse couldn't stop it, his hand at her throat, cracking her head against the wood behind her. "Don't you ever say that again. You were the most beautiful when you looked like this. And you will always look like this for me, do you understand?"

Oh God, he was definitely crazy.

Alyse couldn't breathe with him squeezing her throat. Panic made her nod, and tears flooded her eyes even though she didn't want to cry. She didn't want to show him that he terrified her.

She wanted to be strong, but she wasn't.

Her mind flashed to every moment that Tristan had told Alyse she was beautiful when she was just herself. He didn't need Alyse to be a character, or even polished—he just wanted her. She held on to that.

"Good." He smiled at her tears, letting her breathe again. "We're going to have a perfect wedding night, my love. I even brought the camera so we can always remember it."

Alyse didn't dare ask what the chains were for—it didn't take much to figure it out, and she didn't want to give him any encouragement.

She said the thing her mind had latched on to—the only thing that was keeping the hysteria from swallowing her whole. "Tristan will find me."

Pain flared across her cheek as Garland's fist caught her. "Never mention his name again. You are mine now."

Alyse shoved him away from her, instinct taking over as she tried to run. But her body still wasn't fully under her control, and she stumbled.

She had to get out. *Now. Now. Now.*

Alyse moved in drunken staggers down the hall. The door to the outside was almost in front of her when he caught her around the waist, and she screamed. Alyse fought him with wild swings as he dragged her back toward that room where he planned to strip her of everything that made her who she was.

He slammed her up against the wall again. His eyes narrowed, full of fury, as he put his face right in hers. "You have to be taught a lesson, Alyse. You have to be taught to appreciate who we are together."

He gripped her hair and dragged her forward. Alyse thought he was taking her toward the bed, but instead, he pulled her toward the closet.

"Please," Alyse begged him. "Please, no. Don't do this."

"Mother trained you this way too, didn't she? I know all about your fear of enclosed places and exercise. But we will be doing both daily." He pushed her into the tiny space. She fell to the floor, her legs too wobbly to support her.

"Mother was a horrible person, but her lessons weren't always wrong." He squatted down and reached out, grabbing her throat with his hand again, cutting off her air supply. "I'm smart, Alyse. Smarter than you, smarter than that Neanderthal you let touch your body. You have to be trained. You have to be taught what our life together can be."

Alyse ripped at his hand with her nails, but he didn't release her throat. "The easiest way to train you is to utilize the foundation my mother laid for me. I've read all your sessions with Dr. Elliot. I know your fears, I know your conditioning. I will use them to bring us together."

She didn't stop fighting him, but she was getting weaker. Blackness danced around her eyes to the point that it took her a moment to realize he'd let go. Alyse sucked in air, her own sobs ringing through her ears.

Alyse had no time to appreciate she was able to breathe before he grabbed her hair and dragged her back farther into the closet. Chains shackling her wrists had Alyse sobbing once again. Just like on the bed, the chains were already attached to the wall.

He had planned for this. Known exactly what it would do to her.

Alyse screamed as loud as she could force herself, not caring if it gave him pleasure to know her terror. Not caring if it made him angrier. Maybe there were other houses nearby. Maybe someone would hear her.

Tape screeched as he pulled it off the roll and sealed it over her mouth. Alyse fought to keep herself from drowning in the memories clawing up her spine. She screamed through the tape, tried to kick him—anything to keep her mind there in this moment. But she could do nothing with her hands chained against the wall, and he caught her easily, wrapping more silver tape around her ankles.

He grasped her chin with bruising fingers, speaking in a deadly calm voice that sent chills down her spine. "Let me be very clear, Alyse. You belong to me now. We belong to each other, and we're going to live a long and happy life together. But you're never going to mention Tristan Zimmerman to me again. If you do, I will go out and find him, and finish him off the way he was meant to go in that car crash."

Alyse shook her head.

His smile chilled her blood. "If he comes after you—and I so hope he will—I'm going to kill him, because he's touched what's mine. But I can make it quick. A simple bullet to the brain. However, if you say his name again, when he comes here, I will skin him alive in front of you. I will take him apart piece by piece. You'll never forget his screams. And then I'll make sure he's still alive to see what a loving wife you are to me before I kill him."

He leaned forward and kissed her mouth across the tape, and Alyse recoiled away from him, which made him shake his head. "You *will* learn. Being in here will be your first reminder of what your brain already knows—that you need to obey. In the meantime, I'll make sure everything is ready. I want our first time to be special."

Alyse screamed when he shut the door, the dim light coming in from under it not enough to hold back the panic and claustrophobia enveloping her mind.

She couldn't move. She couldn't breathe. Alyse was trapped once more in the dark, and the only thing waiting for her outside of it was a madman.

And worst of all, Tristan was going to die, because of her. Because she chose to love him. Alyse knew him—he wasn't going to stop until he found her, and when he did, Garland would kill him.

It was too much for her psyche to handle.

Alyse couldn't control her breathing, and tears were pouring down her face. There wasn't enough air, wasn't enough room.

The darkness pulled her under.

Chapter 34

Two hours. Two excruciating hours driving way above the speed limit toward the vague location of the cabin. They'd called in the local authorities and let them know the situation, Callum pulling rank as a federal law enforcement officer to keep them as backup.

The last thing they wanted was locals rushing the cabin. There was no telling what McDowell would do to Alyse if that happened. Callum was sure he wouldn't let her go. He'd rather die.

And take Alyse with him.

Even with them driving at top speed, Tristan was crawling out of his skin. His phone pinged with new updates from Nathaniel and Jenna, any and all information they could find.

And finally, confirmed coordinates. Between all of them, they'd done the near impossible and found the exact location of the cabin.

While they drove, they formulated the plan. They would make a wide perimeter around the property to gather any intel, then push in. Both Callum and Mark looked at Tristan like they expected him to start arguing.

And he was tempted. There was nothing Tristan wanted more than to get to Alyse as quickly as possible. But he knew they had to be smart. McDowell held the upper hand.

The final coordinates took them deep into the wilderness. None of them were surprised. McDowell needed isolation for what he had planned.

Their three-vehicle convoy arrived, their team setting a wide circle around the cabin. They were at a disadvantage since it was the middle of the day, but they couldn't wait for darkness. They stayed out of sight of the cabin utilizing the rocky terrain, low trees, and shrubbery in the area.

They had to move slowly. There was virtually no chance that he didn't have surveillance there. He was too paranoid not to have that sort of security.

Mark gave instructions to the rest of the team. Callum pulled Tristan aside as he checked his weapon. "You ready for this?"

Tristan didn't look up. "Yes."

His face was grave. "It's okay to sit this one out. If you were anyone else, Outlaw and I would pull rank and make you stay here. You're too close. Too emotionally involved."

"No way in hell I'm sitting this out." The words were a growl.

"That's what I figured." Callum nodded. "Let's go."

The three of them moved methodically toward the cabin. The second half of the team would be coming from the opposite direction, the rest setting up a perimeter and waiting for local law enforcement.

It was slow going, looking out for trip wires—and there were plenty of them. Although, unlike the office, none of them seemed to be booby traps intended to maim or kill.

That made Tristan relieved, as well as set off alarms in his head. He stopped when they were within view of the house, Mark and Callum freezing also at his signal.

"Why are McDowell's traps nonlethal out here when he was ready to blow everyone to kingdom come at that office building?" Tristan asked. "That doesn't make sense."

Outlaw studied the area around him. "Maybe he didn't have time."

That didn't sit right either. Everything this guy had done had been with precision and a plan.

"Maybe he didn't want to accidentally kill Alyse if she happened to escape," Callum said.

Tristan nodded. That made more sense. Still, something wasn't right there. His gut was screaming at him, and this time, he was going to listen.

"What?" Mark asked.

"I need to go in alone."

He turned to Tristan. "Are you fucking insane?"

"He knows I'm going to come after Alyse. He'll be expecting me, right?"

Slowly, Callum nodded. "Yeah, I'd say so."

"If we swarm the house, he's going to set off whatever countermeasures he has. But if I go in alone, I can distract him. If we're right, he'll be so interested in hurting me he won't be focused on anything else—including you guys taking him down."

Mark shook his head. "He'll put a bullet in you as soon as he sees you. Being dead isn't going to help this situation."

"No, he won't," Tristan said.

Mark shot an exasperated look at Callum. "Tell him this is a stupid plan."

Callum studied Tristan with narrowed eyes. "I think he's right. McDowell doesn't want to kill him. He wants to torture him. He won't shoot Tristan right away."

Mark looked pissed. "I still don't like it. Five minutes, Pisces. We're not giving you any more time with that asshole."

"That will be enough." His gut felt calm and steady. This

was the right thing to do—Tristan would withstand whatever he had to in order to give the team the chance to take McDowell out.

He knew there were things that could be done to a human in five minutes that you never walked away from. But it would be worth it to save Alyse.

Tristan reached up and removed his comm earpiece. "He'll know."

He kept his weapon. Tristan wasn't about to go in there unarmed, even though he knew McDowell wouldn't let him keep it long.

Taking a deep breath, Tristan nodded at his friends and walked toward the cabin. He felt more at peace than he had since he'd found out Alyse was missing. It didn't matter that he hadn't slept and barely eaten. Tristan was there. He was doing something that would help her.

He steadied his breathing and sank into the welcome embrace of adrenaline and battle mind-set. It was like slipping on a familiar skin.

Holding his gun at the ready, Tristan approached the door.

It wasn't locked, and eerily cheery music assaulted his ears as Tristan pushed it open—some generic pop song. The door opened into a living room. There was no one there, but sound came from the kitchen.

Gun ready, Tristan followed the sound of the music. The man he was looking for was…*cooking*. He was nearly as tall as Tristan was, wiry build with messy dark hair. Tristan recognized him from all the information that they now had on him.

He could take McDowell out now, but Tristan knew that could be a mistake, and Alyse would once again be the one to pay the price.

He looked over at Tristan and smiled as if he'd been

expecting houseguests. "Honestly, Zimmerman, I'm impressed. I thought it would take you longer."

"Where is Alyse?"

He raised one eyebrow. "She's safe. For now."

Garland's calmness was unsettling. Maybe he had resigned himself to his fate? Tristan took a step forward.

"Now, now. Let's not do anything hasty." He drew a wicked knife from out of nowhere and leveled it at him.

The gleam in his eye made it clear he wasn't stable. No big surprise. And they had been right—this man wanted to hurt Tristan very badly.

"I told Alyse, if she was good, I would kill you quickly. But now that you're here, I'm not sure I can keep that promise." He stepped toward Tristan with the knife. "You touched what was mine."

The plan was to stall. Looked like it would be easy enough, just keep him talking. "Alyse isn't a thing. She doesn't belong to anyone."

"She belongs to me!" His roar filled the small kitchen, drowning out the radio. "Put your gun on the counter."

"What are you going to do if I say no?"

The grin on his face told Tristan he was hoping that he'd ask that. Tristan kept watching the knife in Garland's hand, expecting it to fly at him any second. And it did fly, but it went wide to his left.

"You missed."

His smile got more smug. "Actually, I didn't."

Tristan turned to look at what he'd thrown the knife at. It had hit some sort of button on the wall behind him.

"Congratulations. You just killed all of your friends. That button armed every trap I have outside in a two-mile radius." He waggled his eyebrows. "If you leave right this second, you'll have a chance to die quickly instead of slowly."

Tristan didn't move. He wasn't going anywhere without

Alyse. A few seconds later, metal panels closed over all the windows with a resounding thud.

McDowell actually giggled. "Too late now. It may not seem like it, but this is better anyway. With the shutters down, you won't be able to hear your friends scream, and vice versa."

"What is stopping me from putting a bullet in you right fucking now?" Tristan took another step closer. "I'm the one with the gun."

He held up something tiny in his hand. "But I'm the one holding Alyse's life in his hands. You shoot me, and yeah, I'm sure I'll die, but so will she."

"What is that?"

"I press this button, and it releases a toxin into her system through her handcuffs. She'll be dead less than a minute later. Unfortunately, very painfully and messy. Gun, please."

Tristan lowered his weapon and pushed it on the counter toward him. What other choice did I have? "You're not going to make it out of this, McDowell. You have to know that's true."

A small, smug smile appeared. "Of course I will. I now have a beautiful wife, and we're going to live happily ever after. The fairy tale."

"More like a nightmare for her."

Bastard was fast. He flung another knife, at Tristan this time. He slid to the side to avoid it hitting his torso—contrary to popular opinion, Kevlar didn't stop blades. Fire ripped along my bicep as the knife missed his vest but grazed his arm.

"Alyse hasn't come to love me yet, but she will. She will learn. I will teach her."

Blood was seeping through hs fingers as Tristan held his hand over the wound. "Alyse will never love you."

He picked up Tristan's gun and pointed it at him. Tristan

could tell he was fighting not to kill him outright. He was going to use that to his advantage. Tristan couldn't count on help from his team—they were too busy just keeping themselves alive—so he was going to have to take down McDowell himself.

Tristan would use Garland's own weaknesses against him: his desire to hurt him.

"You can't possibly think you're going to make it out of here."

"I'm the only one who'll make it out of here. Well, me and Alyse. I'm the only one who knows all the secrets of this place. Your friends will all be dead soon, and that will buy me more time. But you'll pay for forcing me to start over somewhere else."

"Add it to my tab." Tristan couldn't think about Callum and Mark and the others outside with McDowell's deadly traps. He had to focus on what was in front of him.

"Do you know what I promised Alyse I would do to you if she ever said your name again?"

Tristan didn't answer. He gestured toward the exit to the kitchen, and Tristan walked that way. He reached into his pocket while McDowell was monologuing and grabbed the small transmitter. Tristan used his wound as an excuse, stumbling slightly into the doorframe, and stuck it on.

It wouldn't do much—a loud bang and some smoke, but it was noise-activated. It would go off fifteen seconds after it was activated by the sound of a gun firing.

Now all Tristan had to do was get McDowell to shoot him and not die in the process.

"I told her if she ever said your name again, I would peel the skin from your body, Tristan Zimmerman. And then when you're begging for death, I'll make you watch as I fuck my wife before I finally put you out of your misery. I'm going to make sure every piece of you that touched her is destroyed."

"Has anyone ever told you you're overly dramatic?"

That got Tristan a pistol butt to the back of the head. Now stumbling forward wasn't an act. He fought to keep his vision clear.

He pushed Tristan toward the bedroom, and rage bubbled through his system as he saw the bed with fucking chains on it. Had he used them on Alyse already? Tristan forced the thought out of his mind.

The only thing that mattered now was survival—getting Alyse and himself out alive. Anything else, they'd deal with later, no matter how bad it was.

McDowell pushed him toward the bed and secured one of the chains at the foot to his wrist. Only when Tristan couldn't reach him did he lay down the trigger device.

The bastard was smart. If it had only been the gun in his hand, Tristan would've rushed him and taken his chances. But he couldn't take a chance with Alyse's life.

Tristan yanked at the chain as he walked over to the closet.

He'd put her in a *fucking closet*, knowing full well that had been part of the way his own mother had tortured her. Tristan's heart shattered into a million pieces as Garland opened the door and he got a first glimpse of her.

Tape covered her mouth, and she scooted back in fear as McDowell reached for her. She couldn't get far with her hands shackled and her legs taped.

She'd clawed at her own skin, probably in terror. She was hyperventilating behind the tape he'd put over her mouth.

"Alyse," Tristan called out, unable to help himself. "Breathe, sweetheart. Breathe."

She froze for a second then got more panicked. McDowell didn't like Tristan's term of endearment. He grabbed her by the hair and yanked her to her feet. She was still sobbing behind the tape.

"Leave her alone, asshole." Tristan yanked at the chain again. Alyse's beautiful blue eyes were wide with terror, her chest heaving with an attempt to get air. She was pale, with a sheen of sweat on her face, and she looked like she might be sick. He had to get her calmed down. If she vomited behind that tape, she'd choke and die.

"Alyse. It's going to be okay. Breathe——" Tristan cut himself off before he could call her by an endearment again. "Garland, get the tape off her fucking mouth. You're going to kill her if you don't."

Tristan could feel blood dripping down his wrist from the metal of the cuff, but he ignored it, stretching himself as close as he could get to the closet. "Breathe, Alyse."

He caught her eyes and took an exaggerated breath of his own, hoping she'd follow suit. She did, and it was enough to at least allow the moment of crisis to pass.

But it also pissed McDowell off. He didn't take the tape off her mouth, but he had to release her from the cuffs to get her out of the closet.

His heart rate settled, and his focus became crystal clear as soon as there was no metal touching her body.

Alyse was now out of immediate danger.

It was time for Tristan to get shot.

Chapter 35

McDowell still didn't remove the tape from Alyse's mouth, but Tristan couldn't worry about that now. Since she was no longer chained, he'd wrapped her wrists with the tape then looped a piece around her waist so she couldn't move them. She was huddled just outside the closet door, still breathing too rapidly, but at least not so bad that she might vomit.

He was obviously pissed that she was so willing to listen to him, so Tristan didn't try talking to her again, didn't even look her way. Any connection he could see between the two of them was just going to make him more furious.

Tristan didn't want to give him a chance to regroup. He was too smart. And once he realized that his best way of controlling Tristan was by hurting Alyse, he wouldn't hesitate to use her.

He needed to get that gun in his hand. Tristan was counting on the fact that he would shoot to wound, not to kill him.

Couldn't sadistically torture him if Tristan was already dead.

He was only going to get one chance at this. If he couldn't pull it off, he was going to die horribly.

McDowell spun around toward him, sneer on his face. This was it, his best opportunity. He knew it was going to hurt like a motherfucker, but Tristan dove for him.

The chain immediately yanked him back, blood now gushing from his wrist. Tristan turned back to the bed frame and started yanking and kicking at it. Agony blistered down his arm, but he ignored it.

"Stop, Zimmerman, or I'm going to shoot you with your own gun."

Tristan didn't stop, not even when he heard Alyse's panicked screams behind the tape. He knew McDowell was behind him and had the weapon pointed at him.

The sound hit first, far too loud in this enclosed space, and then the pain from the bullet ripping through Tristan's shoulder, just outside his vest. He'd been right; he hadn't gone for the kill shot.

Tristan let himself go limp, dropping to his knees next to the bed, and silently counted down in his head. He needed him to come closer. He had to be next to Tristan when the charge went off.

"Did you think I wouldn't shoot you?" It was working; he was coming closer. "You're not going to get me to kill you quickly, Zimmerman. You'll wish for it, but—"

Two, one…

The charge Tristan had placed in the kitchen let off a second boom, throwing McDowell's attention away from him and causing him to stumble. Ignoring all the pain in his upper body, Tristan swung himself around and caught him in a roundhouse kick to the head.

He fell to the floor, and Tristan knocked the gun out of his hand, then wrapped both legs around his neck. If he kept himself at this angle, he would have Garland unconscious in just a few seconds. But this wasn't the movies—someone in a choke hold didn't get knocked out for half an hour. McDowell would regain consciousness before Tristan could get them to safety.

His body had already shifted to the second angle before his mind had even come to grips with what Tristan needed to do. He was wiggling in his hold, slamming his hand against his wrist.

Tristan shifted a little more, and with a twist of his knees, snapped McDowell's neck. He fell lifeless to the floor beside him.

For a few seconds, all Tristan could hear was his own breathing. Alyse stumbled over to him, eyes wide, breaths staggered, and he pulled the tape off her mouth.

"Are you okay? He shot you!"

Tristan ran his good hand down the side of her face. It was already bruising. He'd hit her. "I'll be fine, I promise."

That was when they both heard the countdown.

"What's that?" she asked.

He reached over and grabbed McDowell's wrist, looking at the watch he'd been messing with right before Tristan killed him.

"Fuck. He's set off some sort of fail-safe. Probably has this place rigged with explosives." His way to ensure if he couldn't have Alyse, nobody would get her.

They only had sixty seconds. They had to get out of there.

Tristan yanked her close to him and used his teeth to rip through the tape around her waist, at least giving her movement of her arms. "Find the key to the cuffs."

She found it on the dresser and unshackled him, then Tristan used his knife to cut through the bindings around her ankle. They both ran toward the front door, but it was bolted. And all the windows were still covered with metal.

They searched every room, but there was no other way

out. It seemed McDowell was determined to have the last word, even in death.

The closet he'd put her in was the last place Tristan checked. There was something about that tiny space—different, more fortified. It was a long shot, but maybe it would be enough to keep them alive.

Tristan ignored the pain in his shoulder and wrist and cupped Alyse's cheeks. "I know I don't have any right to ask you this, but I need you to trust me. I think the closet may be our only option."

Her face paled, but she nodded. "Okay."

He kissed her then they ran for the tiny room. Tristan could hear her breathing get more labored as he pulled the door behind them, locking them in darkness. But she stayed by his side. He tugged her to the back corner and covered her with his body. It wouldn't be enough if this was the explosion Tristan was expecting, but he had to try.

Then Tristan felt some sort of cool air behind her. He remembered McDowell's words about being the one to know all the secrets about this place. Maybe this was one of them.

He yanked Alyse out of the way. "Feel for a lever. I think there's an opening."

She let out a little sob when she found it, and a door popped open. Tristan immediately pushed her through then crawled behind her. They'd only been outside a few seconds before the cabin exploded into a ball of fire behind them.

The momentum propelled them forward. Tristan felt heat searing his back as he wrapped his arms around her, and they landed hard on the ground.

For a few seconds, the world turned gray, then Tristan pushed the darkness back.

"Are you okay?"

"Yes," she whispered. "What about you? You're shot."

"I'm going to be fine."

They lay there, both trying to catch their breaths. He pulled her close to him. Tristan didn't think he was ever going to be able to let go of her again.

"Tristan!" Mark yelled. He could hear Callum calling for them too. He closed his eyes in relief that they were still alive. McDowell's traps hadn't gotten them.

"We're here. We're okay," Tristan called. "Be careful. Traps everywhere."

"Stay where you are. We're bringing in backup. We've already lost three men," Callum yelled.

Fuck. McDowell had been smarter than some of them.

"Tristan is shot," Alyse yelled. Her voice was hoarse, but the guys heard.

"Report, Pisces," Outlaw demanded.

"Bullet wound to the shoulder, knife wound to the left arm. Significant wrist abrasions. Nothing life-threatening." Tristan looked over at her. "You? Anything…did he…?"

God, he didn't want to ask her any of this.

"No," she said. "He wanted to use his mother's conditioning to help teach me a lesson, so he didn't get to what he had planned in that bed."

Tristan closed his eyes in relief and kissed her forehead.

"Neither of us needs immediate medical attention," Tristan called out.

"Then you're probably best to stay where you are until we get the area cleared of all traps!" Callum yelled.

Lie there with Alyse, knowing they were both safe and the threat to her was gone? He couldn't think of anything more he'd rather do.

"Roger that. We'll be right here."

Alyse leaned her head against his chest, and Tristan knew that he would never take that feeling for granted again. "I'm so sorry for what I did, for putting you in that situation at the restaurant without telling you. So sorry I left you alone."

"You came to this cabin willing to die an awful death for me. I think that gives us a clean slate."

"Good, because I don't think I'm capable of letting you go."

"Even though the job is over now?"

"Woman, I love you. And while I hope you never have another stalker, I will stay by your side and keep you safe for as long as you will let me. Every single day."

She leaned up and smiled down at him. "Oh yeah? I hope that's true for every single night also. Because I love you too."

The last bit of anxiety that had lodged itself in his chest broke free. She had really forgiven him. They had made it out alive. They had the rest of forever to figure out the details of blending their lives together.

All Tristan knew was that it would happen.

He kissed her nose. "One personal protection detail at your disposal, forever. Free of charge."

Chapter 36

One Month Later

A shadow blocked her sun, and Alyse opened one eye to find Tristan standing over her. She smiled. "You're going to make my tan uneven if you stand there too long."

She didn't have to look at him to note the smile in his voice as he sat down next to her on the towel reserved for him. "Or I could ruin your tan entirely and drag you inside."

"Mmm…that's very tempting."

They were on their beach—or what Alyse had come to think of as their beach—on the Channel Islands. Now that the movie had wrapped filming, they had decided to come there for a full week and spend time, just the two of them.

Back home, they already spent a lot of time together. Tristan had never moved back into his house and had permanently moved into her bedroom. After they had a long talk.

Tristan had brought Alyse home from the Garland nightmare, and they took care of each other. Even with his injuries, he absolutely drowned her in love. And she did the same to him.

When Alyse woke with the nightmares of the dark, he loved her back to sleep. And when he was in pain, she did her best to make sure he was distracted by other things. But mostly, they held each other.

It seemed like such a simple act, but it was something that Alyse would never take for granted again.

When they surfaced from all of that, the world had changed. The photos of her at the restaurant—entirely without makeup—had gone viral around the world, as had the details of her time with Garland and how he had been stalking her. To Alyse's shock, the response was nearly the opposite of what she had expected.

Of course there were some negative comments, but most people were…happy. Everyone was saying she seemed far more approachable when she looked "normal."

Women especially said that they could identify more easily with her.

It was a perspective she'd never considered. Alyse might have lost the title of America's Glamour Princess, but she'd gained something far more valuable: being comfortable in her own skin.

Tristan continued to show Alyse just how much he treasured her soul and her body beyond the image. Not once had he made her feel less than whole and perfect since their return, and he'd apologized again for what he'd done. Again and again. Until Alyse had to shut him up with kisses after she'd more than forgiven him.

But they did talk. If they were going to be together, they had to be a team. He couldn't keep things from her, and she couldn't from him.

Tristan stretched out beside her, and Alyse couldn't help but look at him. No shirt, skin shining from his recent swim.

She rolled toward him on her towel and leaned her head on his chest, not resisting the temptation to trace her fingers across his abs.

A few months ago, she never could have imagined this.

"I love you," she whispered to him. She couldn't seem to stop saying it. Now that she could, and now that she knew how precious those words were, she couldn't stop.

His head turned toward hers. "You know I can't keep my hands off you when you say things like that."

Alyse grinned. "That I love you?"

"Yep. Way too sexy." He rolled over her, taking her lips in a kiss that she never tired of. A kiss that made it clear she wouldn't be tanning much longer this afternoon.

"You have a choice," he murmured against her lips.

"What are my options?"

"We can stay right here," he said, slipping his hand up to her neck, where he untied the top of her bikini. "We can go in the water, or I can carry you to our bed, where I'm guessing we won't leave until dinner."

"Mmm, those are all excellent options," she said. "Look at you threatening me with a good time."

He crushed her lips with his and stole all that was left of her breath. "What's your choice, beautiful?"

"Bed, please."

He lifted her off the towel effortlessly, even recovering from a bullet wound. It was healing well, and he would have a new scar, but Alyse didn't mind. It reminded them both of what had happened, and to never forget it.

The entire world had been surprised that America's former Glamour Princess was in a relationship with her bodyguard. But everyone loved the romance of it. Tristan was nearly as famous as Alyse was now.

She wrapped her legs around his waist to pull him closer, and he chuckled. The past week they'd been there, they'd learned more about each other than ever before, and he now knew that was her asking for him to skip everything else and get inside her.

Right now.

He gave her exactly what she wanted, making quick work of their bathing suits and entering her slowly, inch by inch, until she was full of him. It was her favorite feeling, being this close. Here, she never had to worry about any pretenses.

It was just him and her. Nothing else mattered.

Ecstasy rushed up like a wave, both of them chasing that perfect end, and they crashed over the edge together. Tristan pressed his face into the crook of her neck, shuddering with his own release. They rested together for a few minutes, breathing together. Alyse ran her fingers through his still-damp hair, and he dragged his lips up her neck.

He pulled back so they could see each other's eyes. "I love you."

"I love you."

He stroked a finger down her cheek. "I didn't know your father well, but I hope he would be happy to see us together."

Alyse couldn't stop touching him, tracing the lines of his collarbone. "He would have loved us together. I know because he wanted me to be happy, and no one else makes me happier."

"I want to make you happy every single day."

She recognized that look of determination in his eyes, the same one he'd had about keeping her safe. There was no doubt in her mind he was telling the truth.

He would do whatever it took to make their future as bright as it could be. She would do the same.

They may have been brought together under the worst of circumstances, but their forever would be written in the stars.

Bonus Epilogue

Oak Creek, Wyoming

"I guess it's safe to say you Zimmerman brothers are into movie stars."

Tristan's longtime friend Baby Bollinger wagged his eyebrows at him from over his beer, shooting him that boyish grin that charmed damned near everybody when he was trying to.

They were sitting in the large corner booth, along with Tristan's brother Gavin, and Ian DeRose, the founder of Zodiac Tactical. Although since Ian was now married to Wavy Bollinger, that made him Baby's brother-in-law.

Hell, blood, marriage or not...damned near every man in there was his brother. He'd trust them all at his back.

It was a week before Christmas and most of the Linear and Zodiac Tactical employees were there at the Eagle's Nest, Oak Creek's beloved bar, celebrating the season and each other.

And yes, the Eagle's Nest was run by Lexi Zimmerman—

former film star before she fell from grace and married his brother Gavin.

Gavin looked at Lexi like he would move heaven and earth to protect her. Tristan had no doubt his own expression mirrored that when he looked at Alyse.

"Why? You looking to trade in for a movie star?" He asked Baby with his own grin.

Baby glanced over at his wife, same protective expression on his face. "Oh hell no. I'll keep my brainiac professor forever in this life and the next few if I can manage it."

They all raised their glasses in a toast to that.

Most of the women were laughing and dancing out on the floor. Tristan had known Baby long enough to know it wouldn't be long before he was out there too. Kendrick Foster, aka Blaze, was already throwing down crazy dance moves with his lady, Neo—both of them grinning like idiots as they tried to outdo each other.

Sarge and Bronwyn were dancing too...a slow, intimate tangle of limbs, despite the upbeat tempo of the song. Sarge always danced with his wife like that—wrapped around the former Zodiac agent like he would stand against hell itself if she needed him to.

There might be a theme there.

Linear and Zodiac Tactical were made up of a lot of protective men willing to do whatever it took to keep their loved ones safe. Although, not coddling. Never coddling.

They respected all these women for what they were: intelligent, capable badasses in their own right. The women saved them back in as many ways as the men saved them.

Tristan knew Alyse certainly had.

The woman never ceased to amaze him. Her strength, her work ethic, her focus...all made him fall in love with her more. In the past few months, she'd not only continued making films and providing her face and endorsement to products, she'd also moved *behind* the camera.

She'd started a production company with two other of Hollywood's leading ladies to focus on projects that helped promote healthy body images for women. They had a weekly online round-robin talk show where women could share their stories and hopefully help others.

Alyse had gone public with her own body image issues. Although she left out the specifics about her abuse, she'd told the world how exercise had become the enemy to her and how maintaining her perfect image had driven her to depression and anxiety.

And how she wasn't going to live that way anymore.

A few of her more elite sponsors—those who wanted America's Glamour Princess as their spokesperson—had let her go. Good riddance, in Tristan's opinion. Because thousands of women, both young and old, had sent letters and emails and posted messages about how Alyse's honesty and vulnerability had helped them.

Tristan was head over heels—and every other possible cliché—in love with that woman.

He realized his friends around him were laughing.

"What?" He asked.

"You've got the look, man." Ian winked at him.

"Don't worry, we've all had it at one time or another. There's no point in fighting it," Gavin laughed.

"What the hell are you morons talking about?"

They just laughed harder.

Baby leaned back further in the booth. "That: *I can't live without this woman, I'm not even going to try* look."

Gavin held up his beer in a toast. "Seems like there's going to be an addition to the Zimmerman family soon."

"You damned well have that right." If Tristan could talk Alyse into it.

He wasn't her employee in any way any longer. She had her own security team for her daily activities—bodyguards Tristan had picked and vetted himself. Two of the four were women, which Alyse liked even more.

But at night, there in the house when it was just the two of them, Tristan was more than happy to take over the honor of protecting her. Neither of them wanted anyone else around, security professionals or not. They wanted the freedom of doing whatever they wanted, wherever they wanted.

And however loudly they wanted.

Tristan knew they both saw this as forever, but he hadn't made it official yet. He hadn't asked her to marry him although he'd marry her any time she'd have him.

"And there goes the slightly panicked look," Ian said. "Always tends to follow the *oh shit, I'm in love* expression."

Gavin held up his glass again. "Love takes even the best by surprise. The strongest fall the hardest."

Damn it, why had Tristan decided to have his romantic crisis in front of his friends and family? All of them were too damned preceptive for him to be able to hide what he was thinking. Especially when it was practically overwhelming him.

Although this wasn't really a romantic crisis. Yeah, looking over at Alyse now—laughing with new friends, hair loose and falling around her shoulders, very minimal makeup—Tristan felt like his heart was too big to fit his body.

But he wasn't taken by surprise by this feeling. He knew he wanted Alyse Peterson to be his forever. There was no panic about it.

Tristan shook his head. "You guys are right about some stuff, but very wrong about the other."

He dragged his eyes away from Alyse on the dance floor and found them all in various stages of smirking at him.

"Are you going to deny that you're in love with her?" Ian asked.

"Not even for a second."

Baby tilted his head to the side. "Then what were we so wrong about?"

Tristan leaned forward on the table. "That it took me by surprise. Unlike some of you, I'm in touch with my own feelings."

The entire table scoffed at once, all of them taking turns swearing they hadn't been caught off guard by their own feelings when they'd fallen for their women.

But they knew the truth.

Sometimes you couldn't see that the most important thing in your universe was right in front of you until something threatened to take it away.

Every single man at the table—hell, almost every single man currently in this bar—had almost lost the woman he loved.

That sort of terror very quickly taught you not to take happiness for granted.

"I'm going to dance with my woman," Baby muttered.

Ian followed him out to get to Wavy, stopping by the DJ to ask for a slower song. It was just Tristan and Gavin left.

Tristan slid toward the end of the booth. He wanted Alyse in his arms too.

"You really love her, don't you?" Gavin asked.

"With everything I am. Same way you love Lexi."

"And it didn't catch you off guard for real? You've known for a while?"

Tristan reached into his jacket and pulled out a small jewelry box. "I've been carrying this around for weeks, trying to figure out the right way to ask her to marry me. She deserves the perfect proposal."

Gavin chuckled.

"What?" he demanded.

"You'll figure it out, little brother." He got up, leaving his beer on the table. "I'm going to dance with Lexi if I can't talk her into getting off her feet. She needs to take it easy but won't listen to me."

Tristan's eyes widened. "Wait, is Lexi…"

Gavin winked at him. "Don't spoil the surprise. We want to announce it at Christmas. She's eleven weeks."

He jumped up and hugged his brother. "Congrats, man. That's so damned exciting."

As Tristan was pulling back, Gavin yanked him close again. "You already know what perfect is for Alyse. Don't overthink it. Let's have all sorts of good news for Dad next week."

They'd all be having Christmas dinner together at Dad's second home in Reddington City. It was a family tradition. This year, Zac and Anne Mackay were coming too, along with baby daughter Becky.

"Yeah, I don't think I'm going to make a grand proposal happen by then." It wouldn't be perfect enough.

Gavin looked like he was going to say something, then shook his head. "Understood. Now, let's go dance with the two most beautiful women on the planet."

Tristan woke up when he reached for Alyse and found she wasn't in bed with him. Immediately his eyes flew open.

Alyse still wasn't a great sleeper. Sometimes she got up because she had ideas she wanted to jot down or just wasn't tired. But sometimes, even all these months later, she woke up because she had nightmares about what happened with McDowell.

They were staying at a highly fortified cabin on the Linear Tactical property, so he wasn't concerned about safety, even when he became aware Alyse was outside on the deck swing, wrapped in a blanket.

Tristan slipped on his jacket and boots over his pajama pants—needed despite it being a rather mild Wyoming December night—and headed out there himself.

"Got room in that blanket for one more?"

Her smile in the moonlight took his breath away. "Always. As long as that someone is you."

She held out the blanket for him to sit next to her, but instead he picked her up completely and set her in his lap, blanket around them both. "What you doing out here, gorgeous? Bad dreams?"

"No. Looking up at the stars. You never see anything like this in L.A. It's the most beautiful thing I've ever seen."

The most beautiful thing he'd ever seen was currently cuddled in his arms, but Tristan understood the sentiment perfectly. There were nights he'd mourned not having the Wyoming sky spread out above him.

"We can come back here whenever you want."

She snuggled closer. "I liked your friends. And your brother. And Lexi. I knew of her, of course, back when she was in the biz. But I never really spoke to her. She seems really happy."

"Gavin's happy. That's for sure."

"The other people too... the Linear Tactical guys and their wives. And your work friends and their loved ones. There was so much love in that bar tonight. Protectiveness. Possessiveness. Joy."

"Too much?"

"At one time it would've been, for sure. But not now. Because of you." She peeked up at him, head wrapped in the blanket. "Because you love me the same way. And I love you that way too."

"Yes." His word was brief, but it held all the love in his heart.

And suddenly Tristan understood what Gavin had been telling him. Not to overthink it. He did understand what was perfect for Alyse. What was perfect for *them*. It wasn't some big, grandiose proposal that would make social media swoon.

She wasn't America's Glamour Princess anymore. She didn't want to be that.

She was *Alyse*. She was beautiful, kind, and real.

And the perfect moment was now, under the stars of the sky he loved so much. The one she loved too, even though it was new to her.

Tristan slipped her off his lap, setting her on the swing and standing.

"Are we going inside?" She smiled up at him—eyes soft and full of trust. "Back to bed?"

"In just a second." He reached for the ring inside his jacket pocket. "I've been searching for the perfect way to do this. I wanted a grand gesture you would remember forever. But I'm not sure anything could be more perfect than right here under these stars."

Those eyes got big. "Tristan..."

He got down on one knee. "Alyse Peterson, when you walked into my life, I assumed all the wrong things about you. You've spent every moment of every day proving me wrong by just being yourself. Now I want to spend every day for the rest of forever being your protector, your friend, your lover. Being a man you'll be proud to stand beside."

Tears rolled down her cheek.

"Will you marry me? Spend forever with me? We'll work out all the details later."

"Yes," the word was whispered into the gentle darkness. "I'll marry you."

Tristan slipped the ring on her finger. The diamond he'd chosen wasn't ostentatious, but neither was Alyse. She smiled at it then cupped his cheeks in her hands.

"You saw who I really was before I even knew that person existed. The real me."

"I'm in love with the real you. And all the other parts of you. Be mine forever."

"Yes. And you're mine too."

They kissed gently, reverently there under the stars. The first kiss of the rest of their lives.